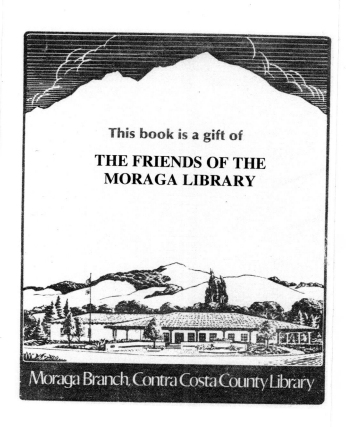

WHITE LINES

WHITE

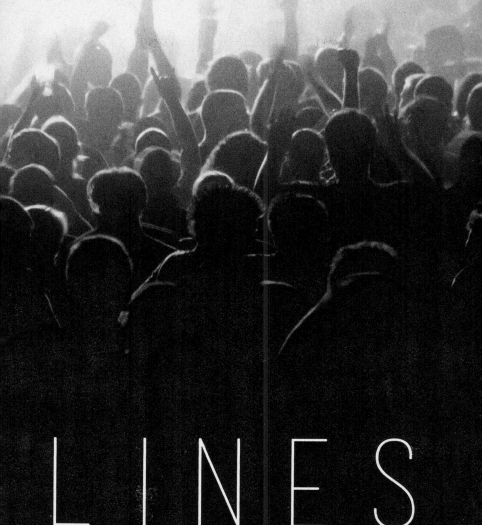

LINES

JENNIFER BANASH

G. P. Putnam's Sons | An Imprint of Penguin Group (USA) Inc.

G. P. PUTNAM'S SONS
A division of Penguin Young Readers Group.
Published by The Penguin Group.
Penguin Group (USA) Inc., 375 Hudson Street, New York, NY 10014, U.S.A.
Penguin Group (Canada), 90 Eglinton Avenue East, Suite 700, Toronto, Ontario M4P 2Y3, Canada
(a division of Pearson Penguin Canada Inc.).
Penguin Books Ltd, 80 Strand, London WC2R 0RL, England.
Penguin Ireland, 25 St. Stephen's Green, Dublin 2, Ireland (a division of Penguin Books Ltd.).
Penguin Group (Australia), 707 Collins Street, Melbourne, Victoria 3008, Australia
(a division of Pearson Australia Group Pty Ltd).
Penguin Books India Pvt Ltd, 11 Community Centre, Panchsheel Park, New Delhi—110 017, India.
Penguin Group (NZ), 67 Apollo Drive, Rosedale, Auckland 0632, New Zealand
(a division of Pearson New Zealand Ltd).
Penguin Books South Africa, Rosebank Office Park, 181 Jan Smuts Avenue,
Parktown North 2193, South Africa.
Penguin China, B7 Jiaming Center, 27 East Third Ring Road North,
Chaoyang District, Beijing 100020, China.
Penguin Books Ltd, Registered Offices: 80 Strand, London WC2R 0RL, England.

Published simultaneously in Canada. Printed in the United States of America.
Design by Ryan Thomann. Text set in Minister.

Library of Congress Cataloging-in-Publication Data
Banash, Jennifer. White lines / Jennifer Banash. p. cm. Summary: In 1980s New York City,
seventeen-year-old Caitlin tries to overcome her mother's abuse and father's abandonment by losing
herself in nights of clubbing and drugs, followed by days of stumbling aimlessly through school.
[1. Coming of age—Fiction. 2. Nightclubs—Fiction. 3. Drug abuse—Fiction.
4. Family problems—Fiction. 5. Interpersonal relations—Fiction. 6. New York (N.Y.)—
History—20th century—Fiction.] I. Title. PZ7.B2176Whi 2013 [Fic]—dc23 2012008725
ISBN 978-0-399-25788-9
1 3 5 7 9 10 8 6 4 2

For Marc Sandy Goldsmith

To whom shall I hire myself out?
What beast must I adore?
What holy image is attacked? What hearts shall I break?
What lies must I maintain? In whose blood tread?

—Arthur Rimbaud, *A Season in Hell*

It's like a jungle sometimes it makes me wonder
How I keep from going under.

—Grandmaster Flash, "The Message"

WHITE LINES

* * * *

IT'S SEVEN A.M., *and the sidewalks are dotted with men in double-breasted gray suits, punks in shades of dust and ash, girls crawling home after a night out, mascara smeared and sticky as tar. The sound of a motorcycle revving its engine mixes with the shriek of a car alarm, too loud, too loud, so I grab the pillow from beneath my head and try to stifle the noise. I am underwater, the sounds of the busy morning receding with every frantic, amphetamine-laced beat of my heart. Skip. Then stop. Skip. Then stop.*

I close my eyes and the world falls away, the VIP room at the club rising up from the dim recesses of my brain, the red velvet drapes whispering as they swing gently shut, the doorway gaping like a rotted tooth. The mirror spread out over my lap in a river of silver, my reflection looming and distorted as I bend toward it, white powder disappearing up my nose, a magic trick, whoops, there she goes again, a rabbit plunging into a black satin hat.

Now you see me. Now you don't.

ONE

I REACH ONE HAND OUT from beneath the warm dark of the quilt and turn off the alarm, the shrillness breaking the early morning silence. I open one eye and the face of Mickey Mouse grins back at me, his hand held up in a jaunty wave, his red lips parted in a grin so cheerful it borders on psychotic. When Giovanni gave me the clock a few months ago for my seventeenth birthday, he laughed, tossing his shoulder-length ringlets away from his face before throwing the box in my lap.

"Darling, it's purrrrrrfect. It's better than Prozac! Think of it—not only will you be able to make it to school on time for a change, but you'll never wake up in a bad mood again!"

Famous last words.

I swing my feet around and tentatively place them on the wooden floor, waiting for the inevitable spins, which I know will be followed by a bout of nausea so intense, I will wish I were dead. Even though I should be used to this schedule by now, it's still a struggle to force my eyes open after four hours of sleep—sometimes less—to move my lethargic body through the morning rituals of teeth brushing and toast. For the next twenty minutes I'll stand in the shower trying to lather my hair with one hand while simultaneously holding on to the wall with the other so I don't fall and crack my skull open. Girl Dies While Scrubbing. News at eleven.

I run a brush through my shoulder-length hair—dyed black this week—flicking droplets of water all over the floor and my feet, and stare at my reflection in the mirror. The circles beneath my eyes the color of bruised plums. The bangs plastered straight across my forehead, glossy as a helmet. My face has all the required features—nose, eyes that are a blue so dark, they look almost black unless you look very closely, and a wide, full mouth that made me the subject of various insults throughout elementary school. But somehow, without makeup, nothing really seems to come together. Even though my complexion is a light shade of olive, without added color I'm as pale and indistinguishable as a ghost. If you walked past me on the street when I wasn't wearing makeup, you might ignore me completely. And most of the time—during the daylight hours at least—it feels like a relief. The only time I'm really comfortable with the feel of eyes gliding over my skin is at night, hidden behind a veil of powder and paint.

I look around the living room, at the clothes I wore last night draped over the back of the green thrift store couch I bought when I first moved in six months ago. It has a few busted springs that squeak when you sit down, but it's comfortable enough. The ceiling in the living room slants down at a sharp angle, forcing anyone over five foot eight to stoop a bit when they walk through the front door, but I love the slightly cramped space. The narrowness of the rooms, the way they're laid out railroad style, one opening onto another like a story unfolding in perfect rhythm—living room, bathroom, and straight back to my bedroom—makes me feel tucked in for the night and safe.

In my bedroom, the windows are covered with heavy black fabric. A huge Joy Division poster hangs over the bed, emblazoned with the image of a marble angel in black and white, wings outstretched, the words LOVE WILL TEAR US APART written in bold lettering across the top. I open my closet, grabbing a black tunic that falls to my knees, and pull on a pair of neon-green tights that bag a little around the ankles, signaling that I've lost weight recently. Stuffing my feet into my favorite pair of motorcycle boots, I grab my leather jacket and shrug it on, throw my backpack over one shoulder and I'm out the door.

I attend Manhattan Preparatory Academy. It's basically a school that caters to rich kids (read: *troubled*) who don't like high school and would rather be doing anything else—which is what I suppose I am. I usually do my homework during lunch, sitting by myself on the front steps of the school, or on the subway, my notebook sliding over my knees. As rigorous as the school is purported to be in the glossy brochures that feature girls smiling wide, their teeth sharp enough to devour the city itself, it usually takes only around forty minutes to finish everything. But it's not like I do the best job, either. Who really needs to know how to do advanced algebra in everyday life? It's not like I'll be at the supermarket someday and suddenly need to solve some complicated algorithm just to figure out whether or not I have enough change for a box of Fruit Roll-Ups.

I turn the corner, walking quickly up Third Street, past the brick façade of the local Hells Angels headquarters and the collection of motorcycles parked outside, and turn onto First Avenue. I stop at the ATM and check my balance, green numbers illuminating the screen. From the looks of it, I'll have to call my father's secretary for the second month in a row to ask for more money. I don't have a set allowance, but my father usually puts enough in my account to pay the rent, buy food and drag my laundry to the Laundromat on the corner once a week. But over the past couple of months the amount has been slowly dwindling. I wonder if this is his usual passive-aggressive way of wanting to talk to me—denying me something until I'm forced to make contact. Of course, it would be so much easier to just call me up on the phone, but my father has never been good with being straightforward. Or with confrontation, for that matter.

A white plastic bag wraps itself around my ankle, and I shake my foot twice to dislodge it, shoving the transaction slip into my pocket as I walk away. Even though Joe's Pizza is closed, the smell of grease still hangs in the air beneath the red awning. The metal grate covering the front is sprayed with white paint that reads DA BOMBE, followed by an illegible symbol scrawled in bright purple—some tagger's signature. It's freaking cold out here for early November, my breath releasing in hot white puffs of smoke, and I wish I'd worn a scarf.

I stop at the bodega on the corner. Inside it's almost steamy, the smell of toasting bread and frying eggs sliding seductively under my nose. The shelves are stocked with canned goods, loaves of Pepperidge Farm and Wonder bread, boxes of Entemann's cookies stacked alongside bottles of Tylenol and rolls of toilet paper. A small glass case at the front of the store holds empanadas, the pale crescents crimped at the edges. Rows of candy bars line the register along with packs of batteries and a glass jar of tough-looking beef jerky. Merengue music plays softly from a boom box behind the counter, and the sound soothes my tired brain, lulling me back to sleep.

The same Dominican guy who's usually working in the morning stares down at me, licking his lips.

"Whatchu wan' today, mami? The usual?"

He's wearing a pressed white T-shirt, sleeves rolled up to expose his biceps. I see a tattoo of a heart on one arm, the anatomical kind, the valves and meticulously detailed chambers pierced with what look like thick metal spikes. He grins at me, pouring a small coffee before I even ask for it. I don't come in here often enough to be considered a regular, but I force myself to smile, my face stretching uncomfortably, and order a toasted sesame bagel with cream cheese. In the club, dressed in yards of satin or tulle, witty remarks slide effortlessly off my tongue, but here I'm unsure, hesitant and tongue-tied. In real life, daylight steals my words like a vampire running from the sun. Which is probably why I've pretty much given up on trying to communicate with anyone at all. As he wraps up my bagel in shiny tinfoil, placing it in a brown paper bag, my stomach growls loudly.

When I was very small, my mother would lean across from me at the dinner table and cut my meat, her silk blouse whispering against my skin, the musk and spice of her perfume overwhelming me. This was before the divorce, when we were still a family. My father drank intermittently from a glass of red wine, his face lit with a gentle smile as if the very sight of me gave him pleasure. When I think about the way he used to look at me, my throat swells with emotion, cutting off the supply of air. Tightening my grip on the brown paper bag in my hand, I blink my eyes quickly to chase away the tears and head back out into the street.

Stupid, stupid, stupid, I hiss to myself as I reach into the bag. *Stop feeling fucking sorry for yourself.* I rip off a piece of warm bread and shove it into my mouth, chewing in time with the slap of my boots against the pavement.

At the corner, I duck into the subway station to catch the train uptown. I drop a token into the turnstile while simultaneously ignoring that same bum who's always begging for a free ride, his big, blackened toe protruding from one of his ripped Nikes.

"Just let me get in behind you," he pleads, grabbing on to my jacket, and I shake my body hard until he lets me go. Last week I gave him a dollar as I slid by, which was clearly a mistake, because he's been lighting up like a Christmas tree at the sight of me ever since.

"Leave that girl alone now," an ominous voice booms over the loudspeaker. I turn around and lock eyes with a small man with white hair working the token booth. His face is weathered, and he stares out at me with concern. He raises his chin in my direction ever so slightly as the train thunders into the station, the cars streaked with black and silver graffiti. The platform smells like days-old urine and the peanut-scented belch of hot exhaust. The crush of schoolkids on the platform reminds me of last night, the crowds of brightly dressed partygoers that pushed at the velvet rope, willing me to let them inside.

I clutch my bagel and coffee tightly as I enter the train, the doors closing loudly behind me. It's crowded, and I hold on to the silver pole with one hand, trying my best to shove as much bagel into my face as I can with the other. Since I moved out of my mother's apartment, my eating habits have been random at best. With no set mealtimes, I'm either ravenous or totally disinterested, with no happy medium between the two. What's the point of throwing food into a pot or setting the table when I'm the only one eating?

"You're so effing lucky," Sara moaned when she first found out I was getting my own apartment, throwing her lanky body down in protest onto the oversized white leather sofa that took up half of my mother's living room. Sara is basically one of the few girls I can actually stand. She always says exactly what she thinks, and her level gaze behind her black rectangular-shaped glasses is unflinchingly honest. She's got this huge shock of white-blond curls that seem to spring uncontrollably from the depths of her skull, and there is nothing in her wardrobe that isn't some washed-out shade of black or gray. When she moved across the street from me in the fourth grade, I wanted to meet her so badly that I stole her bike from in front of her apartment building, hiding it in our basement storage, then watched from the plate-glass window of the lobby as she stood there on the pavement looking confused, hoping she'd come across the street asking if I'd seen it. She never did, and I sheepishly wheeled it back a few hours later and left it with her doorman, taping a pack of M&M's to the handlebars along with a note.

With the exception of Sara and Giovanni, I really don't have any close friends. I'm part of a huge circle of kids who are paid to throw parties—club kids, they call us—but I wouldn't consider any of them real friends. We're more like a bunch of loosely associated lunatics who throw parties with themes like Dante's Disco Inferno! or Iron Curtain Chic! The club-kid scene isn't about forming everlasting friendships or getting real; it's not about having money, though I do make decent cash as a promoter, which comes in handy when I squander away my father's money on magazines, dark chocolate, and records. It's about being on top, where I rarely belong.

"You'll move downtown and I'll never see you again," Sara whined, hurling herself abruptly to the floor, where she collapsed in a fit of fake sobbing. "Good-bye, cruel world!"

Sara goes to Nightingale-Bamford, the school I also attended until last year, when I was "asked to leave" by the headmistress. This may have been because I was basically showing up one day out of five. It also might have been because I was found in the girls' bathroom at the start of the school year, chopping a line on the smooth, granite countertop, a rolled-up dollar bill in one hand. When the door swung open, I looked up at the girl framed in the doorway, her auburn hair the color of burnished strawberries, her legs wrapped in pale pink tights that made me think of pirouettes, a haze of tutus, feathers drifting slowly across a darkened stage. Her rose-colored mouth opened in a wide O, and as she stared at me, her eyes blinking slowly, I froze, gripping the bill tightly in my hand, her face blank and unreadable as the door slowly swung shut. When I was summoned to the headmistress's office the next period during French, I placed my pens and pencils and textbooks carefully into my backpack, my movements slow and deliberate, masking the sinking sense of failure that crept over me like a bad dream.

Even though Nightingale is only fifteen blocks from Manhattan Prep, it might as well be at the other end of the universe, as Sara is in all honors classes and basically lives in the publications lab as coeditor of the yearbook. That's the weird thing about Sara: even though she looks like the bastard offspring of Madonna and the Cure's Robert Smith—all black rubber bracelets, dark eye makeup that she basically sleeps in until it smears artfully and her mane of wild blond hair—people like her, seek her out and want to be her friend. She manages to exist in a space where she cannot be clearly labeled or defined, moving seamlessly from clique to clique, belonging to none of them. If I had even one ounce of Sara's self-confidence and charisma, her solidified sense of self, I could probably rule the world. Instead, I'm the weird girl who goes to a school for "special" kids, that even the other special kids avoid.

"Oh please," I said, smiling at her antics. "Like I won't see you all the time anyway."

"True." She sat up, her eyes sparkling with mischief before her face grew pensive. When Sara shifts gears, it's like watching a wall come down—or go up, depending on what she's feeling at the moment. "Is it because of . . . you know . . . parental stuff?"

The smile faded from my face, and I stared out the window at a garbage truck clanging down the street, not wanting to look her in the eye. "You could say that," I mumble, my voice tight in my throat as if I'm being strangled by my own words.

"I thought things had gotten worse when you showed up with that black eye," Sara said quietly, her eyes on the rug, "but I didn't know what to say. I *never* know what to say."

"No one really does." My voice broke on the last word to leave my lips.

When I think about my mother, I have to stop what I'm doing and just breathe, my brain flooded with images: shades pulled down like eyes slowly closing, the windows shut tight. Wiping the blood and snot from my nose and cleaning the cut that splits my upper lip with hands that won't stop shaking. That feeling of invisibility, the noise of the city closing in around me like a noose.

"What about your dad?" Sara put her arm around my shoulders, leaning in. I could smell her strawberry shampoo and the patchouli oil she always dabs on her neck and behind her ears. It made me think of the industrial-strength cleaning products our maid, Jaronda, used in the kitchen once a week to clean the floors and countertops, that faint medicinal smell she left in her wake.

"What *about* him," I sighed, untangling myself from Sara's embrace. "He's the one who signed the lease on my new place."

"That's fucked up," Sara said, sitting down beside me and twisting her unruly mass of hair into a knot on top of her head. "When they got divorced, I always thought you'd go live with him eventually."

I snorted, rolling my eyes to the ceiling. "I don't think Jasmine would appreciate that."

Jasmine. Long dark hair, tanned skin and liquid black eyes. It was no wonder he fell for her the moment she came to work at his firm. Now they live on seventy acres in Connecticut. My father started his career in the mailroom of Solomon Brothers, working his way up to account executive, cold-calling big fish like Donald Trump for hours at a time, then senior account executive, before finally making partner just before my tenth birthday. Now he practically runs the whole place. After the movie *Wall Street* came out, *Forbes* magazine featured him on the cover, a wry grin plastered across his overly tanned face, his blue eyes staring out from beneath the caption that read THE REAL-LIFE GORDON GEKKO. Sure, there were checks on each birthday, and when the social workers called him last spring, stating in no uncertain terms that I could no longer live in my mother's penthouse apartment on Eighty-Third and Park, he'd signed the lease on the East Village apartment without comment, except to mention that at six hundred dollars a month, the rent was more than reasonable. A steal. But never once did he suggest that I live with him, that maybe it wasn't a good idea for a seventeen-year-old to be fending for herself in the heart of Manhattan's Lower East Side, just steps from Alphabet City, where gunshots popped in the night air like a string of firecrackers and junkies routinely nodded out in doorways.

As I waited for him to speak, to tell me that I was finally and unequivocally coming to live with him once and for all, I could hear Jasmine cooing nonsensically in the background like a demented bird, her tinkling, melodic voice amplified over the wire, and I knew I was lost. *Say it say it,* I thought, concentrating with all of my being, squeezing my eyes so tightly that I saw stars exploding, flowers of red and white unfurling their violent petals. My thoughts echoed in the silence that followed, and the words never came.

I take the train seven stops each way, and I usually like the ride, the narrow series of dark tunnels, the flashing lights that remind me of the strobes that shine down on me in the club, my body illuminated like an X-ray. But today, I'm too nauseated, the whiskey sours I drank last night tumbling around in my stomach like a team of trapped, acidic acrobats. Of course it would help if I could sit down, but there are never any seats during morning rush hour. A man sits across from me reading the *Post,* his face set in grim concentration. The headline for today rises above a large picture of Mikhail Gorbachev and shrieks IS THE COLD WAR OVER? Gorbachev's expression looks worried, his bushy eyebrows knitted together in what might be concern or fear, and I wonder if he knows something I don't. I hang on to the metal pole and close my eyes, wondering how long I can go on this way, how long I can maintain, my blank eyes reflected in the mirror each morning, red-rimmed and wasted. As the train lurches out of the station, I sway back and forth, my fingers burning like icicles, my body frozen to the core.

TWO

"SO, HAVE YOU GIVEN any more thought to your future?"

Ms. Sherman, the guidance counselor, is staring at me over her silver-rimmed glasses, the round lenses magnifying her blue eyes. I've successfully avoided the mandatory weekly meetings, the glossy college brochures and probing questions since the start of the semester, but today, as I was attempting to tiptoe past her office during my free period, she spotted me and called me inside. Her office is plastered with posters of sad-faced kittens featuring cheerful messages scrolled across the bottom—sayings that are probably supposed to be inspirational: HANG IN THERE, BABY! YOU CAN DO IT! But all those furry faces and glib platitudes just make me feel more tired than I already am. I know I didn't always feel this way, so used up and exhausted. When I first started clubbing, even though I rarely got more than a few hours of sleep a night, I moved toward school weightless, feet gliding over the pavement, heels clicking in time with the music coursing through my headphones. This was before I started working the ropes of the VIP room a few months ago, throwing pills down my throat and powder up my nose just to get through the night.

I stare past Ms. Sherman and out the window, concentrating on the cars whooshing past in the street, the fine layer of dust coating the beige venetian blinds. Her office is painted a sunny yellow, the walls way too bright for my bloodshot eyes, a rainbow of pillows covering the dingy white couch.

Ms. Sherman leans forward on her elbows, her red hair frizzing wildly around her pale face devoid of makeup, and rests her weight on the pile of paperwork cluttering her desk. How she's ever able to find anything at all, much less help kids get into the college of their choice, is a complete and total mystery.

"Have you even thought about college? The SATs are coming up soon."

There is a plaintive note in her voice and she holds her hands out in front of her for emphasis. After a moment of silence she sighs loudly, dropping her hands into her lap and sitting back in her chair, watching me carefully.

"Not really," I mumble, clearing my throat and meeting her eyes. The only thing I hate more than waking up in the morning and going to school is being forced to have conversations about my future—or lack of one—before I'm even fully awake. "I still have time, right? I mean, to take the test."

"Well, yes. But you really need to start making some decisions." Ms. Sherman leans forward, shuffling through the papers on her desk until she finds a manila folder, presumably my file. "I'm afraid your grades are going to be a problem." She opens the folder and peruses it intently. "Currently, the only course you're doing well in is English, and yet, back in ninth grade you were an A student."

She takes off her glasses and looks at me, blinking slowly. Even though she's got to be at least fifty, she looks younger without the metal frames, the wan moon of her face as exposed and vulnerable as a baby's. I almost want to give her a hug and tell her it's going to be OK, make her a cup of cocoa. The lines around her eyes are like paper cuts marring the thin, delicate skin.

"I've spoken to your mother, and she said there have been some . . . issues at home. That you've been quite rebellious."

Her voice drifts off into nothingness, and even though I can tell she's trying to be as tactful as possible, my breath halts in my chest. At the mention of my mother, my body goes as rigid as a plank of wood, my fingers curling into fists. I can almost hear her silky voice as she twirls the telephone cord around one thin wrist, grinding her cigarette butt into a crystal ashtray.

You see, Ms. Sherman, I've tried everything. But Caitlin is just completely uncontrollable . . .

As chatty as my mother is, particularly with anyone she wants to either impress or push around, she obviously hasn't clued Ms. Sherman in on the fact that I'm now living alone on the Lower East Side without any parental supervision whatsoever. For one, it's probably all kinds of illegal since I haven't been emancipated. My mother happens to be crazy, but she isn't stupid.

"She wasn't very specific, but . . . do you want to talk about it?" Ms. Sherman asks gently.

My mouth opens, but nothing comes out. I look down at my hands and start to pick at the skin around my nails, which is what I always do when I'm uncomfortable or nervous. I want to speak, to find the words to describe the last seventeen years of my life, but I don't know where to begin, how to describe what it feels like to open the front door after school, afraid of what might be waiting there. How do I explain how hard it is to cover up cuts and bruises with makeup so that the scabs don't show through? How it feels to cry myself to sleep at night, sobs caught in my chest like wads of flypaper. I can hear laughter in the hallway outside Ms. Sherman's office, and a blast of music brings Madonna's "Express Yourself" shimmering into the room for a moment before the music fades away as the volume is turned down.

Come on, girls, do you believe in love . . .

I picture Madonna's haughty face, the blond hair piled atop her head, her defiant stance. Sitting here, afraid to open my mouth and speak, I know I'm nothing like her.

"You don't have to talk to me if you don't want to, Caitlin."

"I can't," I manage to get out. "I'm sorry."

Not to be deterred, Ms. Sherman plods briskly on.

"If you do go on to college, do you know what you might want to study? Mr. Kent tells me you are quite a talented writer."

Mr. Kent is my English teacher, and he gets all kinds of happy if anyone turns in their homework more than once a week. I'd never admit it to Ms. Sherman, but I kind of like writing. Somehow, it's easier to put down on paper what I can't say out loud. Not that I write much anymore, except for school. Two years ago my mother found my diary, read the whole thing from cover to cover, then placed it back in my room, the pages creased with her fingerprints. For weeks afterward, she'd allude to the things I'd written about over the dinner table and as she passed me in the hallways, her silk-clad legs whispering my secrets as she walked by: how I wanted to kiss Brian Fortenoy, how afraid I was that my parents would get divorced, how I hated the silence that hung between them heavy as a wet winter coat. The hopeful look on my mother's face when the phone rang late at night, her eyes hardening as she listened to my father's sheepish excuses. The quiet, palpable rage that simmered just below the surface of her skin, radiating out and infecting us all.

"You better hope we stay together," my mother spat under her breath as she marched into my bathroom one morning, snatching a jar of cold cream from the sink and opening the lid, releasing the powdery scent of roses and chalk in the steamy air. The words hung between us like a threat, and I pulled the towel I was wearing tighter around my naked body, my skin covered in gooseflesh.

"I like English OK, I guess." I shrug like it's no big deal.

"Maybe you might want to think about studying journalism," Ms. Sherman says brightly, happy to have a plan to put into action.

I imagine myself in a busy newsroom wearing a crisp white blouse buttoned up to the neck, my hair cut in a breezy, no-nonsense shag, a pair of tortoiseshell glasses perched on the bridge of my nose. The image makes me inexplicably sad for some reason, and I close my eyes, sighing loudly. What can I really tell Ms. Sherman about the future when I can barely even get through the present? When I first moved into my own place, I thrilled to that first heady rush of freedom, the ability to make myself a peanut-butter-and-jelly sandwich in my kitchen at two a.m. if I wanted to, eating it standing up at the counter, unafraid of what might happen if I left the dirty knife in the sink or forgot to replace the lid on the jelly jar. For the first time in years, I slept dreamless most nights with nothing to fear. There was no one to scream if I walked into the apartment three hours after school let out for the day, to sneak into my room at night, pulling the covers from my bed in a rush of fabric that whistled through the air as it sailed down to the floor. I ate when and what I wanted, and I did my homework most days because I felt like it—not because anyone told me to. I could have Sara and Giovanni over every night of the week, and sometimes I did. But as the months dragged on, it was never enough to erase the ache in my chest when I saw a family on the street, a child balanced carefully on the broad expanse of her father's shoulders, a mother bending over a dark-haired little girl in a stroller, tenderly brushing the hair from her small round face.

The whole idea of college seems hazy and far away as a dream when I'm dragging my clothes up Avenue A to the Laundromat and boiling water for spaghetti for the third night in a row, using an old metal bowl I've punched a hole into for a colander. When you're focused on survival, there's no way to plan for or even think about the future. It hangs there in the distance, as abstract as a Mondrian painting, shimmering just out of reach.

"Well, you're going to have to figure it out sooner or later." Ms. Sherman closes my file, pushing it decisively to one side. "Not to mention the fact that your attendance this year has been nothing short of atrocious. You've missed a total of nine days since the start of the year, and it's only November. I think some detention is probably in order, don't you?"

She raises one eyebrow, looking at me as if she already knows the answer. I hate detention, and so far, no matter how much school I've missed, I've managed to squirm my way out of it. Just as I'm opening my mouth to protest, the phone begins to ring, shattering the moment and making me jump about a mile in my chair. I hate loud, sudden noises. Even the simple, everyday sound of a car door slamming shut can make me flinch sharply and break out in a cold sweat. The only place I am impervious to noise is in the club, the music crashing over me like a wave, sweeping me along and burying me beneath its pounding, relentless beat.

Ms. Sherman picks up the receiver, clearly exasperated by the intrusion. After she says hello, her voice fake and saccharine sweet, she begins listening intently to whoever is on the other end of the line.

"I have to take this," she whispers urgently after putting one hand over the receiver.

I gather up my backpack and stand up, throwing the comforting weight of books over my shoulder, grateful for the chance to escape unscathed.

"Come and see me next week," she says, waving a hand, shooing me out the door. "We'll figure it out then."

I watch as she picks up her glasses, sliding them over her nose, and then swivels around in her leather chair so that her back is to me, her body blocking what's left of the morning light.

THREE

I'M SITTING ON THE STONE STEPS at school, pretending to enjoy an apple that I bought from an Asian grocery a few blocks over, when all I'm really thinking about is how long I have left until I can go home and start getting ready for the club, every stroke of makeup on my skin sliding me further from daylight. I tongue the white flesh and sink my teeth in, wishing the ripe fruit was the tanned blond head of one of the salad girls.

Since Manhattan Prep is housed in a brownstone and has a population of only one hundred students or fewer in the entire school, we don't have a cafeteria. Or a prom. Or dances. Or phys ed. Instead, the Park Avenue girls buy salads at a cafeteria next door and sit in the glass atrium picking at their wilted greens, retouching their lip gloss with sticky pink wands. Even though we are all essentially weird in some way—after all, this is a school for kids who have gotten into some kind of trouble—it's not enough to banish cliques completely. We still have the same bullshit categories as any other school: the jocks, the popular girls, the nerds. And the untouchables. Like me. So I sit on the steps and try to pretend that it doesn't matter, when really, I'd do just about anything to have a friend here. This silent admission makes my cheeks flush with shame. How can I be so weak? Even at Nightingale, I only ever really had Sara, her blond curls hanging over my shoulder, elaborately folded notes tossed at my feet during study hall. Somehow, it was almost enough. But here, with no one to talk to day after day, the loneliness creeps in like an old friend I no longer want to know. Worse yet, it wants to make small talk. *Oh, it's you again? How've you been?*

Across the street, Julian, the new kid, sits on the curb in front of Ray's Pizza, a slice dangling from one hand. As he brings the pizza to his lips, the cheese falls off in one giant greasy slide to his lap. Julian has long dark hair that hangs to his shoulders and looks as if it hasn't made friends with soap or water in days. His skin is the color of café au lait, and there's something about the tilt of his eyes that makes me think he's vaguely Asian. He wears jeans so tight that I'm sure years from now he'll be sitting in some clinic with his frosty blond wife, stammering that he has no idea WHY they've had such a difficult time starting a family. All I know about Julian is that (a) he sits right across the aisle from me in history class, and (b) he transferred from Dalton last week after some kind of scandal involving his ex-girlfriend, and (c) he's totally into the Ramones. He doesn't talk to anyone, and never raises his hand in class, just stares down at his binder and scribbles what looks like pictures of Transformers on the cover with a black pen.

Julian finishes scraping melted cheese off his jeans and looks up, an irritated expression clouding his face. When his eyes meet mine, I feel a rough shock of recognition between us and raise my apple core in a kind of demented greeting, the air suddenly as thick as pudding. Julian tosses me a curt nod and promptly goes back to stuffing the rest of the slice into his mouth, gnawing hungrily at the edges of the crust, watching me all the while. Even though I love staring, and I think that generally other people's lives are way more interesting than TV, I feel uneasy as Julian's eyes lock on to mine. My face burns as he chews the last bite and brushes his hands against his black jeans before walking toward me. I turn the apple core over and over between my palms, my heart careening in my chest as he approaches, glad that my hands have something to do even if the core is damp, sticky, and turning browner by the minute. As Julian moves closer, I can't help but notice how he shakes the hair from his eyes with one expert, jagged motion, how his hazel eyes change from green to brown in the light. His skin is smooth and slightly bronzed, as if he's just returned from some exotic locale. He tilts his chin in my direction defiantly, his eyes flicking coolly over my body, taking me in.

"See something you like?" He raises one dark eyebrow, and I feel like I'm going to spontaneously combust, which is what always happens when someone potentially interesting talks to me in the real world—especially if that person happens to be a guy. And up close, Julian is definitely interesting—though it makes my stomach churn spasmodically to even think the word to myself. People are dangerous, unpredictable. I know this implicitly, and every time I come into contact with them, I become a caged animal, a panther pacing back and forth behind steel bars, wary and agitated.

"Yeah," I stammer, turning redder by the second and wishing that a manhole would just open up and swallow me whole. I look down at my black boots and scramble for something to say, my brain a jumble of images, none that entirely make sense. "Your pizza—I was just . . . hungry."

The minute the words leave my lips, I know they are the truth. My stomach begins to growl loudly as if in agreement, and I look up into Julian's amused face and laugh, my voice echoing in the street, too loud, even with the noise of a passing bus releasing a thick cloud of black smoke. As the sound vibrates through me, jolting me into the present, I realize that it's been forever since I've laughed at something legitimately funny or awkward without being prompted by the ingestion of some mind-altering substance. Still, I can't quite turn off that ever-present voice inside my head, the one that holds up an invisible hand to stop me from going further, from moving closer.

People are dangerous . . .

"Well," Julian says, laughing along with me and holding out a hand, "that's remedied easily enough. C'mon."

I stare at his hand, the long fingers, and look into his eyes.

I toss my apple core to the concrete and take hold of him, ignoring the voice that begins, even now, to protest more loudly, whispering like a flock of ruffled birds, *Don't touch, don't trust.* I draw a deep breath and follow him blindly across the street, unsure of where I'm being taken.

A NIGHT WITH THE SHADES PULLED TIGHT, *the lamp in the corner of the living room filling the space with a candy-colored Tiffany glow. A kiss on the cheek, her painted lips leaving a crimson mark on my skin as her fingers push back the hair from my forehead with a red velvet band.* See how beautiful you look with that mop off your face? *Her voice is low and seductive, a kind of caress, and I shiver at the sound of it, closing my eyes. The mirror looms, gilt-edged and glittering, her reflection directly behind my own. Her dark beauty bewitches the glass while my face charms nothing at all. I don't like red, the color of anger, pain and fear, and my face looks bloodless beneath that sharp burst of color.* My girl, *my mother murmurs, watching my reflection with something not unlike pride.* My sweet, beautiful girl. *She runs her hands through the length of my hair and I swoon under her touch, my nerve endings jangling like bells. The band is tight, and my temples begin to throb uncomfortably. When I open my eyes, my face looks naked, exposed, and I reach one hand up to my head, wincing at the pressure.* It hurts, Mom, *I say softly, afraid to look at her face,*

her features changing even in the brief time it takes for the words to leave my lips. It kind of hurts.

Shut up, my mother hisses as she leans over me, ripping the hair band away and throwing it to the floor. Her hand is raised in the air, her face a mask of fury and bitterness, spittle spraying my cheek where the touch of her lips lingered only moments before. Her gaze flits over to the long banks of windows overlooking Central Park. I don't want the neighbors to hear.

The neighbors. It was always what other people thought that mattered most—the freshly highlighted hair, the Bulgari bangle, the "right" dress. It didn't matter what I did or didn't do, how many A's I had on my report card, whether or not I'd removed all the tangles from my hair that morning. There was no method to the madness, no telling what might set her off, and I lived with my bones shaking like ice rattling in a glass, never knowing when or where it would happen again, knowing only that these episodes were as inevitable as the rain that came to pelt the windows on hot summer nights.

FOUR

"SO, HOW LONG HAVE YOU BEEN HERE?"

I pull at a jagged hangnail and wonder what he's really asking. How long have I been here in New York? At Manhattan Prep? On planet Earth? Sensing my confusion, Julian smiles, his face turning bashful and rosy. Long spiky lashes frame his almond-shaped eyes, flecks of green and yellow dotting the irises. Is he good-looking? I'm not sure. Not conventionally. If he were walking down the street, would I turn and stare? Probably not. Still, there's something in his face, in the way he carries himself, that makes me want to move closer.

"I mean, here, at Prep." Julian's tone is serious, and I look down at my fingers splayed out on the Formica tabletop, my jagged, bitten nails.

"Since last year. I transferred from Nightingale." I shift my eyes over to the slice on the paper plate in front of me, the grease seeping into the paper in a blotchy stain. Even though my stomach is still growling noisily, the cheese, covered with round slices of pepperoni, looks almost diseased, and I have to force myself to pick it up and take a bite. I savor the feel of real food in my mouth, marveling at the fact that, counting my bagel this morning, this makes two meals in one day—a record of sorts.

"Would it be bad form to ask why?" Julian looks down at his own plate, at the remainder of the second slice that is now just a grease splotch and a few random shreds of cheese.

"Probably." I cover my mouth with one hand, wondering if I have any cheese or pepperoni stuck in my teeth. "Well," I say, swallowing hard, "unless you'd like to pony up your own reason for . . . umm . . . relocating."

"Not a chance." He laughs, eyes narrowing slightly as he takes a swig of Dr Pepper. His expression clouds momentarily, and he looks down at the table, nervously tapping the Formica with his fingers before looking up again, the echoes of pain glimmering in his eyes contrasting sharply with his crooked smile. "Maybe when I know you better."

I nod, looking down at my own hands, the fingers pale and cold as minnows. When I was seven, my grandfather taught me to fish upstate in the Adirondacks at a cabin my grandparents rented every summer on Lake Clear. I remember the shy silver trout darting through the cold muddy water, the tuna sandwiches my grandmother packed for us, the sun falling gently on my face, upturned and seeking the light.

"So will I?" he asks.

I blink rapidly, trying not to look stupid. I know it's not normal to drift off into my own head in the middle of a conversation, but sometimes I can't help it. Memories float in at the weirdest times, swirling around me and pulling me ever closer.

"Will you what?"

I am aware suddenly of my own heart, how it pumps along unceasingly in my chest, the muscle squeezing hard.

"Get to know you better." He shoots me a sly smile, and his question hangs in the air; flirtatious, insolent, irresistible. My lips part, my mouth opened in a wide O. Thoughts whiz by, each one moving too fast for me to grab on to any one of them. I know I am supposed to flirt back, to say something witty and charming, but I am tongue-tied, speechless.

What do I say, what do I SAY?

I smile weakly, waiting for the moment to pass. Julian's gaze is locked on my face, his eyes missing nothing. He shifts in his seat, coughing into one hand. His chest sounds full, raspy, like he's getting over a cold.

"So, what do I really need to know about this place besides the fact that everyone seems to have a giant stick up their ass? Present company excluded, of course." Julian changes the subject, and just like that, the tension is defused, the spell broken.

"Oh, naturally," I say, pushing my plate away with one hand. Without missing a beat, Julian picks up my half-eaten slice and destroys it in two bites, chewing noisily. My mouth falls open. It's only a piece of cold pizza, but as far as I'm concerned, the gesture is shockingly intimate—it's as if he's reached across the table and placed my whole hand into the warm cavern of his mouth.

"See those girls over there?" I point through the window at Elizabeth Harris and Alexa Forte, two of the reigning salad queens. They sit on the school steps, cans of Diet Pepsi tucked between their knees, their lips moving frantically. They are everything I'm supposed to be and have failed miserably at becoming—tanned, glossy socialites in training. Their smiles are even and white, their pastel cardigans thrown over slim shoulders. They are living the life that my mother raised me to want, the life I've rejected with my nighttime activities, the multiple holes in my ears and heavy black boots. I swallow hard before continuing as Alexa Forte looks up and meets my eyes, her look burning through the glass.

"They are harbingers of evil and definitely not to be trusted. Plus, they smell like a combination of dusty gardenias, grape Pop Rocks and rancid tan accelerator, so, you know, be warned."

"Warning duly noted." Julian grins, his lips parting to reveal a crooked front incisor. "Anything else?"

"Yeah." I take a deep breath and practically force the words out as Alexa slides a pair of Ray-Bans over her eyes and looks away. "I'm sort of a freak here, so if you want any kind of social life, we probably shouldn't make this a regular thing." I look at the tabletop so I don't have to see the expression on his face, which I'm sure is an ego-flattening combination of pity and fear.

"I happen to like freaks. Besides, social lives are overrated," Julian says after a beat. I look up as he shrugs, the sinew in his lanky arms clearly visible.

"Ha." My laughter comes out as a snort. "Not in my world."

"What world is that?" Julian asks. Unlike most other people, he sounds like he actually wants to know. His fingers are busily shredding a napkin into confetti as he waits for me to speak. I like his hands, the steady, confident weight of them.

"I work over at Tunnel, and sometimes at a few other clubs too. The World. Save the Robots."

Save the Robots is an after-hours spot in the East Village that doesn't open until four a.m. There is nothing more disorienting or exhilarating than walking into its smoky rooms in the dead of night and exiting hours later into the harsh glare of morning sunlight.

Julian looks up at me incredulously. "There's really a club called Save the Robots? Are there actual robots in attendance?"

"Well, club kids can certainly snort lines of coke with robot-like precision."

There is a moment of silence, and I look away, feeling suddenly like I've said too much. When you mention drugs to people who obviously don't do them, there's always this moment of judgment. It's like most people are capable of picturing drug use only as an ABC Afterschool Special cliché, where the heroine "flirts" with pot or booze, then realizes the error of her ways and goes to rehab, where she is miraculously cured. These hour-long specials usually end with an annoying freeze-frame of the heroine jumping up in the air to show her newfound freedom—but it just makes her look completely psychotic. It goes without saying that shows like these generally make me want to stab myself in the eye with a pencil. But Julian doesn't seem judgmental, just a little sad.

"Aren't our teenage years supposed to be spent being as lazy as possible, stuffing chips in our faces and playing Nintendo?"

Julian smiles, showing that tooth, and runs his hand through his hair, fingers catching on the tangles at the bottom before he yanks them free.

"Well, I guess there is *that*." I laugh nervously, hoping I don't still look like a bloated, hungover corpse. "But it's not really work, you know? I basically just throw parties, and sometimes work the door of the basement."

"The basement?" He looks at me quizzically.

"The club's split up into a few different rooms," I explain, my face flushing. "There's the main dance floor, the Chandelier Room, and on the bottom floor is—"

"The basement," he finishes with a grin. "Makes total sense. And I suppose the Chandelier Room is full of . . . chandeliers?"

"Bingo."

"So, you are the cruel and evil force who decides who gets in?"

I nod. "Basically. It's not that big of a deal, though."

I spew the words out quickly, like I'm trying to rid myself of them as fast as I can. I don't know what I hate more, listening to most people's petty bullshit or talking about myself. It feels illicit, dirty, like bragging, my entire body ballooning to the size of the Empire State Building.

"Would I make the cut?" he asks, testing me.

"Hmm . . ." I tilt my head and pretend to scrutinize him, taking in the dirty black jeans, the ripped Converse sneakers on his feet, the Ramones T-shirt and his black leather jacket slung over the back of his chair. "For you, I *might* make an exception," I say, shoving my straw down to the bottom of the plastic cup and breaking up the ice. "Maybe."

A wave of giddiness runs through me, and I'm aware for the first time how *normal* this all is, how simple it is to talk to him. I'm sitting with a boy I like in a pizza parlor, just like any other girl in the world, my problems receding into the distance with every shy, awkward glance. I want to stay here for the duration, cozy in this warm room, Julian's foot accidentally bumping against mine under the table, my belly full and happy. *Normal.*

Julian brings one hand to his chest like he's just been shot, feigning injury, his eyes closing momentarily. As I watch him, I'm aware that for the first time since I came to Manhattan Prep, I'm not impatient for the day to end. For this one small moment, I'm content to stay right where I am, sheltered by the windows beginning to fog over with moisture and heat, the scent of meat and cheese hanging heavily in the air, sitting alongside a boy I barely know.

FIVE

I AM PENCILING BLACK LINES around my eyes with a fat stick of kohl when Giovanni walks through the door, the buckles on his boots jangling noisily. Giovanni thinks that everything in the world belongs to him—my apartment included—and treats it as such. Not that I mind.

"You are behind schedule," Giovanni remarks in veiled annoyance, one hand on his hip, a cascade of curls framing his round face. Perpetually waging a battle with those last five pounds, Giovanni routinely disparages his slight double chin while demolishing an entire package of Oreos. I lean into the silver glass, covering the dark circles beneath my eyes, sweeping a brush loaded with translucent powder over my skin, the hairs tickling my cheeks. A gunmetal gray dress slithers from the back of the couch to the floor, where it pools on the dark wood. My living room walls are painted a deep Chinese red, and at night, I love the warm pulse of color. But in the unforgiving light of day, it's sometimes like being trapped in an abattoir, the scent of death hanging in the air like a cloud of noxious heavy perfume.

"How many times have I told you, no powder under the eyes? It's aging!" Giovanni pulls the brush from my fist and drops it onto my vanity table with a satisfying *thwack,* his sudden movement knocking my French textbook to the floor. The girl on the cover is seated at a sidewalk café and grins like a lunatic, a yellow beret placed jauntily on top of her head. I realize that I've forgotten to do my French homework yet again for the fifth day in a row, and wonder if it's still even possible to pass now, given that I never speak in class and that I've practically failed the last three tests. Even though I knocked all the rest of my homework out hours ago, I seem to forget about French on a daily basis. Maybe because it's so boring—not to mention the fact that as skills go, it currently ranks somewhere between "obsolete" and "useless."

"Oh my God," I drawl, staring at Giovanni's face in the mirror. I begin to smile in spite of my annoyance. "I'm only seventeen! How old could I *possibly* look?"

"Every minute counts, honey," he snaps with a flick of his fingers. "Now shove over and let me do my job." I dutifully make room on the white velvet bench I've had since I was ten. Giovanni sits down and picks up a tissue, saturating it with makeup remover, and wipes away the dark lines surrounding the wide eyes I think are my best feature. Right now they just look tired. The silver bracelets on Giovanni's wrists tinkle as he moves, and I shut my eyes at the comforting feel of his hands on my skin. Tonight he is wearing a black Stephen

Sprouse jacket covered in multicolored sequins that shines like an electric bulb, and black pants of his own design with a line of metal grommets climbing up one leg. His hair is impeccably coiffed, and his skin glows smooth and lineless in the light from the red lantern hanging overhead, making him look younger than his nineteen years.

I met Giovanni a year ago when I was first starting out in the scene, when I was still living with my mother. I had just begun working the ropes of the Tunnel basement, and already I'd become an expert at sizing up the crowd, my face a mask, eyes sweeping impassively over the bodies gathered in front of the velvet rope, their hungry gaze searching for signs of recognition or empathy. I liked the club kids who pushed through from the back of the line, the flurry of their double-cheeked kisses as they placed their hands on my shoulders and leaned in, their pupils spinning like disco balls. There was Mitzi, with her pink-and-black teapot hat and black ball gown. Roger in an aluminum space suit, waving his silver-clad hand jauntily as he stepped through the ropes. Maia in a dress of electric blue so bright that it seemed to pulsate under the lights, her face painted blue to match. Manny, in his signature white jumpsuit, a pair of gossamer wings strapped to his back. I liked the way I was envied by the other girls in the scene, how they depended on me to get in, for drink tickets, for recognition. When they looked at me, eyes shining with covetousness, it was the only time in my life I could remember feeling important.

Giovanni was known around the club scene for three things: his gift for fashion, and his appetite for cocaine and boys—not necessarily in that order. We bonded over getting high. It was one of those nights that never seem to end, when the blackness stretches on forever, the sun a distant memory hiding in the murky sky, stars like spilled glitter. I was in the VIP room at The World, seated on a long velvet bench, when Giovanni sat down next to me, tossing his curls and flashing me a smile. In the rose light he resembled a Spanish prince stranded on foreign soil. Weeks later when I told him as much, he shrieked in horror, tossing a pillow at my head for good measure. "I'm Puerto Rican! Not some fucking Spaniard!"

But that night all I knew was that he was beautiful, and that, for whatever reason, he had chosen me.

"I know you, you know." Giovanni leered, leaning into me slightly, the heat from his body seeping into the space between us.

"Oh yeah?" I mused, eyebrow raised. I was bored, but not bored enough to have to sustain mindless conversation.

"You're Caitlin," Giovanni said, taking a sip of what looked and smelled like a rum and Coke. "I'm Giovanni." He held out a hand bejeweled with silver rings, his fingers closing around mine. "I'd like to dress you."

"You know, I'm perfectly capable of dressing myself," I said with a smile, dropping his hand and pointing to my outfit.

Giovanni took in the black unitard, the black-and-white polka-dotted Betsey Johnson crinoline skirt that puffed around my waist like a cloud, the wide black elastic belt cinching my waist, and the high-heeled patent-leather booties on my feet with a disparaging glance, his mouth curled into a grimace. "Not in my opinion," he answered, his lips relaxing into a grin. "Besides," he said with a wave of his hand, "I've decided we should be best friends."

My mouth fell open, my eyes bulging from their sockets. Was he drunk? (Definitely, I would learn later on.) High? Why else would anyone make that kind of a reckless declaration, flay themselves open, exposing a tender pink belly, a rapidly beating heart? This kind of effusiveness was unheard of in clubland, especially where I was concerned. People liked me in that saccharine, artificial way you pretend to like visiting relatives or distant acquaintances, but I never let anyone get too close. Close was scary and unpredictable. Close was a racing pulse, hiding under the bed while praying for footsteps to recede. Most of all, closeness, I knew, meant eventually disappointing the people you loved best. My mother, who always wanted a different daughter. Even Sara, who, as much as she loves me, cannot understand why I do the things I do, why the club has become such a huge part of my life. Without missing a beat, Giovanni reached into the interior pocket of his jacket, producing two white pills that glowed like moon rocks in the palm of his hand.

"Want a hit of X?"

I hesitated, but only for a moment before I popped the capsule into my mouth, picturing the white powder coating my stomach, my intestines, the very tissues of my body. Before that night, I had done coke a few times, and basically drank my weight in booze, but this was the first time I'd tried anything that came in a pill, the first time I'd surrendered to what the universe offered me, hands outstretched. As the X made its long, arduous journey down my throat, I shivered once hard, my shoulders shaking as the capsule dropped into my stomach.

Thirty minutes later, the drug began its slow seep into my bloodstream, my limbs loose and pliant. A wave of nausea bent me in two, sudden light flashing behind closed eyes. I raced to the bathroom and sank to my knees, one hand on the cold white porcelain of the toilet, shoulders hunched. I returned to the VIP room, sheepish and spacey. As soon as I sat back down, Giovanni grabbed one of my hands and began tracing designs on my palm with his long, pointed pinky nail. From a faraway distance, looking down at myself, I knew that it was madness, letting someone I didn't even know touch me, sit this close, take my hand in his own and cradle my flesh as if it were a newly born child. I braced myself for the familiar feeling of panic, that need to get up and run until the breath came ragged in my chest, until I was light once more and clear of all attachment. Maybe it was the drugs racing through my body, lighting up my limbs like a pinball machine. Maybe it was Giovanni himself, his soft chuckle in my ear, the purr of his voice telling me, *Slow down. Stay for a while* and *stay with me*. So for once I did.

"Did you puke?" he murmured with a soft giggle.

"Well, yeah," I answered, grabbing his rum and Coke and taking a swig, the frothy bubbles clearing the scum and bitterness from my mouth. My head warm and light, as if it just might uncork itself from my neck and float away. "But you haven't. Why is that?"

"Honey," Giovanni said, smiling, "I'm a professional."

I blink rapidly, jolting myself back into the present. A thick layer of mascara now coats my lashes, and I stare at the girl reflected in the glass, her dark eyes shadowed and mysterious, a beauty mark penciled on her right cheek, her lips coated in a film as shiny and red as plastic.

"Let's get you dressed, dollface." Giovanni steps back to survey his work, squinting critically at my freshly painted face before throwing the eyeliner pencil down and wiping his hands on a tissue. I stand up and pull my dress over my head, kicking my tights off until I am standing there in my bra and underpants, my skin rising into goose bumps. I don't know much about Giovanni's daytime world—he told me once that he's studying fashion design at the Fashion Institute of Technology or, as he puts it, Fags in Training, but he never talks about school or assignments, or has to wake up for anything during the day, so I highly doubt it's the truth. Even I, pathetic excuse for a student that I am, have to adhere to deadlines every so often. All I really know about Giovanni is that he lives in a one-bedroom apartment in Chelsea with four slightly psychotic drag queens who sometimes steal the clothing he makes, selling it to secondhand stores in the East Village. I don't ask questions, just let him crash when he needs to. In this way, Giovanni and I understand each other without ever exchanging a word. Our lives exist for each other only at night, when the air is charged with shadows. But even with all I don't know about him, Giovanni is my closest friend in the scene, and for some strange reason, I trust him. Maybe it's because of our nightly ritual of satin and lace, the glittering pins placed next to my flesh, points sharp enough to draw blood.

Giovanni watches over me, protective and paternal without being overbearing. Each night he turns me gently under his hands, his fingers light on my waist. For Giovanni, every night is a blank slate, a chance to begin again.

Giovanni pulls a mass of white tulle from his bulging overnight bag and begins carefully draping it around and across my body, his mouth full of pins that glint in the light. I think of piranhas, of reptiles with sharp teeth as the frothy material swirls around me, pulling me under.

SIX

THREE A.M., the room spinning under the flashing colored lights, tulle banked like a snowdrift behind me, making it impossible to sit down. If midnight is the witching hour, three a.m. is the dark, fathomless abyss of the soul. If I were home by myself right now, I'd probably be completely freaked out, the clock ticking loudly in my ear, every rumble of the pipes or creak in the floor making me jump with uneasiness and fear. A pile of unopened textbooks heaped on the bed, a makeshift barricade. The covers pulled over my head and the television tuned to a late-night talk show, the murmur of voices providing the illusion that I am not alone. But instead I'm on top of a large speaker on the main dance floor, hands raised over my head, the sounds of Soul II Soul pumping through the air. The bass hits me squarely in the solar plexus, making my entire body vibrate. *Keep on movin', keep on movin', don't stop, no . . .* It's my favorite part of the night, when I can just lose myself in the melody streaming through the speakers like hot honey, reality off in the distance, hazy as a half-forgotten dream.

The first time I went to a club, I was a few months shy of sixteen and still living at home. I scuffed my feet against the pavement outside Tunnel on a warm spring night, the kind where everything seems full of possibility, buds hanging in the trees like earrings. Sara had gotten an invite for a party in the Chandelier Room from some senior she knew whose brother went to NYU—freshmen playing at being promoters for a night. Sara sighed loudly as the doorman's eyes passed over our ripped jeans and black coats, his passive gaze gliding past the invite she held above her head like a flag. We went because we'd never been to a club before, because we were bored. Mostly we went because Sara thought it was a good idea, which was pretty much the reason I did anything in those days.

Earlier in the afternoon, we'd ridden the train down to Times Square, swaying as the car rocked us from side to side, grunting occasionally as we fell against the tangle of arms and legs that surrounded us. Forty-Second Street was a fever dream, the smell of roasting nuts mixed with the wail of sirens as an ambulance hurried down the street, the neon façades of XXX theaters and strip clubs floating against the sky. We'd just started to wear black, to line our eyes in broad swaths of charcoal. Sara paused momentarily, kicking her new motorcycle boots against the curb to dirty them, to break them in. I'd stopped wearing the clothes my mother bought me at Nieman Marcus, leaving them in my closet with the tags still on. I'd begun to rip my T-shirts, spray paint my boots, to shop in thrift stores for long skirts and vintage leather jackets. Sara's mother never cared about what she wore, but my mother's

45

expression got tighter and tighter each time she looked at me, a wire coiling beneath the perfect bones of her face. Surface tension.

A man near the subway entrance had set up a metal table littered with stuffed animals, and as we passed, he yelled out something incomprehensible, holding a blue dinosaur triumphantly above his head. Pimps strolled along the pavement, their pastel suits bright as candy. Hookers stood on street corners, their taut abdomens bare, legs extending from miniskirts so tiny, they were more like bandages stanching a wound, their eyes shadowed and hard.

Sara grabbed my arm, pulling me into a store with a bright yellow awning that read KODAK: PHOTOS, IDS, SOUVENIRS. We walked past rows of I ❤ NY T-shirts, miniature plastic models of the Statue of Liberty, the Empire State Building, plastic globes that imprisoned the deco opulence of the Chrysler Building, its metal frame surrounded by flakes of falling snow. A glass counter at the back of the store held various kinds of identification: driver's licenses and state IDs. The rows of identically laminated smiles looked back at me smugly, as if they could somehow foretell my future, as if they knew what might happen next.

"Why do we need IDs anyway?" I asked, looking around the store as a burly guy dressed in a blue Adidas tracksuit came striding toward us.

"In case we get carded," Sara mumbled under her breath. "Dumbo."

Sara was terrified of getting carded. I was more terrified of being humiliated in public, which is why I went along with the whole thing in the first place.

Thirty minutes and one trip to the photo booth later, where we tried to look both older and serious behind a yellow plastic curtain as the camera clicked and whirled, we held in our grasp the IDs, still warm from the lamination machine, IDs that said we were, laughably, twenty-one years old.

"Even if we DO get carded," I pointed out as we made our way back toward the subway, "no one will ever believe we're twenty-one. Not in a million years."

"Look." Sara pushed her mop of blond curls away from her face in exasperation. "Think of this as insurance." She held her ID out in front of her for emphasis. "We'll probably never even have to take them out of our wallets."

Scarily enough, she was right.

That night when the bouncer finally lifted the velvet ropes high, the door girl, her nose in a clipboard, barely looked up as we approached the entrance, giving us a cursory glance as she plucked the invite from Sara's fingers. Suddenly, we were inside, and the pounding beat of the music rushed through me, starting at the soles of my feet and tingling up the length of my body. All around us were kids our own age, some a bit older, silver glitter on their faces and exposed limbs, bright red lips, dressed in clothing that seemed to function more as a costume than anything else. There was a feeling in the air, a kind of adrenaline that went beyond the insistent beat of the music driving me onward, pulling me deeper inside. I moved as if in a trance, needing to get to the core of it.

Three of the most beautiful women I'd ever seen passed by, their bodies swaying gently beneath tight black dresses. Drag queens, I knew immediately, the most gorgeous of illusions. I watched them, transfixed by their delicate, feline features as they pushed through the crowd, their skin shining under the colored lights, their long-limbed bodies that seemed so much more well developed than my own achingly flat chest. The music bubbled, screams of jubilation rising from the dance floor as the DJ segued into the next track. I was spellbound, glued to the floor. This was a world that bloomed at night like a black orchid, its petals unfurling luxuriously, a place that had nothing to do with the tight smiles and expectations I'd left behind on the Upper East Side. If this was tumbling down the rabbit hole, my senses stunned with blinking neon, then I wanted to keep falling at breakneck speed, never hitting bottom.

A guy ran by, a pacifier hung around his neck like a whistle, his bare legs exposed in short, billowing bloomers, black suspenders crossing his bare chest. He pushed through the crowds as if the room was his, as if he belonged there, his child-like limbs belying his real age, which must have been around nineteen or twenty. As he moved, the pointy nub of his elbow dug into my side, and I yelped in pain. He turned around, his impish, quizzical face opening, a penciled black star outlining one eye, his hands full of drink tickets. He ripped off a sheet of ten or fifteen and held them out.

"Here," he said with a grin. "I'm Sebastian. Come and hang out for a while."

He nodded toward the set of red ropes just off the bar up

ahead, a series of large crystal chandeliers dripping from the ceiling like melting icicles. I was stunned, mouth open. No one had ever picked me out of a crowd before. As if I were special. As if I could somehow belong.

Once we'd made it inside, the objective of the evening was pretty much over—at least for Sara, who smiled thinly, yawning into one hand. I couldn't have been less tired. After Sebastian had dragged me out on the dance floor a few times, where I moved stiffly, a marionette with wooden limbs, we made our way back to the couch. He refilled our plastic cups of champagne, but I wasn't drunk. My blood frothed and bubbled with excitement, the possibility of a new world unfurling before me like a magic carpet. The room spun with chatter, music and laughter, and I wanted to be a part of it, to belong here and nowhere else. The pain, the mix of regret and determination in my father's eyes as he walked out of our apartment for the last time, my mother's bottomless rage: I wanted to leave it all behind me, the past as dry and useless as dust.

Sebastian leaned in to me and said, under his breath, "You should come to my next party—but only if you leave your boring friend at home." One blue eye closed slowly in a wink, his mouth ruby red. And at that moment, my fate was sealed.

Giovanni appears below me, shaking his fist in the air to get my attention, and climbs up onto the speaker, spilling half of his whiskey sour on my white patent-leather boots in the process. There was an open bar earlier in the night, and Giovanni has clearly taken full advantage—he looks as though the slightest breeze will send him toppling off of the speaker and into the teeming crowd below—and I grab on to his wrist, steadying his movements. I take his drink and perch it near the edge of the speaker, then take his hands in mine and raise them above our heads. Our torsos touch, bodies grinding in time to the synth beat as New Order's "Bizarre Love Triangle" begins, eliciting a manic shout from the packed floor as sweat begins to run in rivulets down my sides. It's times like these when I feel at one with the world, part of the universe in a way I rarely, if ever, do during the daylight hours. I am connected to each person in this crowded, overheated room by an invisible gossamer rope, my chest tightening with happiness. I can see the sweat shining on the smooth skin of Giovanni's forehead, and I watch as he throws his head back, howling into the darkness. When he looks back at me, raising one eyebrow in a kind of dare, I mirror his ecstasy, tilting my head back until the lights blur my vision, and release a scream into the waiting night. My voice sounds free and loose above the pulse of the music, and when the song segues into Rob Base and DJ E-Z Rock's "It Takes Two," chaos erupts from the dance floor once again, and I feel like I could scream forever, Giovanni's palms sweating against mine, head filled with an electric current of joy, a happiness so pure, it feels almost like love itself.

Or maybe it's just the drugs.

We're not allowed to let the known dealers into the VIP room. Actually they're not supposed to make it past the entrance, but a few always sneak through the cracks. In exchange for admittance, they make sure to press a few rocks of blow, expertly wrapped in plastic, into the palm of my hand as they pass under the velvet rope. It's the way things work around here. I turn a blind eye in exchange for nose candy, and they get into the VIP room where the prime customers pack the tiny dance floor with their voracious appetites. Sometimes I give my stash away at the end of the night to Giovanni or a random club kid—there is no shortage of people who will covet such a windfall. Sometimes I do a line here and there, when I'm bored or super-tired. But lately my consumption is becoming more and more frequent, to the point that I've begun to associate going out itself *with* cocaine, the two intricately mixed together in a way I'm not sure I know how to separate anymore. I'd been clubbing for just a few weeks when Sebastian offered me a line in the bathroom, the white tiles smudged with the imprint of hundreds of pairs of shoes, a drag queen in front of the mirror pouting at her own reflection. Sebastian didn't even bother going into a stall, just pulled a small vial from his pocket, unscrewing the top and holding the vial beneath his nose, sniffing loudly.

"You want?" He held out the vial in my direction, leaning into the mirror to check his nostrils for traces of powder. I turned the vial over in my hand, terrified of his immediate dismissal if I refused. I stared down at the white powder that looked as innocuous as the fake snow that crusted our tree at Christmas. I uncapped the vial, holding the little black spoon under my nose, plugging the other side with my fingers the way I'd seen Sebastian do it. My hands felt clumsy, too big for my body, and I was panicked that I might drop the vial on the floor, spilling the presumably expensive contents all over the dirty tiles. When I inhaled sharply, there was a sensation like kindling suddenly catching fire, a fleet of Roman candles exploding behind my eyes in flashes of pink and blue. Jagged white lightning. Diamond dust. The unease I'd been feeling moments before evaporated completely, swept away on a tide of euphoria and well-being, and when I smiled at Sebastian in the mirror, my teeth seemed coated in silver, my tongue glittering with crushed glass. And ever since then, it's never been quite the same. The high is there, but only for a few moments before it slides away from me, moving elusively out of reach.

From my vantage point above the dance floor, I see Christoph out of the corner of my eye, his blond ponytail grazing the back of his neck. I raise my hand in a wave, wondering if he'll be pissed that I've abandoned the VIP ropes to dance on a speaker like some bridge-and-tunnel lunatic. He nods, raising his chin in my direction, his eyes catching the light. Even though I've been working here nearly nine months now, Christoph still scares me a little. I think he's around forty-five, though his chiseled, overly tanned features make him seem much older. Or maybe it's the fact that I'm seventeen, and forty-five just seems impossible on so many levels. Christoph was briefly married to Jemma Jill, the reigning queen of Studio 54, and when that relationship fizzled, he became the creative director at Tunnel and proceeded to turn a cavernous, run-down space in a pretty undesirable location into a playpen for club kids and lunatics.

"He totally has a crush on you!" Giovanni whispers excitedly.

"I know," I moan, rolling my eyes and grimacing uncomfortably. Ever since I'd shown up in his office last year wearing a black baseball hat with the word SEX running across the top in mirrored lettering, Christoph has, as they say, "taken an interest" in me. The hat was a gift from Giovanni, who bet me five bucks that I'd never wear it outside, much less to a meeting with Christoph. It may have been why he not only hired me on the spot, but also handed me five hundred dollars for "expenses," which I promptly shoved into the toe of my black combat boot and later spent at Betsey Johnson, sacks of glitter and sequin-studded tulle trailing in the street behind me.

Besides the fact that he scares the bejesus out of me, I can't decide how I feel about Christoph, except that he's way too old for me. Christoph is just so *intense* about everything: the club, money, his hair, me. Sometimes I catch him staring at my face as if he's contemplating a world takeover or a coup. He's just so *adult,* and that terrifies me more than I can say. I already live the life of a grown-up in so many ways—I cook for myself, do my own laundry—and these things are already a struggle without adding a fortysomething boyfriend to the mix. Plus, Sara would kill me if I even so much as contemplated a relationship with him. But still, I'm not always one to take my own—or anyone else's—advice. Even Sara's. There's something that thrills me whenever I catch a glimpse of his vaguely feline face, some sort of magnetic force that draws me closer. *Might be interesting,* my inner self whispers when I show up at his office each week to be paid in cash, my breath stopping in my chest when his eyes lock on to mine. *Might be trouble,* I usually hiss in response.

"You should go talk to him!" Giovanni screams over the music.

"You are full of bad ideas," I mumble, dropping to my knees and out of Christoph's line of vision. I sit on the edge of the speaker, my feet swinging out into space. Christoph keeps walking, but throws a look back at me over one shoulder, and I quickly close my eyes and pretend to be lost in the music, my eyelashes so heavy from Giovanni's overzealous mascara application that my lids feel like they're being pulled down by a pair of impatient hands.

Sebastian steps out of the crowd, an impish grin on his cherubic face, blue eyes sparkling under his signature bowl cut. Tonight he's wearing blue-and-white-striped knee socks, white satin shorts, his chest bare and smeared with white paint and glitter. His cheeks are sprinkled with penciled-on freckles, and he holds a brightly colored Jetsons lunch box in one hand. If the scene had a Pied Piper, Sebastian would be it, dropping ecstasy pills behind him as he skips away, club kids following in his wake like rats. Nobody really knows where he came from—somewhere in the Midwest, if you believe the rumors—but since arriving in New York he's pushed himself into the scene with the ferocity of a toddler throwing a temper tantrum. Still, as obnoxious as he is, it's hard to dislike him. Maybe it's because he was one of the first to invite me to breakfast after the clubs closed, stuffing our faces with eggs and bacon before we cabbed over to Save the Robots. We huddled together on the smoke-filled dance floor for hours before exiting, stunned by sunlight, into the early stillness of the day, the crowd parting around us as Sebastian, wearing only a jock strap and black boots, jubilantly skipped down the street. Creeping in to my mother's apartment, my breath catching in my throat until I closed my bedroom door behind me.

Sebastian is lucky enough to have the kind of charisma that would make most people follow him into a burning building without a second thought. Even though he's the force behind some of the most awful parties in the history of the club—like the time he filled the entire Tunnel basement with raspberry Jell-O, which was pretty unhygienic, to say the least—he's managed to charm his way to the very top level of party promoters in the city. I'm still not even really sure how he managed it. One minute he was this weird kid in diaper, strutting through the club blowing a whistle he wore on a string around his neck, and the next he was hanging out with the crème de la crème of Manhattan nightlife, staging three-legged drag queen races accompanied by bowls of ecstasy punch, and turning busboys and random clubgoers into superstars.

I have a strange allegiance to Sebastian, even though I don't completely trust him. I've seen him destroy some defenseless bridge-and-tunnel club kid wannabe with a few carefully chosen put-downs, a rolled eye, or, worse yet, complete ambivalence. After all, there's nothing worse than being ignored.

"What are you doing up there with that fat Puerto Rican queen?" Sebastian screams, one hand on his hip, his eyes wide under the makeup.

The animosity between Giovanni and Sebastian is long standing, and no one's sure exactly how it started, but it's safe to say that they despise each other. Someone told me that Sebastian stole Giovanni's last serious boyfriend, Hector, a design student from Parsons, and then dumped him un-ceremoniously in the basement before eighty-sixing him completely from the club, effectively breaking his heart and forever earning Giovanni's hatred. The real story, like every-thing else in the world, is probably a little more complicated.

"I'm not trying to hear that," Giovanni mutters, pulling a compact from his pocket and inspecting his face, ignoring Se-bastian as he shines the mirror on his skin and purses his lips, enthralled by his own reflection.

"Play nice," I say sweetly, a warning just below the surface of my voice. These two have been known to come to blows if they get agitated enough, and I am not in the mood to pull them off of each other if things get too heated. Sebastian moves closer to the speakers, and I lean down so that I can hear him over a break in the music.

"Well, I just came *over* here, Cat, to ask if you wanted to be on the invite for this outlaw party I'm throwing next week. You see, we're going to get this giant truck, and pack as many club kids as we can on it, along with huge speakers and a DJ, then drive around Lower Manhattan . . ."

Did I mention that Sebastian often has the worst ideas ever?

"Yeah, count me in," I say casually, trying to act like it's no big deal to be included on an invite with Sebastian, when in reality it's a position that any one of the nameless club kids trailing behind him would beat each other to death with a pair of stilettos for. Maybe he's choosing to include me just to piss off Giovanni, or maybe he's high. Whatever the reason, there's no way I'm going to say no.

Sebastian beams so hard that I can almost feel the heat radiating off his body. "Fabulous!" he screams, throwing his lunch box over one shoulder and stalking off across the floor, the posse of kids behind him all jockeying for position, pushing each other to try to get closer to his diminutive frame.

"Well, little Miss Mover-and-Shaker," Giovanni says lightly, "I hate to be a party pooper, but don't you have school in a few hours? Or are you ditching . . . *again*?"

Ugh. School. Now that he's invoked it, the word hangs between us like a threat. Then I remember Julian, and a warm feeling begins to grow in the pit of my stomach, gathering strength as the embers ignite. Maybe tomorrow won't be so bad. And after all, it is, or was, Monday, and Monday nights usually end early anyway, so I wouldn't be considered *completely* lame for going home now . . .

"Yeah, you're right," I say with a sigh. "I really should go home."

"Home?" A sardonic smile coats Giovanni's face. "Where's *that*?"

Underneath the sarcasm, I can see the pain in Giovanni's eyes, the way they mist over and look away from me, coated with a film of tears so delicate and subtle that most people wouldn't even notice. My stomach begins to ache a little because I know exactly what he means.

"Right here," I say, leaning in and whispering the words in his ear. "With me."

"Love you, girl," he says, reaching over and squeezing my hand tightly, his face uncharacteristically naked beneath the pressed powder dusting his brown skin. I look down at the floor, afraid to meet the sincerity in his eyes. I never know what to do when I'm confronted by a show of real emotion. It's like some necessary part of me was turned off long ago and a numbness has slowly crept into my veins, moving through my blood like a silent killer and turning it to ice.

As if on cue, a song by Information Society begins blaring out onto the dance floor, and Giovanni grabs my arm as the insistent beat makes the speaker throb below our feet. Giovanni hates Information Society, along with all other mainstream bands he refers to as "mall music."

"OK, now we really *are* leaving."

* * * *

SOMETIMES, MY MOTHER SPENDS *a whole day with me. A "girls' day out," she calls it. On these days, I am in love with the red velvet interior of the Russian Tea Room, the gilded paintings on the walls, in love with my mother, who throws her blond mink coat over the back of her chair and orders me a Shirley Temple with a wave of her hand. I am fascinated by the gleam of the crystal, the ginger ale somehow made fancier by the bloodred cherry floating blindly in its depths. Her elegant hands grasp the silver serving boat of sour cream, placing a graceful dollop beside her caviar blini. My own plate holds chicken Kiev, and I watch openmouthed as the waiter pierces the flesh with a knife, releasing a stream of golden butter that pools along the edges of the fine china. There are trips to Rumplemayer's after ice-skating lessons at Rockefeller Center, the gaggle of brightly colored, googly-eyed stuffed animals and year-round Christmas lights flashing brightly overhead as my spoon plumbs the depths of a hot fudge sundae. My fingers are sticky, and I wipe them frantically against my tights when she's not looking, afraid even then of my constant imperfection.*

My mother's eyes flicker with approval as I blot my mouth on a napkin, leaving behind the dark, immutable stain of a kiss.

SEVEN

IT'S WAY TOO EARLY to be awake, and all through history class and a discussion of the Vietnam War, my eyes struggle to stay open even though Mr. Cass is showing a film featuring images so horrific and violent that when my eyes do flutter open, I'm greeted by the sight of a wailing, naked Vietnamese boy, his flesh streaked with dirt. Bodies are piled behind him, the flesh charred, unrecognizable, a small hut in the distance reduced to a plume of smoke. I close my eyes, letting the blackness wash it all away. When I open them again, a soldier is crossing a burned-out field, a human head held in one hand by a shock of black hair, its mouth distended in a silent scream.

I raise my hand and ask for the bathroom pass, and as I stand up, I realize that I'm shaking. My organs are vibrating beneath my skin, and there is a rolling in the pit of my stomach. I walk quickly to the girls' bathroom hoping that no one's inside, and push the door open.

The pink tiles sparkle in the early morning sunlight coming through the bank of frosted windows at the far end of the room, and a tap drips insistently, the sound comforting in its repetitiveness. I walk to the sink and turn the cold water on full blast, place my wrists under the rushing stream and try to breathe deeply. It's a good thing I didn't stop for a bagel this morning, because it would already be strewn all over the spotless floor, mushy and unrecognizable.

I bend down, cupping my hands together and filling them with water, slurping noisily as I drink. I stand up and look in the mirror, wiping my mouth with the back of one hand as the bathroom door swings open and Alexa Forte enters the room, her blond, waist-length hair wrapped around her body like a cashmere sweater. At the sight of me she stops dead, her boots clicking on the tile, her green eyes surveying my face in the mirror. She stands immobile only for a moment before walking over to the stalls, locking the door behind her with the sharp sound of metal kissing metal. I know I should probably leave, but I still feel awful, my stomach uneasy, my feet riveted to the floor. From inside the stall I can hear the sound of retching, and I wonder if my queasiness isn't a preview of several horrible sick days to come. Worried, I put a hand to my forehead, but the skin is cool, if slightly clammy. The flushing of the toilet interrupts my thoughts, obliterating them in a ferocious rush. When Alexa exits the stall, she seems composed, business as usual, as she approaches the sink and turns on the tap, lathering her hands vigorously, steam obscuring her face in the glass.

"Ms. Sykes brought doughnuts today. I fucking hate doughnuts." She switches the tap to cold, cupping the water in one hand and rinsing her mouth out, spitting delicately into the sink.

I could explain Alexa Forte in detail, but I probably don't need to. There's an Alexa Forte at every school and they're all the same. Long glossy hair, perfect skin, bodies that are effortlessly thin and curvy, or so I'd thought. My mother absolutely adores Alexa—along with everyone else on the island of Manhattan—and we had the misfortune of living down the block from her family for three whole years. Alexa was basically my mother's image of what an Upper East Side debutante should be, and for a few years I was constantly compared with her. "Why can't you be more like that Forte girl?" my mother would sigh in exasperation, her eyes sliding over my tattered black skirt, striped tights and black platform boots before they glazed over entirely. That was before Alexa was caught at her last school in the supply room making out with her physics teacher, a recent Columbia grad rumored to be pretty easy on the eyes. Her parents promptly freaked and sent her here, hoping that a transfer would help to expunge the incident from her record or at the very least make it less noticeable—or so I've heard. Lost in my own thoughts, I scramble for something to say before Alexa becomes disgusted with my muteness and flees.

"So why eat them?" Somehow, miraculously, I've found my voice. It sounds tinny and strange bouncing off the tiles, reverberating in the small room.

Alexa wipes the steam from the mirror with one hand and regards her face in the glass, wiping the corner of her heavily glossed mouth with one pinky.

"Why do you do anything that's bad for you?" she deadpans, her eyes moving over my face, reading me. "You're Caitlin."

I nod wordlessly and turn back to the mirror, gathering my hair in a low ponytail and securing it with an elastic band. She doesn't introduce herself. Why would she? Everyone knows who she is.

"I hear you hang out downtown a lot."

"I guess," I mumble. "I mean, I live there now, so . . ." I have no idea what to say next. I don't like Alexa Forte, and she's never treated me even vaguely like a human being since I transferred here, but I'm slightly freaked out over the fact that she is not only talking to me, but trusting me with her eating disorder, as I'm already assuming this isn't the first time her stomach has spontaneously rejected a selection of baked goods. The question is, why?

"I've never been below Fourteenth Street." Alexa pulls a brush from her monogrammed Louis Vuitton shoulder bag and begins to brush her blond mane with long, careful strokes. "My parents say it's dangerous down there." She rolls her eyes apologetically, the whites shining in the glass.

"Not if you know where you're going," I answer. "I could take you sometime—if you want. We could go shopping or something." Anxiety rises in my chest, cutting off my breath, my hands tingling with numbness. *Shopping?* Had I gone temporarily insane? I could no more see Alexa Forte downtown, lost among the Goth freaks, club kids and punk rockers, than I could see myself running away and joining the circus.

Alexa reaches into her purse and pulls out a pen. "What's your number?" As I stammer my digits at her, I wonder what the hell I'm doing. In what universe could Alexa Forte and I possibly hang out? Maybe I should've stayed home sick today . . .

"I'd say talk to me at lunch"—Alexa throws the pen back into her bag, my number written in black ink on the inside of her wrist—"but I think we both know that's not going to happen."

Right. I'm still a freak. The lowest freak on the totem pole in a school of total freaks. Just in case there was any confusion.

Alexa smiles regretfully, her cheeks rosy and flushed, and I find myself marveling that this is the same girl who just willfully emptied the contents of her stomach into the toilet moments ago. She's not as perfect as she seems. So what? *So, this might be interesting,* I tell myself, *as long as I don't take it too seriously.* Without another word or a backward glance, Alexa heads for the door, her hair swinging behind her.

I take a deep breath and look at myself in the mirror, my stomach quieted now, face still pale beneath my bangs. I have my mother's face, her pointed jaw, the same widely spaced eyes that make me look vacant as a porcelain doll, skin the yellowish hue of slightly curdled cream. "Who are you?" I whisper at my reflection, my voice hushed as if I am kneeling in church, the silence deep and viscous. I lean in to the mirror, one hand on the glass as I search my face for some kind of answer. The water drips mindlessly from the tap, and I hear my mother's voice in my head, that low, seductive purr I know so well.

I made you. You belong to me.

I flick my eyes away from my reflection, stomach aching, wipe my hands on a paper towel and head back to class.

EIGHT

"SHE DID *WHAT*?"

Sara's white curls bounce in the afternoon breeze, and she kicks her booted foot repeatedly on the iron leg of the bench we're sitting on outside of Gus's Deli, across the street from Nightingale. Sara has a free lunch period today, and since this happens so rarely in her ridiculously overcommitted life, I've walked over to meet her. Part of me wonders if Julian is sitting on the steps outside our school, a slab of pizza in one hand, a Coke in the other, if he even thought about me at all once the bell rang. When I passed him in the hall this morning, he looked down at the floor in the very definition of the word *awkward*, his eyes sliding away from my face, a small smile of recognition twisting the corners of his mouth. Needless to say, I did not take this as the most encouraging sign in the universe, so I'm glad to get out for a while and avoid any potential lunchtime weirdness. I don't know what I expected. I didn't exactly think Julian would throw me to the floor and start whispering declarations of love in my ear or anything, but I didn't bank on complete and total nothingness, either. My chest feels heavy, disappointment filling my throat, the taste of lemon juice mixed with dirt.

Sara is picking at one of her many bizarre salad bar creations—a heap of lettuce studded with mandarin oranges, tuna fish, almonds and black olives. The result makes it seem like she cruises the salad bar blindfolded. Just the smell makes my stomach turn over again, and I take a sip from the cup of black coffee in my hand, the bitterness steadying my nerves, caffeine shooting through me like lightning. It would be amazing if I could somehow get through the day without chemicals, caffeine included, but with the amount of sleep I get—or don't get—it's not even close to an option. I try to remember what it was like to wake up excited for the day to begin, to need nothing but my own momentum to propel me from one activity to another, but every time I close my eyes and search for that feeling, I come up blank.

"It was definitely weird," I say, placing the hot cup between my thighs to warm them.

The wind is rocking through the trees above us like it means business, and I almost can't wait for the first snowfall of the year, the whole city suddenly clean, blanketed under drifts of white dust, how silent it will feel. I didn't tell Sara everything that happened in the bathroom—just that Alexa Forte had asked for my number and hinted that she'd like to hang out downtown. Somehow, what went on in that stall, the food that was violently ejected from her perfect body, doesn't seem mine to recount, so I'm staying quiet about it.

"God," Sara muses, taking a bite of tuna, "do you really think she'll call?"

"Who knows?" I shrug, pulling my black leather jacket closer to my body. "I'm not exactly holding my breath."

Sara's laughter is a snort, her cheeks stuffed with lettuce. With her white hair and nose pink from the cold, she reminds me of a bunny rabbit, the furry hood on her vanilla-colored down coat adding to the illusion. "Are you working tonight?" She swallows hard, wiping her mouth with a napkin. "Or can I come over?"

Sara hates clubs and can't understand why I choose to spend every night in them. The one time I persuaded her to give the club a second chance and took her to work with me, she was yawning five minutes after we got there, and I ended up putting her in a cab an hour later. She maintains to this day that nightclubs give her narcolepsy, and that everyone who frequents them is pretentious and totally full of themselves. That's the point, I tell her, rolling my eyes.

"Working. But you can come over this afternoon if you want."

Sara takes one last bite and closes the plastic top to the salad bowl, placing it on the bench next to her black tote bag, a row of metal safety pins running up the shoulder strap. "Can't," she says, still chewing. "Yearbook."

"Why don't you just move a bed into the pub lab and be done with it? That way you can arrange senior pages in your *sleep.*"

"Good idea," Sara says, swallowing hard. "Imagine all I could accomplish. I could really get things *done.*"

One of the reasons I love Sara is that we totally get each other—same completely sarcastic sense of humor. Sara is so deadpan that most people can't even tell when she's kidding. Especially her teachers, who mostly think she's some kind of mad genius when she's not totally annoying them with her smart-ass remarks.

"You look thin," she says out of nowhere, scrutinizing my legs covered in black leggings, her eyes moving up to search the bones in my face. "And tired. You're working too much."

"Not really," I say, brushing her comments aside. "But why beat around the bush? Why don't you just tell me I look like shit?"

Sara rolls her eyes and nudges me in the side with her pointy-ass elbow. "Relax! I'm just worried about you, moron." She smiles and her tone is playful, but I can tell that beneath the veneer of lightness, she's dead serious.

"I just . . . think maybe you're partying too much. I mean, after the whole fiasco at Nightingale, I think I have the right to be a little worried, you know? Doing lines in the bathroom? That's not like you, Cat."

Her eyes mist over with tears, and she looks away from me and out into the street, the grin slowly evaporating from her face, fading into nothingness.

"Look," I begin, trying to keep my tone reasonable so that I don't burst into tears or fly off the handle. Her concern infuriates me. I don't want to be questioned or cross-examined. She's supposed to be the one person who understands me completely, the one person I don't have to defend myself to. "I *told* you what happened. I got home really late the night before, and I was practically falling asleep in class. I was just doing one little line to get me through the day, and if that idiot freshman hadn't walked in, no one would be any the wiser. We wouldn't even be having this conversation."

"Wouldn't we?"

I'm silent, crossing my arms over my chest. Somewhere deep inside me I know she's right, and it needles at my skin like a million tiny jolts of electricity. I know things have to change, that I can't keep stumbling through the darkened landscape of my life, but I don't know where to start. It's like I'm running a race, weights strapped to my ankles, the clock ticking down minute after minute. Merciless.

"Cat, I'm only saying this because I love you, but you're fucking up. Big time. And what's worse is that I think you know it. So be as pissed at me as you want." She turns and looks at me, and the pain in her eyes almost breaks me apart. "But I'd rather have you be angry with me than continue down the path you're on, because sooner or later you're going to end up in the goddamn hospital. Or the morgue."

There's a moment of silence in which I can hear the sound of my own ragged breathing mixing with the noise of the traffic, the cacophony of buses and pedestrians, the sound of Sara's heart beating solidly next to mine.

"For God's sake, Sara, stop being so dramatic," I snap, trying to brush off her words, but they stick in my brain, anchoring there with surprising force. "I'm not going to die," I say more quietly now, looking down at the leaves that blow past my boots, wondering how I can be so sure.

"Maybe not," Sara says quietly. "But I don't want to take that chance. I don't know why you're so willing to."

Sara's voice breaks and she looks away again, her eyes distant as she stands up, walks to the curb and tosses her half-eaten salad into the trash. A woman walking an arthritic beagle passes slowly by, the dog dragging its hindquarters as it meanders slowly down the street. Tears swim in my eyes, blurring my vision, and I bring my fists up to my face, rubbing my eyes as if I want to blot them out entirely. When Sara gets like this, the only thing to do is change the subject.

"So . . . ," I say when she sits back down, taking a deep breath, unsure if I should tell her about Julian but suddenly unable to stop myself. "I met this guy yesterday. Julian. He's new." The words come out in a rush, and I'm aware of my face flushing stupidly. It's been so long since I've had a crush on anyone that I feel like everything I'm saying sounds ridiculous. Sara's mouth falls open and she waits for me to finish. "We had some pizza together yesterday at lunch, and today he just kind of . . . ignored me."

"Wait . . . ," Sara says slowly, her brow scrunching into a mass of wrinkles above her shock of white hair. "He used to go to Dalton, right? Julian Lee? Worships the Ramones? Has a lot of dirty black hair? Looks Japanese or something?"

"Yeah," I say, nodding, "that's him."

"Oh, Cat," Sara says quietly. "You got off easy."

"What do you mean?" I take one last gulp of my coffee, wincing as the now cold liquid hits the back of my throat. I hate cold coffee. I'm feeling shaky and unhinged from all the caffeine, like I might break apart at any moment. My wrist aches, and I rub it absentmindedly with one hand as I wait for Sara's response. It broke in two places last year when my mother decided that a B on a science test was unacceptable and slammed my hand in the door of our Town Car the night before I was supposed to see Depeche Mode at Madison

Square Garden. I inwardly cringe, remembering the pain, the impact of metal on bone, the crunching sound as my wrist shattered into pieces, the high-pitched scream that left my lips, and my own bewilderment. *Who's that?* I thought as my voice echoed through the air, shrill and unfamiliar, one part of myself watching, disconnected and weirdly observant.

"You don't know about him?" Sara crosses one leg over the other, angling her body toward me, her polka-dotted red-and-white tights a beacon in the weak fall sunlight. "His girlfriend tried to kill herself last year by taking an overdose of Xanax, and she left behind some kind of note blaming him."

I nod slowly, taking it in.

"I mean, she was probably screwed up to begin with, but still, he is *so not* boyfriend material."

"I never said I *wanted* him to be." I can hear the defensive tone in my voice, and suddenly I feel like I could sleep for a million years. "I don't want to deal with anyone right now anyway," I tell her, the words sounding hollow and empty. It's true—the idea of having a boyfriend scares me silly, and even though I can't imagine being in any kind of relationship, I'd be lying to myself if I didn't admit that I wanted to get to know Julian in some way, that I'd felt a kind of connection between us yesterday rising up over the table, some invisible thread pulling us closer. A car screeches down the street blasting the new Duran Duran song, bass kicking, and Sara briefly nods to the beat. Sara is a sucker for pretty boys with highlighted floppy hair and early eighties New Wave wardrobes, and Duran Duran more than fits the bill as far as she's concerned.

"Well, that's good, because he would be a seriously

questionable choice, and I don't want to see you get hurt. He's the last thing you need right now, Cat."

My stomach turns over at her words, and I wonder if for just once in her life, Sara is completely and totally wrong.

"Don't worry. Like I said before, he totally ignored me today."

"Good," Sara says with a snort. "Let's keep it that way."

The trouble is, I'm not sure I want to. I stare out into the street, my eyes blurring and losing focus as I think of his face, that grin as he stared at me across the table, and my heart flops useless in my chest, trying to find its way out. But now that Julian's ignored me, the ball has been firmly tossed into his court. If he wants to talk to me, he'll have to make the first move. There's no way I'm risking the total humiliation of walking up to him between classes and having him act like I have some kind of bizarre flesh-eating disease that will instantly infect him if he so much as breathes one word in my direction. Maybe I scared him away with that whole stupid speech about being a social pariah, but what else could I do? He would have found out the truth eventually. Everyone always does.

I watch as a pigeon pecks at loose crumbs around the trash, its dirty feathers touching the ground as it bobs its delicate head toward the sidewalk. I wonder if it knows something I don't, that maybe I should learn to be satisfied and stop expecting a banquet instead of a life full of stale, dry crumbs. The leaves above shake in the wind, and I look up at the sky for some clue about what happens next, some kind of answer. Instead, there are only clouds rolling across the horizon.

NINE

I'M WEDGED BEHIND the velvet ropes that lead to the Tunnel basement, and although I'm supposed to be sitting on top of a high stool, lording my power over the crowd and looking as bored as humanly possible, I'm antsy. The music is making me want to dance, even though the black, knee-high boots I'm wearing are cutting into my toes and making me cranky. So when Sammy, one of the club's biggest dealers, pushes to the front of the line, I'm almost relieved. He raises a pale eyebrow at the rope hanging between us, and I open it with a click, letting him in. He leans in for a double-cheek kiss, resting his hands lightly on my upper arms. Like most of the serious dealers, he's wearing a black suit with a T-shirt underneath, and shiny shoes. Nondescript and boring. Sammy's got to be in at least his late twenties but seems younger with his buttery blond hair and smooth, unlined face.

"How are you, Cat? You're looking fabulous as usual," he marvels, his eyes sweeping the length of my body, taking in the black leotard, black-and-white patterned tights and high black boots, a white piece of fur knotted in my hair, lips stained bloodred. I feel like some kind of demented superhero in this outfit, but Giovanni was insistent as usual, so here I am, standing behind a rope the exact color of my parted mouth, one hand on my hip. I would die of embarrassment if I had to wear this outfit on the street in broad daylight, but the club is a place where I am most often someone else entirely, and where anything is possible. Sammy takes my hand, and I can feel the weight of a plastic bag being pressed into my palm. He winks, his eyes catching the light overhead before he walks down the long set of red-carpeted stairs.

It's scary to admit to myself that in the last few months, whenever Sammy presses that plastic bag into my palm, my pulse races, my eyes glitter in anticipation, the feeling of the sticky plastic under my fingers accompanied by a sudden dampening under my arms. As soon as Sammy leaves, I motion to Giovanni, who is leaning against the wall behind me chatting with a very young-looking boy wearing a white tutu, and ask him to watch the door for a minute while I run to the bathroom.

"Can I abuse my power?" Giovanni raises one eyebrow, already sizing up the crowd with a Machiavellian grin.

"Totally," I say, laughing. "Have at it."

Walking away from the crush of people surrounding the velvet rope, I feel a wave of relief to be done with them for a few minutes, their intense scrutiny and high-pitched laughter. The cavernous bathroom is on the second floor. Hair products are lined up in a row on the counter along with perfume bottles and tonics. Marla, a fat Polish woman with bleached-blond hair, presides over it all, a metal basket on the counter in front of her filled with bills. There's a rumor that the bathrooms at Tunnel are the partially converted locker rooms of the train workers of the early 1900s. In fact, the club is actually built on the site of an abandoned train tunnel, the tracks running from the back of the Chandelier Room into obscurity. Sometimes there are private parties thrown right there on the tracks, strobe lights flickering, turning faces to fragments, stilettos sinking into the dirt and gravel.

"What's up, kitty cat?" Marla has a big, booming voice, and it bounces off the tiles and reverberates through my head. I walk over with a smile as she reaches to enfold me in her fleshy arms, practically cutting off my circulation with her cleavage. "Taking a break?"

"You got it," I say as she releases me. I walk over to the stalls and lock myself inside and sit on the closed toilet lid. Taking a break. Is that what I'm doing? Because I don't know anymore. As I reach into the plastic bag with my pinky, scooping a bit of white powder under my fingernail and holding it to one nostril, inhaling deeply, my eyes close and I try to ignore the sinking sensation in my stomach that lets me know I've gone too far. *There was a time,* I think, *when drugs added to the night more than they took away. When you were happy just to be here, in this crazy, fractured world, dancing all night beneath the lights, sweat breaking on your skin like holy water.*

I remember that feeling of bliss, and there's a twinge in my gut now where it used to reside, especially since I know I've been faking it in the past few months. Tears well up in my eyes, and my mouth fills with bitterness as the drug works its way into my system. I repeat the process on the other side, breathing in hard, then rub the excess over my gums. The taste in my mouth is slightly unfamiliar, like dirt, but weirdly soapy at the same time, and as I begin to wonder why, the room begins to quickly slide away from me. *There's something . . . missing in me,* I hear myself murmur, the words slow and thickened.

Missing . . .

A lush, elongated feeling lengthens my muscles as I fall to the floor, my body useless and limp, my bones hijacked. I reach out for the door, my hands scrabbling at the lock, my body moving forward into empty space, fingers scratching at the metal as the room swirls away in a cyclone of red and black.

TEN

CAITLIN! WAKE UP!

I swim in and out of the light. My eyes glued shut, head stuffed with wet cotton. I feel a sting on my cheek. *Who let bees in here?* I try to raise my arm, but my skin sticks stubbornly to the cold tile. My eyes flutter open, false lashes scraping my cheeks. Giovanni's face looms above me, huge and frantic, drops of sweat beading his forehead.

"Cat, are you OK? Should we call someone?" His eyes move back and forth over my face, and using what feels like all of my strength, I reach one hand up and touch his cheek, his skin like yards of satin beneath my fingertips. I lie there, marveling at the feeling of fingers on flesh. If I've ever felt this good before, I've blocked it out.

"No, no," I say, and my voice, when it leaves my mouth, is a croak, hoarse and raspy. "I'm OK. I think I'm OK." Giovanni moves behind me and helps me to sit up as a warm wave moves through me, flooding the core of my being. I look around and realize that I'm sitting in the middle of the bathroom floor, the lights overhead screaming like a group of meth-addled cheerleaders, Marla and Giovanni huddled around me, their faces tense.

"When you didn't come down after a few minutes, I came up to get you, and when I walked in, Marla was pulling you out from the toilet."

"Well, I heard you go down," Marla jumps in, "but the door was locked, so I had to reach under and drag you out of there." She smooths back my hair, checking for permanent damage. I reach one hand up to my head, the skin sore beneath my fingers. For the first time I realize that my head is throbbing with a slow pulse, a record played at the wrong speed. *Ka-THUMP, Ka-THUMP* . . . But even as my body registers the pain, the feeling immediately recedes, moving into the distance like a car pulling away from the curb and out of sight. A wave of pleasure floods my body, and I let out a low moan.

"You must've hit your head on the door when you fell," Giovanni muses as I try to move away from his probing fingers. "What HAPPENED? You were only up here for ten minutes. Did Sammy give you something?" He peers into my eyes, holding me by the jaw. "Your pupils are like goddamn baseballs."

"Yeah," I croak, the room floating before me. Somehow, Marla's never looked so beautiful, her hair so flaxen, almost transparent in the light, and Giovanni could be an angel, the ruffled white shirt against his skin glowing like a searchlight . . .

"Cat?" Giovanni is annoyed now, his eyes looking for answers.

"He gave me a bag," I say slowly, "and next thing I know . . . this . . ."

I seem to be incapable of speaking in complete sentences, and every word that falls from my lips feels like a massive effort. I close my eyes briefly, and I feel arms on either side of my body, shaking me roughly awake.

"OK, you need to stand up and walk." Giovanni and Marla pull me up, propping me against the wall for a moment. "Let me see the bag," Giovanni commands, holding out a hand.

"I've got it," Marla says reluctantly. "She dropped it when she went down." Marla reaches into the top of her shirt, rummages around in her bra for a moment and pulls out the bag, slightly crumpled now. Giovanni grabs the bag and dips a finger in, bringing it to his lips, testing, tasting.

"This isn't coke—it's D."

"Are you suuuuure?" I slur, my tongue thick and bloated between my teeth. D is what we all call heroin, as most bags are sold out of abandoned buildings on Avenue D, four blocks away from my apartment on the Lower East Side. D for downtown, D for drowsy, D for deadly. I've heard that the batch making its way through the clubs right now is particularly lethal, and if how I feel right now is any indication, I'd say the rumors, for once, are true. It's as if my whole body has been completely submerged in a vat of hot honey. I've always been too scared to try heroin even though it's been offered to me more than once. Now I know why—if I ever did so much as a line of this stuff ever again, I'd never want to stop.

"Cat, why would he give you this anyway? He knows you don't do this shit!" Giovanni's dark eyes are narrowed with anger, and he stuffs the bag in his pocket with one hand, still holding me up with the other. "C'mon," he says, pulling me along. "Let's go find him."

We stumble through the crowd, my eyes spinning in their sockets like twin pinwheels, the lids fluttering closed, then snapping open again as I am jostled and moved through the club and down the stairs, Giovanni's arm around my waist, steadying me. My feet feel like they're floating across the floor, the blisters on my toes forgotten, and as we make our way down the basement stairs, I stumble and fall, my heel catching on the carpeting. Giovanni pulls me to my feet, and the world swings by me in a dizzying swirl as I lean against him, upright once again. Just as I'm catching my breath, Sammy passes by us on the stairs, his face split into a wide grin until he sees my expression, my unfocused stare. Giovanni grabs Sammy by the arm, pulling him over to us.

"What the fuck did you *give* her?" he hisses through closed teeth as Sammy's eyes widen in their sockets. "You know she doesn't do any fucking D!"

"I didn't," Sammy stammers, looking confused. "I wouldn't . . ."

"You DID," Giovanni says menacingly, his grip on Sammy's arm tightening. Giovanni drops my arm to better deal with Sammy, and I lean against the wall, my head lolling on my neck. It's so hard to keep my eyes open, even though a small crowd has gathered to watch the drama, the air filled with the sound of whispers mixed with the synth crash from the DJ booth below us. Somehow nothing seems to matter—not my fucked-up family—or lack of one—not my plummeting grades, or the fact that I haven't even begun to think about college, SATs and what I want to do with the rest of my life. All I want is to be at home, safe in my bed, quilt pulled up to my chest, the scents of fabric softener and the Nag Champa incense I sometimes burn drifting sweetly through the air . . .

"Caitlin, wake *up!*" Giovanni is shaking me, his hands on my shoulders. My eyes crack open, and I struggle to keep them that way, blinking slowly, trying to clear my vision.

"Look, man," Sammy says quietly, his voice measured and pleading. "It was a mistake. I must've gotten the bags mixed up." He gestures emphatically with his hands, palms open. "It'll never happen again."

"Get the fuck out of here," Giovanni snaps. "Before I beat the living shit out of you."

Giovanni may be gay, but he'll kick anyone's ass all the way around the block if he's angry enough. He's always pulling back the sleeves of his shirt to show off his stupid biceps. It's totally annoying.

Sammy smirks at Giovanni as if to say "Yeah, right," cocking one eyebrow in disbelief. I don't blame him since tonight, Giovanni is wearing a fishnet long-sleeved shirt and a black silk sarong he whipped up this afternoon. With his eyes outlined in black liner and a pair of long sparkling earrings hanging from his ears, he doesn't look like he could beat *me* up if I challenged him to a fight, much less Sammy. Sammy shoots me an apologetic look while mouthing the word *Sorry,* and then makes his way up the steps, hungry eyes following his every move as his blond head grows smaller, then disappears entirely.

"C'mon, sweetie," Giovanni sighs, grabbing me firmly

around the waist, my body leaning heavily into his side. "Let's get you out of here."

"I can't leave the door," I mumble, my head resting on my chest like a broken flower.

"Fuck the door!" Giovanni snaps, pulling me along, my boots scraping on the carpet.

We stumble up the stairs and out the front door of the club, then down the steps as rain shines wetly on the streets, making them glisten like black ribbons, and tumble into a yellow cab waiting on the corner, engine idling, white plumes of smoke drifting in the night air. Once in the backseat, shivering from the cold dampness on my skin, I lean against Giovanni, my head resting on his chest as the streets blur past. My eyes flicker once, twice, candles sputtering out, then slide firmly shut as the world slips away, my dreams punctuated by the sound of windshield wipers swishing across wet glass, the whine of the engine and the beat of Giovanni's heart.

I AM TWO OR THREE YEARS OLD, small and slightly round, a mop
of blondish-brown hair standing up all over my head in defiant
cowlicks, mystified by socks, unable to get the tight cotton over the
unwieldy annoyance of feet. I count my toes, forcing them clumsily
into white anklets, one . . . two . . . three . . .

A sudden noise behind me, a flapping of wings, warm air moving over my skin.

Give me that!

Hands reaching out, grabbing the soft cotton from my grasp,
her fingers nipping my skin like the mouth of an angry swan, socks
thrown to the floor as she raises my body up and I fall into the refrigerator, my head banging against the metal door, body sagging
like a discarded doll. It's not the first time it happens, her angry
hands on my skin, but it is the one I remember first.

Why can't you DRESS yourself?

Her face close to mine, a mirrored reflection, my features super-
imposed on her face, looming large and monstrous. Daddy will be

home soon, *I tell myself.* Soon Daddy will be home and maybe she won't be mad anymore.

What is WRONG with you, Caitlin?

Hands on my shoulders, red talons, the nails digging in, and the shaking, my brain rolling around in my skull like loose pieces of a board game, unmoored in a box, my bones splintering beneath the smooth covering of my flesh.

ELEVEN

I WAKE IN A COLD SWEAT, my hair sticking to my cheek, the sheets damp and bunched up beneath me. I push the quilt off of my lower half and swing my legs around, resting my bare feet on the floor, wincing at the cold air on my toes, the room spinning wildly. My leotard and tights from last night feel plastered to my body, and the thought of a hot shower, the steaming water washing away the grime with the jasmine soap I buy in Chinatown, almost makes me groan aloud with longing. I stand up and sway in place for a minute before walking to my bedroom door and opening it with a loud creak, making my way slowly, carefully into the living room.

Giovanni is asleep on the couch, one hand thrown over his face to block out the light that peeps in through the black tarps. There is a half-eaten tuna sandwich and an untoasted strawberry Pop-Tart on the floor beside him, our shoes kicked off in a pile at the front door. I vaguely remember Giovanni making the sandwich when we first got back from the club, standing at the kitchen counter chopping celery, the room filling with the browned scent of toasting bread as I lay on the bed hugging my pillow to my chest, my eyes heavy as stone.

As water sluices over my body, images from last night flash through my brain, disjointed and out of sequence. The high is long gone, replaced by weakness and a slight nausea. I sit down in the tub, my knees drawn up to my chest, arms wrapped around them tightly until the queasiness recedes like a bad dream. By the time I emerge a few minutes later, I feel steady enough to stand underneath the heat lamp embedded in the ceiling above my head, towel-drying my hair. When I wipe the mirror over the sink down with one hand, pushing away the condensation, my face stares blankly back at me. There are black circles around my eyes, hollow and dirty with smeared eyeliner, the sockets sunken into my face like a naked skull, and I avert my gaze as I brush my teeth, scrubbing the inside of my mouth like I'm eradicating some kind of contagion. Things have got to be different today, somehow. If I can just start the morning off on the right foot, maybe it's not too late to turn things around. I remember the cold tile against my back in the Tunnel bathroom chilling me to the bone, my skin a bluish-white. I shiver, drawing the towel more tightly against my body, and I have to sit down for a moment to make the image recede, my hands shaking.

I pad back into my bedroom, the huge black-and-white Joy Division poster over my bed looming over me. The marble angel beckons with tightly closed eyes, and I have to look away. My feet leave wet prints on the floor, and I rummage around my closet looking for anything that's even remotely clean. I've missed the first three periods of the day, but with any luck, if

I hurry I can make it to history. After last night, it feels important to go to school, to sit in class and dream out the window, hand cupped under one cheek, the dry, woodsy scent of paper and pencil shavings tickling my nose. All of a sudden I want someone to make me scrambled eggs for breakfast, the napkin folded just so, toast cut in precise triangles. I want someone to tuck me in at night with a warm blanket, a cup of cold milk waiting placidly on the nightstand. I long for a mother's hand on my forehead, the soothing knowledge that everything will be OK, even if it won't.

I step into a pair of ripped jeans and top them with a black sweater, pull on my boots, the leather broken in, comfortable as a pair of slippers. I wrap a knitted scarf around my neck, pulling my wet hair back in a ponytail. I do all this without really looking in the mirror, not wanting to confront what I know I will find there, the vacant eyes of a dead girl.

I scrawl a note for Giovanni on the back of an old invite for one of Sebastian's parties, and after placing it on top of the half-eaten sandwich next to the couch, I grab my leather jacket and my knapsack and close the door quietly behind me. What is left behind on top of the sandwich looks like this: "See you later. Thanks for last night. I love you. C." I'm really capable of saying those three little words only in writing—never out loud. Even writing them makes me feel like I'm squirming uncomfortably inside my own skin, trying to get out of my body before it's too late. But when I think of the way Giovanni held me over the toilet, pulling my hair back so the vomit wouldn't get all over me when the waves of sickness began, how he sat with me on the bathroom floor for hours, propped up against the wall of white tile, his hand looped tightly in mine, I know those words belong to him. I don't think I've even said them to Sara. It's become kind of a joke between us. Whenever she leaves for a vacation with her parents, or for some summer program for gifted rich kids, she'll hug me while I usually stand there like a piece of furniture, awkwardly bringing my arms around her torso to hug her back, patting her between the shoulder blades like I'm burping a scrawny bird. When she says, "Bye, Cat. I love you," I quickly blurt out, "Me too" before scampering away so I don't have to watch her figure recede as she walks away from me. For a while, Sara even started calling me Me Too, just to annoy me, as in "Hey, Me Too, want to go get Tasti D-Lite after fifth period?" Or, "Hey, Me Too, can you come over Saturday night?" Still, it's all a pose—Sara knows I love her without my having to say a word. At least I hope she does.

I used to see this therapist on Eighty-Third and Park who told me that I probably associated touching of any kind with being hurt in some way. The therapist had flaming red hair and wore matching red rectangular glasses that reminded me of Sally Jessy Raphael, and every time I went to a session, I secretly suspected that she was doing the *New York Times* crossword instead of taking notes. Her expression, when she lifted her eyes from the paper in front of her, was cloudy and unfocused, as if she didn't know who I was. But she was right about the touching. As far back as I can remember, I've had this tendency to flinch when people move toward me too quickly—even if it's only for a hug. I'm like some freak that was raised by a pack of wire monkeys, scared of human contact.

By the time I get out of a cab in front of school, I'm beginning to think that coming all the way to the Upper East Side today maybe isn't the greatest idea I've ever had. My nose is running, and I have that spacey feeling I always get the morning after I've partied way too hard. As much as I shake my head to try to clear my vision, my eyes feel disconnected from my skull. It's as if some vital piece of connective tissue has been severed and my eyeballs are just rolling around in their sockets like so much loose gravel.

As I exit the cab, tossing a wad of crumpled bills at the driver, I sway in the cold air, grabbing on to a metal trash can for support, and lean in, the smell of rotten, decomposing food rising up to meet me. I double over, retching, wiping away strands of bitter-tasting bile with one hand while passersby ignore me, their eyes sliding quickly away. When I feel well enough to stand up straight, I stay motionless for a minute, building up the strength to move forward until I can make my way up the stone steps and through the swinging doors.

The lockers are at the back of the first floor, and I trudge toward the rows of gray metal. With every step I feel increasingly unsure, my sneakers coated in lead. I'm shoving some books into my bag when the bell rings and bodies begin pouring into the hallway, surrounding me like fluttering, spastic wings, their chatter an insistent buzzing. I hold on to the door of my locker, the hall swaying around me, when a voice cuts through the nausea, and Julian's face appears in front of mine. Today he's wearing an olive-green T-shirt with the Smiths album cover *The Queen Is Dead* on it. His hair is dirtier than ever, his eyes deep as graves.

"Hey," he says, looking me up and down, his eyes coming to rest on my face. "Are you OK? You're not looking so good."

"Great," I manage to mumble tonelessly, swinging my locker door shut with a bang. "Whatever."

"Wait," Julian blurts out in obvious confusion, his forehead creased. He places one hand on my arm, his touch burning my skin. Some kind of alarm goes off inside my skull, and I bristle, shrugging off his hand and pulling my knapsack over one shoulder, the sudden weight steadying me. Julian takes one step closer and I back up, the room spinning. "Cat, I didn't mean it like that—I mean, you always look nice." He stops, blushing deeply before continuing on, two high spots of crimson coloring his cheeks. "Look, I was just trying to see if you were—"

"Listen," I snap, "why don't you just go back to pretending I don't exist, all right?" There is a moment of silence in which I am aware all conversation has stopped, and that people are watching us with fascination that borders on glee. A whispering, the sound of paper catching fire begins, crackling through the silence. I catch a glimpse of Alexa Forte out of the corner of my eye as she walks by with one of her minions in tow, and the sound of their hushed voices burns my skin like a thousand paper cuts.

Julian coughs once, and clears his throat with a raw, ragged sound. "No problem," he says in a voice that sounds half strangled, his eyes now slightly distant, frozen over. Now it is my turn to fall silent. I swallow the words that sit heavily in my chest unsaid: *Wait, no, but, so* . . . Even as I stand there motionless, I know I am making a huge mistake, that things are unfolding fast, way too fast to stop them, to take it all back and start from zero. There's nothing I can do, so I choose to do the simplest thing, the thing I do best—I leave.

I push through the crowd with sharp elbows, not caring if I hurt anyone, my face scorched with embarrassment. I think of miles of sand dunes, red and black rocks shimmering in the heat, my anger reflected in the barren landscape, those violent colors. Without turning back, I know that Julian is watching me. The quick staccato steps of my boots reverberate in my ears, and I breathe a sigh of relief as I turn the corner, his eyes falling away.

* * * *

THE PLINKY-PLONKY SOUND of the ice cream truck rings through the hot summer air, thick as the tar melts on the rooftops above my head, and the truck makes its way down the block, filling the neighborhood with a lingering music. The air, heavy with summer blossoms, is soft and languid, caressing my bare arms.

Vanilla and chocolate swirl drips onto my palms, hot concrete under my legs. I sit with my father on the front stoop outside our building, before we moved all the way uptown, before the money, the divorce, when the word SoHo meant "home."

My mother exits the front door, pushing her sweat-dampened hair back from her forehead. She sits down next to my father, taking his hand in her own and bringing it up to her lips, softly kissing the skin of his palm, her eyes closed. Inside, there is dinner waiting: a roast chicken fragrant with lemon and herbs, mashed potatoes to soak up the delicate juices. A decanter of white wine sparkles in the setting sun streaming over the scarred wooden table.

My father listens carefully, nodding as he licks at his double cone, the mirror image of the one in my own small hands, interjecting

*a series of hmms and oh reallys as I chatter on happily, my whole
world reduced to simply this: the sun burning red and hot orange
along the tops of tall, concrete buildings, the feel of ice cream soft
and cold on the heat of my tongue, my father's low voice a rumble
in my ear as color flies across the darkening sky, the lights of the
city resembling a strand of gemstones, shining and brilliant, as they
whisper my future into the gathering night.*

TWELVE

I DUCK INTO THE SUBWAY on the corner of Seventy-Seventh and Lexington, descending into the hot, stale mouth of the station. My stomach still feels queasy, and I take a sip from the bottle of iced tea I bought at the newsstand on the way to the train, trying to clear away the lingering taste of bile. I need to go to the club and pick up my money for the week from Christoph and run an idea for a party by him, something I could easily have done when school let out, but the thought of having to eat lunch by myself again among the whispers and sideways glances was enough to propel me downtown without thinking twice. Every time I close my eyes, there is a flash of Julian's face, and a feeling of regret swoops over me so intense that I almost turn around and walk back to school to find him. Maybe I should have given him a chance to explain instead of just cutting him off and walking away. My stomach sinks to my boots, and I sigh as the train pulls into the station, the rushing movement of the cars lifting the hair from the back of my neck.

When I exit the station on Eighth Avenue, I turn on Twenty-Seventh Street, heading past the familiar rows of empty warehouses that precede Tunnel, my pace quickening. I climb the front steps, ring the buzzer for entrance and step inside. I stand for a moment in the instant nightfall, waiting for my eyes to adjust. I make my way upstairs past the dreaded bathroom and into Christoph's open office, light flooding in from the two big windows that face the street. I feel my pupils contract, and I blink like I'm coming out of a stupor.

The walls are painted the gray of storm clouds, and the room is full of black lacquered furniture that looks like it comes alive and stomps around the office in the early hours of the morning. Christoph is seated at his desk, bent over what looks like a stack of bills, wearing a pair of steel-rimmed glasses I've never seen before. His blond hair, which I can see in the light is shot with streaks of gray, is pulled back in his trademark ponytail, his perpetually tanned face only half visible. I watch as his head comes up, alert, his posture rigid. His face relaxes as he realizes that it's just me, and he runs a hand over the top of his head, smoothing his hair down, then pulling his glasses off and throwing them onto the desk in one fluid motion.

"Ahh . . . Cat," he says, grinning, pushing a stack of paper off the high-backed chair next to him and patting the seat, motioning for me to sit. "To what do I owe this unexpected pleasure?" Christoph says the word *pleasure* like it's something illegal, rolling the word around in his mouth and savoring it like wine, a valuable and rare vintage.

I sit down, crossing one leg over the other, my face frozen

in a smile. I never know what to say to Christoph and I can't really figure him out. There's something impenetrable about him that makes me afraid to look him in the eye. He's old enough to be my father, and in real life I'd be completely grossed out, but somehow, over the past few months, my life has slid far away from anything approximating real, and so Christoph, like everything else in the shadowy dream world I inhabit when the lights go down, has somehow become a possibility.

"I just came by to . . . umm . . . get paid," I blurt out. "And to talk to you about this idea I had for a party in the basement." I take a huge gulp of air and then keep talking, afraid to stop, of the dead air that will rise between us. "I was thinking of doing a petting zoo—you know, club kids body-painted as zebras and tigers, suspended in cages over the dance floor, hay everywhere . . ." Christoph is squinting, his eyes the palest shade of blue, like jeans that have been washed a hundred times in a caustic mix of bleach and lye. I've thrown only two other parties, which both kind of tanked, so I'm nervous, afraid he won't give me another chance.

"That last one wasn't too . . ." Christoph's brow wrinkles, and his voice trails off into nothingness.

My cheeks flush and sweat breaks out under my arms. The last party I threw was pretty sparsely attended, most likely because I still haven't gotten the hang of actually getting out there and promoting. After a year, even though I'm well known in the scene at this point, I still have to force myself to approach people, a fake smile on my face, my lips curling awkwardly away from my teeth. I want so much to be like

Sebastian, gliding across the dance floor instead of standing in the corner all night thrusting invites at any random stranger who passes by, but I can't seem to get the hang of it, no matter how hard I try.

"I know," I say. "But it takes a while to get established, and I think this petting zoo thing could be really . . ."

My voice trails off as I notice Christoph's eyes traveling along the length of my body. He leans back in his chair, hands folded behind his head, holding my eyes with his own.

Please don't let me fail at this, I think, whispering the words over and over in my brain. So far I've failed at being a daughter, a student and probably a friend. I can't bear to fail at anything else, and these parties, as meaningless as they are, this place, is all I have left.

"Aren't you on the invite for Sebastian's outlaw party next week? That thing with the truck?" Christoph smiles a half smile, as if the thought of Sebastian amuses him. He's wearing a soft black sweater that looks like cashmere, and a pair of jeans so broken in that they're almost destroyed, the legs frayed open artfully at the knee and thigh. He seems absurdly comfortable with his body, as if he lives in his skin as effortlessly as his jeans.

"Yeah, I'm on it—he asked me a few nights ago." I look down at the ends of my scarf, wrapping the red strands around my fingers and choosing my words carefully. "But I was thinking of doing this one a week after—I'm not trying to compete with Sebastian or anything." The truth is, I *can't* compete with Sebastian. I'm just some little upstart who's thrown two little parties in the Chandelier Room, which, because it's so small, is where Christoph puts all the promoters he's not sure about yet, who sometimes works the door of the VIP, and Sebastian is fast on his way to becoming a downtown legend. Whether Christoph is aware of this fact or not, I'm certainly not going to bring it up.

"Let me think about it," he says brusquely, picking up his glasses and bending toward the stack of papers on his desk, which I take as my cue to leave. I stand up, throwing my knapsack over my shoulder, and wait there awkwardly, unsure if I should remind him about the money he owes me or if I should just leave and worry about it later. Just as I'm turning to leave, Christoph lets out a large sigh and mumbles something unintelligible in German. Every time I show up to get paid, it's always a production. I can never tell if he remembers exactly why I've come in the first place, and sometimes I just stand there uncomfortably before he unlocks the drawer and counts out a pile of crisp bills. In this way, Christoph reminds me of my father.

"Wait, Cat, I have your money," he says, raising one finger in the air, then leans back and reaches into the front pocket of his jeans, retrieving a gold ring that jangles in the air. He opens the top right desk drawer and removes a large, green metal box, unlocking it. He reaches in and grabs a stack of hundreds, counting out five with a series of brisk movements, the bills falling from his hands as easily as a bank teller. He holds the money out, leaning toward me with a smile.

As I take the cash, Christoph grabs my wrist, gripping me tightly, his fingers closing around my flesh, his expression curious as he registers my surprise, the way my eyes widen at his touch. His eyes restlessly roam my face like they're looking for something that has been lost, and my stomach is tense, pulse revving the way it always does when I'm surprised or touched without warning. I don't *want* Christoph to be touching me, but at the same time it's *all* I want, to be touched, and I can't untangle my own response enough to make sense of the wave of fear and excitement that rips through me. I want to run, but my feet are nailed to the floor, my tongue swollen and wordless. After what seems like years pass, he releases my wrist and settles back in his chair as if nothing has happened. He returns to the stack of papers on his desk and begins scribbling something with a fat gold Montblanc pen that reminds me of a large expensive crayon, his pen moving determinedly across the page as if I'm no longer there at all.

I turn around, dazed, as if I've walked out of a movie theater into afternoon sunlight, and shove the money into my pocket, crumpling the bills as if to annihilate them completely. Although the paper is crisp and new, the bills feel slick, almost dirty in my hand. As I retrace my steps out of the club and push open the front door, I'm hit by a wave of exhaustion so intense that I want to sit down right there on the dirty metal steps strewn with champagne corks and cigarette butts, and cry.

The money bulges in my pocket, pushing against my skin uncomfortably, but the weight of it is somehow reassuring, slowing my pulse. Tonight I will order in from the Thai place in my neighborhood, the scent of lemongrass and cilantro wafting like spicy, exotic incense from the open plastic containers. I will go to the grocery store and pull items from shelves: dishwashing liquid, soap, a bag of apples, a jar of spaghetti sauce, and when I reach the cashier and pull the thick wad of bills from my pocket, I will feel worn out from the effort and so much older than my seventeen years. I will watch as mothers push their children down the aisles in metal shopping carts, noticing the way their small legs dangle down into the open air, how one mother will draw her little boy to her breast, gently wiping his upturned face. Her movements will be both tender and delicate, and my heart will constrict in my chest as I force myself to turn away and concentrate instead on a display of ramen noodles, a shrink-wrapped package of juice boxes, a bag of Twizzlers. Despite my earlier efforts in the day to get up and do what is expected of me, to do something *right,* nothing has changed. As I stand there in front of the club, I'm aware that I'm on a treadmill, my feet traversing the same patch of dirty ground again and again, heading nowhere at all.

The thought of going back to school, of sitting in class and trying to stay awake, pretending I'm interested in epic battles or the vast intricate codes of geometry, seems pointless, and I raise a hand in the air as a cab, yellow and pulsing in the afternoon sunlight, makes its way down the street. I climb into the backseat and lean my head back as the buildings flash by, replaying the past ten minutes in my head and wondering just what Christoph was thinking when he reached out for my hand, his eyes locking on mine.

THIRTEEN

WHEN I GET BACK to my apartment, it's blissfully empty, a smiley face and a series of xxooxx's scrawled below the note I left for Giovanni this morning. The building is quiet and still, the bed made, pillows on the couch plumped. The bed looks so inviting that I immediately pull off my boots and fall into it, pulling the blanket up under my chin, and plunge into dreamless sleep, the day disappearing in a rush of blackness that sweeps me under its wide, comforting wings.

I wake to the sound of the phone ringing loudly on the bedside table, and I half open one eye, glaring at it. I snatch the receiver from the cradle to quiet it, hugging the piece of hard plastic to my chest before raising it to my ear and whispering tentatively into the receiver.

"I see *someone's* taking a nap," a girl's voice chuckles softly, seductively. The voice is unfamiliar, delicate and sarcastic all at once, and I sit up, rubbing my eyes with one hand. "I also see that someone never made it back to school this afternoon. *Tsk tsk.*" She makes a sharp clicking sound with her tongue, voicing her obvious disapproval, the noise echoing through the wires and producing an instant headache.

"Who is this?" I ask, clearing my throat and coughing lightly as I lean on one elbow, squint and peer at the clock, which reads 4:45 p.m.

"Don't tell me you've forgotten me *already*."

There is a moment of silence as I flip through my mental Rolodex, coming up completely blank, and then the answer appears like a sudden jolt of electricity to my brain, shocking me into wakefulness.

"Alexa." I don't know why I didn't realize it sooner—maybe because I was in a sleep so deep it practically qualified as a coma.

"In the flesh." She laughs softly on the other end of the line, and I sit up a bit straighter, leaning against the white wooden headboard I've had since I was ten, trying to focus. My head feels like it's full of static, white noise, and my thoughts are meandering through my brain as if they have all the time in the world to sort themselves out. "Well. So to speak."

"What do you want?" I ask her, the irritation in my voice plain. I'm tired and grumpy, and I hate being woken up by a ringing phone more than anything in the entire world. It could be President Reagan on the line, and I'd probably tell him to call back later.

"Well, *that's* not a very friendly attitude, now, is it?" Alexa's tone is playful, but I can also hear the steel in her voice, a line of metal spikes beneath the candy floss of her words.

"Hey, I never said I was Little Miss Sunshine." I laugh, trying to pass my brusqueness off as a joke.

"I'm calling to see if you want to go shopping downtown tomorrow after school," she says, getting right to the point.

I imagine her on the other end of the line making a list on a yellow pad, her handwriting filling the page with feminine, perfect script. Things to Do Today: Call weird girl and invite her shopping. Mani/pedi at 5.

"I can have my car take us."

"What?" I laugh. "No subway for you?" I close my eyes and try to picture Alexa walking among the homeless guys pissing on the tracks, stepping nimbly over piles of trash as rats run at her feet, the punk rockers on Astor Place ogling her pastel skirt and sweater sets, the wide cloth headbands she favors, and I giggle to myself silently.

"Let's take it one step at a time, OK?" she snaps. Then, after a second or two of dead silence, "Why? You think I couldn't handle it?"

"You said it," I say evenly, knowing it will drive her crazy, "not me."

"Fine then," she says, the challenge implicit in her tone. "We'll do it your way." Then, like a general barking orders, "Meet me in the atrium at three."

She's referring to the glass-topped food court right next door to the school where the salad girls buy their lunch every day, chewing mindlessly on huge green leaves the way cows mouth their cud, staring into space, their eyes vacant.

"See you then," I say, my only answer a sharp click as she hangs up the phone, the connection severed, a dial tone buzzing loudly in my ear. As I replay the call in my mind, hearing her voice reverberating in my thoughts, I'm completely mystified, my brain spinning as I consider the possibilities. What does she want with me? Is she just slumming? Trying to lay a veneer of downtown cool over her glossy uptown perfection? What could I have that she might want to dig her manicured nails into?

I lie back down and curl up, pulling the soft blanket around my shoulders, grateful I'm not working tonight, that the evening will stretch luxuriously before me in a haze of bad TV, spring rolls and tom yum soup, the jumbled sound of canned laughter and commercials putting me slowly, gently to sleep. As I drift off, I see Alexa's face rising up out of the sweet slumber that rushes over me. *Dork,* she whispers affectionately, almost lovingly. *Loser.* Her eyes are ominous as a fortune cookie, her smile the last thing to disappear.

FOURTEEN

I'M TAPPING MY FEET against one of the wrought-iron café tables that litter the inside of the light-filled atrium, watching as groups of girls parade in front of me, cups of frozen yogurt clutched to their chests, their giggles echoing through the room. The freshmen all look so pure and unspoiled that it almost hurts to look at them. They all seem to have the same mouthfuls of metal that glint in the light, making them self-conscious as a herd of baby deer, skin so translucent that I can almost see blood beating below the surface. They make me think of pails of milk, church bells, of the early morning dew coating the grass in Central Park. I turn away, bringing a Styrofoam cup of coffee to my lips and blowing on the surface to cool it, steam flooding my face.

I slept for twelve hours last night. No movement, no dreams. Just an empty void. I've felt fuzzy all day, like I've somehow managed to overdose on dopamine, my brain slow and plodding as I fumbled with my locker combination and tried to follow along with Ms. Sykes as we read aloud from

The Picture of Dorian Gray, my eyes heavy-lidded, my tongue thick in my mouth.

A rush of movement and Alexa suddenly appears, throwing her huge pink purse onto the metal table with a thud. "Sorry I'm late," she says, sitting down in the chair beside me and crossing her legs, clad in neon-pink tights that perfectly match the wide cloth headband holding her hair back from the angular planes of her face. "Ms. Newman was being a total bitch, and I couldn't get away."

Today, Alexa's also wearing a black miniskirt and a black jersey top that clings to her torso, the tights, purse and headband interrupting the monotony like a punch to the face. It makes me smile to think of her planning this outfit so carefully last night, trying, for once, to fit in. For the record, I've never seen Alexa Forte in anything but pastels. Her color palette usually reminds me of an Easter basket. Or a nursery.

"Was she ignoring the bell, as usual?" I ask shyly, afraid that I will spook her like a wild horse if I say the wrong thing. Ms. Newman is our French teacher. She makes a habit of babbling on endlessly, which generally makes us all late for our next class. Alexa is unlucky enough to have French as her final class of the day, which means she gets out at least fifteen minutes late on a daily basis.

Alexa nods, reaching into her purse and pulling out a pack of Gauloises, extracting a black cigarette with a gold band around the middle and lighting it, filling the air with the pungent scent of tobacco. The smell makes me wish I were sitting at a café on the Left Bank, the bustle of the Paris streets moving before me in a parade of expertly tied scarves and yapping little dogs. When I was nine, my mother took me to the spring collections. I remember the rain-soaked streets, how even the dampness felt welcoming and glamorous on my skin. The crunch of a croissant melting under my tongue and the discreet eyes of the waiters as they refilled my mother's wineglass, the diamonds on her wrists and fingers sparkling beneath elaborate chandeliers. How her eyes narrowed as I reached for a second pink *macaron* during high tea at The Ritz, and the scratch of her nails against my hand, tearing the skin. *Just one,* she hissed, then looked around the room to make sure no one was listening, her face tense and watchful.

"So," Alexa says, exhaling smoke in a white cloud above my head, "are you ready to deflower me? I mean, this *is* my first time downtown and all."

I laugh, throwing my head back. Who knew Alexa Forte was funny?

"Don't worry," I say, standing up and throwing my backpack over one shoulder. "I'll be gentle."

A half hour later we are walking down St. Marks Place, Alexa glued to my side, though she seems a bit more relaxed now that she's off the train, her eyes no longer glazed over in fear. During the subway ride, her thigh pressed into mine as she looked blankly ahead, afraid to make eye contact with the group of Hispanic boys who stood in front of us, swaying as they held on to straps that hung from the ceiling, their eyes searching her body, lingering at length on her chest, smiling lecherously as she ignored them and stared into space. The car was mostly full, bodies pressed together in the steamy heat, the car packed with people getting off work early, playing hooky, looking for trouble in Washington Square Park, on their way to classes at NYU, or simply because, like me, they happened to live there. Spray paint streaked the outside of the train, smearing the metal with black lines and bright color that crept inside the car like a disease. I tried to explain, very gently, that the E train was a safe line, and that it was broad daylight outside, not three a.m., but Alexa stayed rigid for the entire ride, smile frozen in place, her "downtown" outfit thrown into high relief by the cigarette butts crushed out on the dirty subway platform, the break-dancers who moved through the train stopping in front of us, Day-Glo sweatbands around their foreheads, the zippers on their jackets catching the light as their limbs spun in a movement that was somehow more than dance.

We walk past Trash and Vaudeville, a punk store on St. Marks Place, the Jesus and Mary Chain's *Psychocandy* album blaring from the doorway, filling the street with the electric whine of grating guitars. We stop at one of the many folding tables set up on the edge of the street, vendors hawking everything from socks to sunglasses. Alexa plucks a pair of huge neon-green shades from a table and slides them over her face, obscuring her eyes completely. The Jesus and Mary Chain segues into Jane's Addiction's "Jane Says" as a group of punks pass by, safety pins in complicated patterns gracing their leather motorcycle jackets, buckles glinting silver in the late fall sunlight. One girl, her hair on end in a bright pink Mohawk, does a double take as Alexa slides the glasses over her placid blond features, the Mohawk girl's expression slightly amused, her lips curving into a smile.

"Are they me?" Alexa asks, face expressionless. She looks like a green bug, or an extra from a Human League video, her face whitened by the extreme color as if she's been video-edited. Washed out. Either way, she decidedly does not look like Alexa Forte, which is, in and of itself, pretty funny.

"Yeah, *totally*," I say with a snort, pulling the glasses from her face and throwing them back down as the Jamaican guy manning the table glares at me, yards of yellow cloth wound around his head in some kind of complicated headdress, dreads falling out of the bottom.

"Watch the merchandise, mon," he mumbles, reaching out to straighten the display of sunglasses, patting them into place.

"C'mon," I say, grabbing Alexa's arm, pulling her away from the table. She giggles nervously, following me obediently as a toddler as I lead her back into the crush of people, the street pulsating with life. A group of skaters glide by, their skateboards covered with brightly colored stickers, their pants so baggy that they wouldn't stay up at all if not for the belts pulled tight and low around their hips. The rush of wind pulls the hair away from my face with the force of gravity, and all at once I'm aware of how weirdly, inexplicably happy I am. The bright blue fall sky overhead, red and orange leaves crunching underfoot, the voices of the vendors melding together in a companionable chatter, Alexa's hand on my arm as I lead her more deeply into what is foreign territory for her but achingly familiar for me. I want to wrap all of downtown up in a big red bow and hand it, arms outstretched, to the next person I pass who looks unhappy or just plain tired. On days like these with the crisp wind at my back, the electric-blue sky, I am in love with New York, in love with the burnt-orange glow of autumn.

By the time we walk around the corner to Love Saves the Day, Alexa doesn't seem scared at all anymore. Inside, I watch as she flips through a rack of vintage dresses from the sixties with her usual confidence, pulling out a black sheath and holding it up to her slender frame, turning a critical eye toward the mirror. She holds the dress up to her body with one hand, using the other to pile her hair atop her head. Watching how comfortable she is with her beauty, her ease in flaunting it, I can't help but wonder if I will ever feel so at home in my own skin. Alexa sways gently in front of the mirror, seemingly entranced by what she finds there, and I'm aware that even the clerk with the huge Afro tagging jackets behind the counter has put down his pen and is now staring at her rapturously as she walks into the fitting room, flinging the pink velvet curtain shut behind her. A sudden hand on my shoulder jolts me out of my thoughts, and I spin around, eyes wild, ready to strike.

"I *thought* that was you," Sebastian says triumphantly, his face cracked in a smile, but I detect a bit of nervousness underneath his bravado. His eyes widen under smudgily applied blue liner as he gauges my reaction, the way my hands harden into fists in spite of myself, and he takes a small, tentative step back. "I was just coming over here to say hi! I saw you through the window." He points to the plate glass behind him, then grins impishly, biting his bottom lip.

As I stand there staring at him, I realize that I've never really seen Sebastian in the daylight. Stumbling out of clubs at eight a.m., yes. But never in the middle of the day, out on the street in real life. I'm shocked at how normal he looks without the feathers, the blue-and-white polka dots painted on his skin. He's wearing faded jeans with huge, clunky black shoes and a navy sweater, a very long red-and-blue-striped scarf wound around his neck, his short blond hair combed back from his face, a black messenger bag slung over one shoulder. But beneath his eyes are matching purple circles, and his complexion would be considered beautiful only to a family of skeletons.

I relax my hands, my pulse slowing as my vision realigns itself. I twist my face into a smile, trying to regain what's left of my composure. "Yeah," I say weakly, "it's definitely me." We stare at each other for a moment in that weird silence that crops up when you run into someone from the scene on the street, far from the dusky confines of the club. He looks me up and down, and I know he is thinking the same thing I am. *So this is what she looks like.*

"What are you doing down here?" The question I really want to ask is, How are you even *awake* at this hour? But I don't really have to—Sebastian's manic shuffling feet and relentless sniffing provide the answer without my having to say a word.

"Just doing a little shopping for the outlaw party. You're definitely coming, right?" His face scrunches up in mock worry, but I know Sebastian well enough to know it's all an act—no one misses Sebastian's parties, especially if, like me, they are lucky enough to be included on the invite.

"Definitely," I say, reaching out and squeezing his arm, trying to sound more excited than I really am. Sebastian's parties, though usually fun, are also chaotic and exhausting, the kind of evenings it can take days to recover from, and I know this truck thing will probably be no exception.

Just then Alexa glides over wearing the sheath dress, her hair piled on top of her head with two black lacquered chopsticks she must've pulled out from the bottomless depths of her tote. Sebastian looks her up and down, his grin widening further as he takes in her long, tanned legs that extend from the hem of the dress, her rosy heart-shaped face, and eyes that survey the scene coolly.

"What do you think?" she says, turning around so that we can see the dress from every angle.

"Fabulous," Sebastian gushes warmly, flitting around her like a bird. "Totally fierce." And then to me in mock horror, "Cat, where have you been *hiding* this gorgeous creature?"

I open my mouth, but before I can speak, Alexa holds out one hand in Sebastian's direction. "I'm Alexa," she says with a smile, taking his hand in her own and shaking it gently.

"Sebastian, Alexa, Alexa, Sebastian," I say in a drone, gesturing in the air between them, aware that my night and day lives have just messily collided in a vintage store on Second Avenue amidst the dresses of satin and crepe, the air permeated with the faint smell of mothballs mixed with incense, heavy as dirt. I feel dizzy, and I take a deep breath, filling my lungs. This is my world. *Mine.* Alexa is beside me shimmering like a gorgeous mirage, and I wonder if bringing her into my life was a huge mistake.

"So, how do you know each other?" Alexa sounds genu- inely curious, and as she waits for one of us to answer, she reaches up with one hand, pulling the chopsticks from her hair, the golden weight of it tumbling to her waist. It's a flaw- less move, and I can almost feel the molecules in the room re- arrange themselves around the curves of her flesh. It's a movie moment, and I wonder how long she's been practicing it in the mirror.

"We met at Tunnel," Sebastian says with obvious pride.

A look of confusion flits across Alexa's face, and she clicks the chopsticks in her hand against each other uneasily, her brow scrunched like an accordion. Perpetual insider that she is, Alexa is clearly uncomfortable with being on the outside, even for a moment.

"Tunnel?"

"The *club*?" Sebastian answers, a faint note of disbelief col- oring his voice. He looks at me as if to say, Where did you find this girl? I shrug, rolling my eyes at him apologetically and hoping Alexa doesn't notice.

"We're promoters," I say, trying to make it sound more le- git than it probably is. It definitely sounds better than the truth, which is that we get paid to go out and dress up, to scarf drugs like an unruly pack of two-year-olds at an all-you- can-eat birthday cake buffet. "We throw parties at Tunnel," I explain, shrugging like it's no big deal, and to someone like Alexa Forte who attends galas at the Met wearing couture dresses from Dior on a regular basis, it probably isn't.

"You should *totally* bring Alexa to the party!" Sebas- tian squeals, digging in his messenger bag for an invite, and handing Alexa a fluorescent-yellow scrap of paper. "Open bar till midnight. It would be so much *fun* if you could make it!" he chatters on, reaching out and squeezing both of Alexa's hands in his own, chopsticks and all. In spite of the fact that Alexa is, well, Alexa, and therefore cooler than I will ever be, it's clear that she's flattered by Sebastian's effusiveness, blushing prettily and squeezing his hands in return before he releases them.

"Yeah, maybe," I mumble, catching a glimpse of myself in the full-length mirror and wishing that everything was somehow different—my washed-out oval of a face, my straight dark hair, my ripped jeans and black pea coat—my entire life. My conversation with Sara in front of the deli haunts me, the way she stared out into the street, her face expressionless. Vacant. The store is overheated, and my stomach turns wildly beneath my clothes as I begin to panic. Why would anyone be interested in me when they could have even a smidge of Alexa's attention? Watching Alexa and Sebastian fawn over each other, a wave of jealousy sweeps through me with a force that almost brings me to my knees.

"See you later, Cat!" Sebastian calls over his shoulder as he skips out the front door, bells ringing at his back.

"Well, you're certainly a dark horse," Alexa muses, looking in the mirror and running her fingers through her mermaid hair. She turns around to face me, her lips gently curling in a smile so light that I may be imagining it. I stand there and weigh the possibilities, shifting from one foot to the other. She stares at me with those questioning eyes, her cool expression, and I know that jealousy or not, I have no choice. Despite myself, Alexa's appearance in my life has disturbed the order of things, knocked me half out of my insulated little world, my body hanging in a kind of freefall. I've opened a door and let her squeeze inside, into the life I've made for myself. And I want to see how it all plays out, even if it ends up hurting me. Or her. Now there's no turning back.

* * * *

BLOOMINGDALE'S, IN LATE AUGUST, *the smell of new leather, soft cashmere the color of overripe grapes, the ringing of bells as the elevator announces its arrival. My mother grabs a purple sweater, holding it up against my chest, her head tilting to the side, surveying me like an artist finishing a painting, bending the canvas to her will.* I like it, *I say, hoping I sound helpful, grateful, biting my lower lip as she tosses the sweater down on the heaping table and selects one the color of the lemon ices my father used to buy me on hot summer nights, small cables running across the chest. Shopping is one of the only things that seems to make my mother happy, her cheeks pink as a newborn's each time she releases her credit card from the confines of her Louis Vuitton wallet and hands it over.* We'll take both, *she says decisively, tucking the sweater under one arm and grabbing my hand, her red nails scraping the flesh of my palm in a familiar rasp.* For my beautiful daughter, *she says in a saccharine voice, smiling at the salesgirl, clearly reveling in the adoring-mother role that she loves to perform whenever we are out in public together.*

As I watch her hand the sweaters across the counter, her cheeks glowing like coals, I am learning something about excess, the language of desire, a sick feeling in my stomach every time I watch my mother make and remake me, my pale, unadorned body never enough.

FIFTEEN

I'M STANDING OUTSIDE TUNNEL, gaping at the enormous semi truck parked at the curb, at speakers the size of icebergs being loaded into the back end. The cobblestones are still slick from the light rain that fell a few hours earlier, abandoned cars parked at the curb among two Ferraris—one of them Christoph's—and a silver BMW. I haven't seen Christoph since that afternoon at his office, and my heart palpitates violently when I consider the possibility of running into him tonight, and what he'll say. What I might say back. There's something about him that exerts an irresistible pull, the way things that are dangerous draw you ever closer, whispering into your ear with their slow, seductive murmur. Chocolate. Tequila. Cocaine. The rush I get from being around Christoph mirrors the feeling of disappearing into a bathroom stall with Giovanni, hands shaking as I unwrap a tightly folded triangle of paper to reveal flakes of soft white powder. When I first started clubbing a year ago, I lived for that feeling. Now it makes me feel as if I'm on the edge of a cliff, the night sky hiding the jagged rocks lying in wait. Now I'm not sure I like it at all.

On the corner, a collection of bums stand around a fire they've made in a trash barrel, warming their hands above the orange flames while less than ten feet away, two women in full-length fox fur coats pat their teased manes of hair into place before marching up to the velvet ropes. Three hours from now they'll most likely be on the main dance floor alongside a couple of guys wearing pinstriped dress shirts, tiny glasses and red suspenders—the delineated markings of arbitrage or investment banking. As the club gets more mainstream, the scene will ultimately shift somewhere else, but for now, the yuppie impact is still negligible. I watch as they tap their stiletto heels against the pavement, waiting for the rope to magically be lifted. Maurice, who is working the front door tonight, stares straight ahead, a headset clipped to one ear, his arms folded over his massive chest. I know without even sticking around to watch that they will be granted admittance eventually. But not without a fifty-dollar entrance fee.

DJ Haruki is setting up for the night, his arms flexing as he bends over the turntable. I watch his minions unload massive crates of vinyl, sliding them toward the makeshift DJ booth at the back of the truck. Haruki is Sebastian's on-again, off-again boyfriend, and knowing how volatile their relationship is, it's a total crapshoot whether they'll be making out in the corner by the end of the evening or throwing beer bottles at each other's heads. The scene is complete pandemonium, club kids clamoring to get on board the party truck, waving yellow invites in their hands and dancing in the street to the music of oncoming traffic, their heels clicking against the stone like some kind of code only a band of drug-seeking, house-music-loving maniacs could decipher.

It's a chilly night, and I'm wearing a nude slip from the 1920s trimmed in frothy beige lace that's slightly yellowed and covers my knees completely, and a short, white faux fur jacket that Giovanni made last week. I pull the soft material around my body, shoulders shivering. Against my better judgment, Giovanni has slicked my hair back in a ponytail and attached a long extension, securing it with an elastic band so that my hair now appears to hang past my waist. In fact, it's pulled back from my face so tightly that my normally round eyes now have a curiously upward tilt, and my mouth is colored the red of a field of blissed-out poppies. When I finally look in the mirror, I don't recognize myself.

"What time was she supposed to be here?" Giovanni asks, pulling the sleeve of his jacket back to reveal a chunky silver watch with a heavy black band. The moon glows above our heads, filling the street with benevolent light. It is fully round and so huge that it almost looks as if we might reach out and pet its craggy contours.

"Ten," I say, squinting as a taxi approaches, stops to gawk at the madness and peels off down the street. "Maybe she's not coming." I let out a sigh, as if I'm horribly disappointed or inconvenienced, but the truth is that I'm feeling slightly relieved. I half suspected that she wouldn't show up anyway, that when it came right down to it, nerves and fear would probably get the best of her.

Sebastian appears, flanked by two highly impressive drag queens wearing short gold lamé dresses and enormous platinum-blond Marie Antoinette wigs, their towering hair almost overpowering their intricately made-up faces. Tonight Sebastian is wearing white shorts with bright red suspenders crossing the skin of his naked chest. His face is painted with a collection of blue and red dots, and the large, chunky black shoes he's wearing reduce his feet to leaden blocks. He looks like a demented clown who just escaped from the gayest circus on the planet, and I can't help but smile at the sight of him. I raise my hand in greeting, and his face lights up as he saunters over.

"Oh good, Cat, you made it!" His voice is breathy, as if he's been running up a flight of stairs. He looks at Giovanni, who shoots Sebastian a simpering smile. "So, where's your *friend*?" Clearly he does not mean Giovanni. Sebastian's eyes turn all squinty as he scans the crowd.

"Not sure," I say, prepared to begin making excuses, but knowing full well that after Sebastian's had his first hit of X, maybe a few lines of blow, he won't remember that Alexa didn't show. Actually, knowing the quality of the drugs he routinely procures, he probably won't remember Alexa even exists on planet Earth, much less that she dared to snub his party.

Just then a black limousine pulls up directly behind the truck, and a chauffeur in a black cap gets out and opens the passenger door. A leg appears, highly sculpted and ending in a neon-green patent-leather pump with a heel the width of an ice pick. I tap Giovanni on the shoulder and point toward the car, his mouth falling open at the sight of her body sheathed in the short black dress she bought at Love Saves the Day, hair falling to her waist in the kind of soft waves that are created only with a certain degree of expertise with hot rollers. Her lips are red, her hands sheathed in black fingerless fishnet gloves. She extricates herself from the limo with a kind of grace I've seen only in old movies, and nods curtly to the driver before walking over to us, her shoes tapping lightly on the stones. Although her heels are high and the ground is uneven, she walks fluidly, a coat of white fox fur thrown over her shoulders.

"Hey, Alexa," I say, my voice coming out as a squeak, still in shock that she's actually here, at an outlaw party, so far downtown that she might as well be swimming right now.

"You made it!" Sebastian squeals, leaning over to air-kiss her on both of her tanned, impeccably made-up cheeks.

"Alexa, this is my friend Giovanni." I gesture toward Giovanni, who is busily sizing up Alexa's wardrobe from head to toe, silently reading her.

"Charmed, darling." Giovanni reaches out and presses his lips to her hand with a romantic flourish. I giggle at Giovanni's theatrics while Sebastian glowers on the sidelines, rolling his eyes in disgust.

"So great to meet you," she purrs. "Is that the truck?" Alexa points at the semi, pursing her lips while skeptically raising one eyebrow. Somehow I cannot picture her smushed into the back end, pressed up against a collection of random body parts. Alexa looks as if her temperature rarely rises above tepid, and I wonder again what exactly I've done in bringing her here.

"Jesus Christ," Giovanni mutters, staring at the truck. "What about ventilation?"

I see his point. Once the back doors are shut, there are no windows, and with a hundred sweaty bodies packed in, things have the potential to get pretty unpleasant.

"Ventilation schmentilation," Sebastian scoffs, dismissing Giovanni's comment with a wave of his hand. "We'll just leave the back open!" Sebastian moves decisively toward the truck and we follow him like children, his suspenders blooming against his chest like a shotgun wound. Alexa's hand rests lightly on my arm as she glides across the cobblestones.

Once we step onto the semi, it begins to move, lurching down the street with a frenzied shout from the crowd, fists raised in the air, drinks sloshing over the sides of cups. I know that sooner than later, the floor will be so tacky that it will take enormous amounts of effort just to extricate a platform heel. We are pushing toward the back, Alexa's hand wrapped tightly in mine. I turn to look at her face and her expression is blank, affectless, but when I catch her eye, there is a sudden flash of panic as she takes in the teeming crowd, the half-naked club kids strewn across the back of the truck.

"I don't . . . ," she whispers, her free hand moving to her throat and hovering there for a moment.

"It'll be fine," I say, staring into her eyes. "*Really*."

I try to put as much emphasis on that last word as I can, imploring with my whole being that she's safe here, although I know the truth is much more complicated. And just like that, the fear slides away from her face and is gone, her expression aloof.

Sebastian shoves his body up to the front of the makeshift bar, which is nothing more than a couple of coolers pushed together, and after talking briefly to Ethan, whom I recognize from the Tunnel basement where he's a barback, Sebastian returns with two frosty bottles of champagne tucked under one arm, grinning widely as he pops the corks, white froth falling over his heavy black shoes. We pass the bottles around, sucking greedily as the liquid rushes up to fill our throats. The music crashes around us, and I watch as Haruki peels off his black leather vest, his skin glistening with sweat, the truck vibrating as it takes a sudden sharp turn and we fly past the water, the moonlight washing over us.

Alexa turns to me, her face animated from the champagne. "Let's dance," she yells, throwing her coat to the floor, swaying gracefully to the beat. I mirror her movements, the wind rushing through my dress as the truck slows for a stoplight. All at once, Alexa wraps her hand around my waist, pulling me close, her torso pressed flush against mine. Her face is so close, her skin is as smooth as vinyl. Do I want to kiss Alexa Forte? Not exactly. It's more like I want to be subsumed by her body, a place I imagine to be perfect and problem-free, though in my rational mind, I know better. The truck rams over a pothole in the road, the floor jolting beneath our feet, music grinding momentarily to a halt, and Alexa and I stumble, breaking apart and stepping back with nervous laughter, our eyes sliding away from each other.

"Let's go and sit down," I yell as the truck rights itself and the music begins again, a heavy beat. I point to the far corner of the truck. Giovanni is already seated on the floor like a pasha presiding over the festivities, Alexa's coat thrown over his shoulders.

"What's up, lezzies?" Giovanni says with a smile as we approach, and I reach out and clock him in the shoulder, grinning from ear to ear.

"Bitch," Giovanni says lovingly, rubbing his arm as Alexa and I flop down, curling our legs under ourselves. Alexa sits up so straight, it looks like she has a metal rod rammed up her spine. I, on the other hand, have no problem with slouching most of the time; my shoulders are so round that I'm practically C-shaped. The movement of the truck has slowed, and the rocking sensation is vaguely pleasurable, like swaying in a hammock.

"Where's Sebastian?" I ask, scanning the crowd for his impish face and coming up empty.

"Who cares?" Giovanni answers flatly, flicking open the top of his vintage onyx poison ring and lifting his hand to his nose, closing his eyes as he breathes in. Snorting coke from a plastic bag is way too déclassé for Giovanni, and pulling out a mirror would attract unwanted attention. I watch as Alexa surveys Giovanni with obvious interest as his eyes open again, noticeably wider now, taking in the lit-up buildings in the distance, the World Trade Center coming up on the left.

"Want some?" he asks amiably, holding out his hand in Alexa's direction. She hesitates for a moment, only a moment. In fact, I'm not sure Giovanni even notices, and even though I'm thinking all the while, *Don't do it* as she reaches over, scooping a hit under the pinky nail of her right hand, I stay silent as she brings her fingertip to her nose, inhaling deeply as her eyes close.

"Cat?" Giovanni holds out the ring expectantly, and as I bend over and breathe in, the drug rushes through my body like Christmas, a holiday in my head, the rush before the fall off a tall building, a swan dive into the night. I close my eyes, silver sparklers dancing in the blackness, and open them only when Alexa begins to speak.

"Who's that guy?" Alexa points one slim finger at Ethan, the muscles in his arms bulging against the tight black T-shirt, his wavy shoulder-length hair the color of toasted almonds. Ethan is a dead ringer for Michael Hutchence, the lead singer of INXS, and it's a rare weekend when girls aren't crowding the bar of the basement, flirting suggestively with him. Sometimes I find myself staring at him, wondering what it would be like to have someone that gorgeous as a boyfriend, but when he looks up from the bar with his gentle questioning gaze, I always look away. There's something about Ethan that reminds me of Julian, the way Ethan moves, the hair falling in his face coupled with the determined set of his jaw. I wonder where Julian is tonight. I stare off into space and picture him in his room, the Ramones blasting from the stereo. Is he thinking of me at all? Or am I now just another crazy girl who freaked out on him with no warning?

"The barback?" Giovanni wrinkles his brow, flipping the lid of his ring closed with a flourish of his wrist. "I think his name's Elvis, maybe?"

"It's Ethan," I say, rolling my eyes in exasperation. "Why can't you ever remember anyone's name?"

"I remember yours, don't I?" Giovanni says sweetly, taking a pull off the champagne bottle he's managed to sequester over here.

"Only because you see me practically every damn day."

"In any case, he's tasty," Giovanni answers dreamily, his brown eyes liquid and soft as they follow Ethan's movements. As if he can sense us talking about him over the crashing din of the music, Ethan looks up, his eyes stopping on Alexa.

"I think I need a drink," Alexa murmurs, her eyes locked on Ethan, and, as if in a trance, she moves gracefully to her feet and disappears into the crowd that breaks over her like a wave, her blond hair shining before she evaporates completely.

"Girl," Giovanni croons under his breath, his mouth agape, "your friend is *trouble*."

"Don't I know it," I murmur, watching her smile engagingly once she captures Ethan's attention, whispering in his ear and pushing the mass of his hair back with one hand. It's obvious from the way he leans into her touch, his lips curled into a smile, that he wants her. And who wouldn't? I cross my arms over my chest, hiding the small amount of flesh that Giovanni is forced to push together and manipulate with corsets and tape in order to look even remotely substantial.

After about an hour of driving around aimlessly, the truck lurching from side to side like a drunken party guest, people begin throwing up, and Sebastian directs the truck back to Tunnel, where we pile out on the curb, dazed but intact. As we move through the doors and down to the basement, I look over my shoulder for Alexa, catching sight of her walking arm in arm with Ethan, her face uplifted and turned toward his, her eyes shining. Noticing me, she raises one hand in greeting, but she doesn't leave Ethan's side, her blond mane mingling with his light brown curls. I seem to have lost Giovanni as well, but am not worried. This is how the evening usually goes—we split up at some point to get a drink, schmooze and dance wildly, and are usually reunited by two a.m. or so, giggling in a corner somewhere or bent over Giovanni's poison ring in a bathroom stall.

Once in the basement, I collapse on a sofa in the corner, sighing heavily, my feet twitching spasmodically from the coke. I'm lost in the labyrinth of my thoughts when a voice cuts through the jumble of static and I look up to the sound of my name, Christoph looming above me. He smiles, and suddenly I feel very small. I jump to my feet, teetering unsteadily on my heels, and fall halfway into his arms, blushing furiously as he places his hands on my shoulders, righting me. My pulse races crazily at the touch of his hands on my skin.

"What are you doing here?" I ask the moment I am standing straight, looking at the concrete floor before lifting my eyes. Christoph rarely sets foot in the basement, preferring to receive updates on the night's festivities from the cushy confines of his office. The bass thumps all around us, and I can feel it in my feet, seeping through my shoes and climbing up my legs in a fit of delicious tickling.

"I work here," he says, his eyes flashing with amusement.

"What a coincidence," I say nervously. "So do I."

We are silent for a long moment, and I can feel my heart galloping in my chest. The minute Christoph gets within ten feet of my body, my palms turn clammy and I begin to sweat.

"So," Christoph says, coughing once and looking away briefly before his eyes return to my face. "I would like to take you to Florent tonight—when I'm done here."

Florent is a diner in the Meatpacking District that's open 24/7 and is usually filled with an assortment of night owls who generally resemble the cast of a Fellini film, or the long-term residents of a maximum-security mental ward. Take your pick.

"You mean tomorrow morning?" I quip, raising one eyebrow. I don't know what's wrong with me. Whenever I get insanely panicky, I fall into joke mode. I'm sure it's horribly annoying, but Christoph doesn't seem irritated. He looks down at me with something not unlike interest, his eyes so light, they are almost colorless. A pack of club kids I don't recognize push past, wearing what look like birdcages on their heavily teased and lacquered hair, their spacey, blissed-out expressions a clear indicator that they're probably on the new drug, Special K, which I have never tried. From the way these kids are falling all over each other like a pack of uncoordinated toddlers, I have no plans to, either. Their movements widen the space between Christoph and me, their shouts and giggles reverberating over the insistent drone of the music so that I can barely think. I feel dislocated, as if I've just landed on some alien planet, and Christoph is still staring at me, waiting for an answer.

My throat is as dry as paper, and to my own amazement I can hear myself saying yes the way I say yes to coke, to staying out until five a.m. on a school night, to the tide that pulls at me again and again, sucking me into the soft, wet sand. I am thankful for the loudness of the music enveloping us, because my voice sounds more like a croak than anything resembling the sounds produced by an actual living being. Christoph leans toward me, trying to hear over the crowd that closes in on us, the heat, the din, the light that bathes our bodies in a red-and-blue haze, light that feels almost holy as I say it again, sounding more sure than I know I will ever feel about anything at all.

SIXTEEN

I SIT ACROSS FROM CHRISTOPH, stirring cream into my coffee, the inky-black surface lightening to a pale mocha. Outside, the four a.m. sky is still pitch black, and birds have begun nestling in the trees, waiting for daylight. It is totally out of character for Christoph to leave the club so early in the evening, but when he appeared at my side, I hesitated only for a moment, stopping at the bar where Alexa was leaning across the polished wooden surface, trading kisses with Ethan. As we approached, her eyes swept over Christoph, missing nothing.

"You OK?" I asked as she pulled away from Ethan, crossing one long leg over the other.

"Totally," she said with a smile, her teeth glowing phosphorescent. Her hair fell across her eyes, obscuring them, a curtain falling after a performance, and she turned back around, lighting a cigarette.

My spoon scrapes against the porcelain cup as I spin it round and round in an attempt to calm my nerves, even though after the coke I've done tonight, coffee is the last thing I need. I stare into the dark liquid to avoid Christoph's eyes, how they seem to take in everything—my inexperience, the chipped silver polish on my bitten nails. Finally, I look up. One hand rests beneath his chin, his own untouched cup on the red paper place mat in front of him.

"You look nervous," Christoph says slowly, as lazily as if we're on a beach somewhere, hot sun shining down on our half-naked bodies, a glass of rum punch in one hand.

"Well," I say, aware that I'm stammering a little, "I guess I am."

I die a little inside when I realize that my cheeks are probably bright red. Could I seem any more like a stupid high school girl? And if that's what I am, why is he here? *Why are you?* the little voice inside my brain pipes up. *Why are you here?* Alexa's voice trickles through my mind like water, the half smile in her voice: *Why do you do anything that's bad for you?* I'm afraid to know the answer to that question, so I push it out of my mind, erase it before it can take root, sinking its black tentacles into the spongy mass of my brain.

"Do I make you nervous?" he asks, reaching out and placing one hand over mine.

I'm aware that I've stopped breathing. When his fingers grasp my own, the warmth of his hand is as comforting as a basin of warm water, his touch quietly seductive. Not *right* exactly, but not altogether wrong either. Christoph is the last person on the planet who should be having this effect on me, but at the touch of his skin, a heat runs through my body, a dry wind, and I realize all at once just how lonely I've been these past few months. All my life, really.

He squeezes my hand for a quick moment and releases it, smiling as he picks up his coffee and takes a sip, his eyes never leaving my face.

"Maybe," I manage to squeak out, feeling like all the air in the room has suddenly been sucked out by a giant vacuum while I wasn't looking. Maybe? Saying Christoph *maybe* makes me nervous is like saying that coke makes me just a *bit* antsy. I'm so on edge that my heart is ready to make its eminent exit through my mouth.

"Why is that, do you think?"

I watch the hostess walk behind the counter, her hair falling down from her carefully constructed bouffant, the skin over her cheeks stretched shiny and taut as plastic wrap.

"Maybe because you're my boss?" It comes out as a question, my voice raised at the end of the sentence. I look out the plate-glass window behind his head and at the rain that has started to fall lightly on the pavement, the sidewalks slick. Across the street, graffiti covers the brick façade of an apartment building, the bright yellow letters rising out of the dark: REAGANOMIKS SUX.

"What if I wasn't?" Christoph asks, jolting me back to the moment.

"Wasn't what?"

"Your boss."

I manage a half smile, every beat of my heart strained. "Are you firing me?"

"If that's what it takes."

Now Christoph smiles, his teeth slightly crooked, and leans back in his chair and loosens his ponytail until his hair falls around his face.

"You like working at the club, don't you."

He sounds like he cares, like he actually wants to know, so I lean forward on my elbows, my jacket creaking like an old chair as I rest my weight on my arms.

"I think I have trouble dealing with reality."

As soon as the words leave my lips, I realize just how true they are. Why I'm saying this to Christoph right now in the early morning in this greasy diner is really anyone's guess. I feel the blood rush to my face as I speak as the tension that forms in the space between us deepens and stretches taut.

"What do you mean?" he wonders aloud, the crease between his eyes more prominent. "Isn't *this* reality?" He gestures to the room before us with one hand, the punks with blue and pink Mohawks sitting at a table in the corner, the chains on their boots jangling, the pack of gays from the nearby drag bar dressed in mesh tank tops and ripped jeans, and I begin to fear the dawn that will sneak up in the sky, streaking the room with the first flush of blue light as the sun moves higher, eradicating the cool freshness of early morning.

"This? Not really. It's still dark out, for one thing." I reach for my coffee cup and wrap my hands around it protectively, grateful to have something to fidget with. "The club kind of exists in its own alternate universe, you know? It doesn't really have anything to do with the daily routine of school, subway, homework . . ." I concentrate on the music moving scratchily through the speakers overhead, some grating Muzak version of Hall and Oates's "Private Eyes" among frantic handclaps and a syrupy orchestration, afraid that I've said too much.

"What about your family? What do they think of you spending your nights in some grimy nightclub?"

"Isn't it a little late for you to be concerned now?" I ask sarcastically, taking a sip of coffee. As soon as the hot liquid hits the back of my throat, I wish I could spit it out, my tongue coated in an oily bitterness. Christoph laughs, and his face relaxes. "Besides," I add, "I don't live at home anyway, so my parents don't have much to say about it."

"Good to know," Christoph says lightly, reaching into his pocket and throwing a five-dollar bill on the table. At the sight of the money, my heart plummets. He's obviously bored with me if he wants to get out of here so quickly. What I don't understand is why I actually care. It's not like I wanted to hang out with Christoph all night. In fact, the very idea fills me with a kind of terror I've previously only read about in Stephen King novels. All at once, I'm sweating, my temples damp, and I reach up and smooth my hair back with my fingertips, trying to compose myself. What if he tried to touch me somewhere a lot more . . . friendly? Or, God forbid, kiss me? *Maybe it wouldn't be so bad,* my inner voice interjects, annoying me. *He held your hand and you didn't exactly run for the door, now, did you?* Still, there is a huge difference between someone holding your hand across the table, and placing their lips over your own, your breath mingling together until your mouth opens, willingly or not.

"I have to be up in a few hours." Christoph smiles apologetically. "I have a meeting with some investors. But I would like to take you to dinner some night soon if you're free."

"Dinner?" I am dumbfounded. I can't imagine sitting across from Christoph at a table, ingesting actual food and making small talk at the same time. My brain might explode from the strain of having to cut my food into proper bites while not spilling any on the tablecloth or myself, and at the same time trying to impress him with my witty repartee.

"Yes, you know—that activity people engage in when they are hungry." Christoph's slight accent is like the sound of stones skipping on a lake, the music of rippling water.

"Umm . . . ," I stammer, hoping for time.

"You do eat. Don't you?"

"Sometimes," I finally answer. "Rarely, if I'm being truthful. But I might be willing to make an exception this one time."

"How wonderful of you," Christoph answers, his blue eyes flashing with amusement. "Have you been to Chaos yet?"

Chaos is a new club that opened a few weeks ago. I went to the opening-night party but left early to try to study for a history exam that I ended up barely passing anyway. Sometimes I have no idea why I even bother. I should just drop out of school and be done with it, but Sara would probably hunt me down and kill me. The best thing about Chaos is the rooftop terrace and dance floor, but it opens only after three a.m. It's full of Eurotrash zombies and models who shop for their structured, all-black ensembles exclusively at stores like Armani or Charivari, who think living dangerously is being out past midnight on a Thursday. Needless to say, it's not really my scene.

"I was there for the opening, but I didn't know they served food."

"They don't, normally. I've arranged for a private table on the roof. I was hoping you'd be free a week from today—next Saturday."

"I work on Saturday," I answer automatically, knowing the moment the words fall from my lips just how totally absurd they are. Christoph owns the club, so Christoph can do as he likes with everything he presides over—including me. Especially me. Looking at his face, at how casually he's suggested this evening, I wonder for the first time if that's all it is to him, if he's summoned me forth with the same arrogance with which one might order a fine meal, snapping his fingers for champagne and knowing that it will appear, the bottle beaded with moisture, the silver bucket shining and packed with ice. I imagine myself spread out on a platter, edible flowers strewn through my hair as a waiter hands Christoph a carving knife. I know that I am much like Christoph's red Ferrari, like all his women parading in and out of the club swathed in tight black dresses: an object to be won and collected. That I am as different from these women as is imaginable is not important, nor is the fact that I'm only seventeen. The fact remains that if Christoph wants me in this way, even if I am one of many, it must mean that I am something of value—at least to one person in the world.

It occurs to me that Christoph, in some strange way, reminds me of my mother. The same imperiousness and certainty of worth, of absolute rightness. Entitlement.

This is mine, and this and this and this . . .

"What's your favorite food?" Christoph asks, pulling on a tan leather jacket, the highly glossed patina shining under the fluorescent light.

"Pizza," I blurt out without thinking, but also knowing there's nothing I can really do to sabotage this date, to keep it from happening. Most likely I will be sitting on that rooftop next Saturday stumbling through an atrocious amount of small talk and trying not to spill wine down the front of my dress. There is a look of desire in his eyes, brimming there, the space between us as electrically charged as the air before a thunderstorm, the smell of ozone in the air, a yellowed sulfur. Still, even though I know I have the power to cut this whole scenario off before it really has time to begin, I'm frozen in place, my hands clutching the sides of my chair.

When I nod my assent almost imperceptibly, with only the slightest move of my head, Christoph smiles slowly, and I wonder in that moment if there was really any choice at all.

* * * *

THE APARTMENT IS HUSHED AND QUIET, *and I turn fitfully in my sleep, the bed a prison, trapping me in dreams that make me shake upon waking. My teeth chatter like a mouthful of old bones, like I've been grinding them down to gravel all night long. In my dream, the door opens and my mother steps inside, her body clothed in a black peignoir, her toenails painted a brilliant red that shines against the white carpet as she pads purposefully to my side, my eyes opening groggily at the sliver of light from the hallway. The smell of her perfume fills my nose with its harsh and acrid scent.* Jean Patou, *I can almost hear her say conspiratorially in my ear.* Jean Patou 1000.

I've gotten your report card, *she hisses, holding up the offending yellow slip of paper so that it floats in front of my face.* It won't do, Caitlin. It won't do at all. *At this point in the dream I begin to toss in my bed. Sometimes I yell out, as if by screaming I can somehow alter the trajectory of events, wake myself into the present. The stiff paper drops to the floor, and my blood thuds in my ears as my mother's other hand comes out from behind her back, the blade of an ax glinting in the streams of fractured light filtering in through the open door.*

Put your head in my lap, Caitlin, *she croons, her voice more soothing than chamomile.* Put your head in my lap. *Almost against my will, I move silently, tears running down my cheeks without sound. I feel the warmth of her thighs under my face, her flesh burning like ice through the thin fabric. Her free hand runs through my hair softly, gently as the ax swings down.*

SEVENTEEN

I SIT UP IN BED, gasping for breath, the air closing in around me like a cloak I can't shrug off. The clock ticks insistently on the bedside table, alerting me to the fact that it's 6:59 in the morning, and that I have been asleep for approximately one hour. The dream is always the same, waking me in the early morning hours unfailingly, no matter how many drinks I consume or pills I throw down my throat. I push my hair from my face with a damp palm and realize I am thirsty, so thirsty, it is as if I'm on a sand dune, the ground hot and arid beneath me, the unrelenting sunlight battering my body.

I reach over to the bedside table, knocking the clock to the floor with a sharp clattering sound that sets my teeth on edge, and feel around until my hands close around a glass of water that's probably been there at least two days, maybe more. I chug it down, wincing at the stale, dead taste in my mouth.

I reach for the phone, the room swimming before my eyes. Even in the dimness of the room, my practiced fingers move clairvoyant over the keypad. When I hear Sara's voice in my ear as if through a veil of hazy smoke and gravel, my panic begins to recede. I manage to spit out the words *dream, again, scared, now, help* into her waiting ears, and the relief I feel when she tells me to just come over is so intense that tears squeeze out from the corners of my eyelids and begin their slow descent. The early winter sky outside the window is a leaky ballpoint pen, stars obscured behind patchy clouds that glow opaquely in the light of the moon that's fading away.

When the cab pulls up in front of her building, Sara is waiting in the lobby, slouched in a huge black leather armchair, watching the revolving glass doors with sleepy eyes. She's wearing a black hooded sweatshirt and a pair of pink pajama pants with giant martini glasses embossed on the fabric in black ink, her feet obscured by furry slippers. Her hair is a mass of tangled blond curls that look like they're trying to make a run for the Canadian border. At the familiar sight of her, I feel my heart begin to stop the bizarre skipping and stopping thing it always does after the dream ends and I awaken, the hard muscle of my heart bumping clumsily against my ribs.

"You OK?" she says as I get closer, taking in the black leggings I pulled on hastily and the thin white T-shirt that covers my torso, my skin scattered with goose bumps in the morning chill. Her brow crinkles with concern, her eyes damp pools, and at that moment my gratefulness is so huge that I want to pull her body to me and hang on for dear life.

"Better now," I say as she stands up, placing an arm around my shoulders, which I realize now are shaking. "Better here."

I know that I sound completely unhinged bordering on unintelligible, but I also know that Sara has seen me like this before more times than she can probably count, and that I don't need to be more embarrassed than I already am. There's something about the dream that always paralyzes me, throwing an icy blanket over my soul and squeezing it with dead fingers. I guess some might call this a panic attack, but all I know is that if this is just panic, then I have no idea what I'd do if there was a real emergency. Probably curl up in a ball and hyperventilate until I die.

We ride up seventeen floors in the elevator, my head light, and slip silently into the apartment. Sara's left the door open a crack so she doesn't have to ring the bell to get back in with me, and I follow the familiar terrain of the long hallway as we pad softly down the carpet to her bedroom, my hands holding on to the walls for support. Once inside, I feel the last remaining traces of fear begin to slide away as I look around at the room I know as well as the lines crossing my own palms: the broken Betamax that Sara got for her eleventh birthday thrown in a corner, a VCR and TV set up along one wall, the posters lining the fuchsia walls, the Cure, Bauhaus, Pet Shop Boys, Depeche Mode, Duran Duran, the Sisters of Mercy, the motley crew of tattered teddy bears and fuzzy, dilapidated penguins strewn atop a queen-sized mattress on the gray carpeted floor. The large windows that overlook Park Avenue are shrouded in swirls of heavy black material that makes the room seem cavelike, despite the early morning light threatening to streak the sky and belie the impending rain. I would know this room if I were blindfolded—the cloying purple scent of the Aussie Sprunch spray Sara liberally applies each morning, the smoky incense that smells of green tea and cedar that she buys in bulk on

w streets of Chinatown, and the scent of Sara her-
rk musk mixed with the cleanness of lemons and the
psychedelic haze of patchouli. An old New Order tape plays
softly on the red boom box on top of the dresser. The track is
"Your Silent Face."

Sara throws herself on top of the bed, pulling the white
comforter up to her chin with an audible groan that signals
me to climb in next to her and rest my head on her shoulder.
Her blond springy curls tickle my face, and I push them away
gently with one hand, patting them down on the pillow like
I'm consoling a small child.

"What brought it on this time?" Sara whispers sleepily.

"Not sure," I answer with a deep sigh as my body begins to
let go and relax. "Nothing. Everything?"

"Uh, can you maybe be more specific?" Sara says with a
giggle.

"Alexa came out with me last night. And I went to breakfast with Christoph. Before that, I partied on a semi truck
that drove around downtown packed with about a hundred
screaming club kids who were blitzed out of their collective
minds. So one of those things, maybe? All of them?"

Sara sits straight up in bed, and the whites of her eyes
and her platinum hair glow in the dimness of the room. "I'm
sorry," she deadpans. "I think I just hallucinated. *Alexa Forte*
partied with you on a *truck*? Did she run away screaming into
the night?"

"Hardly," I snort. "I think she went home with a barback,
actually."

"Slut," Sara says, giggling.

"Totally."

"And how did you end up with *Christoph*?" Sara cannot keep the note of revulsion from creeping into her voice, and at the sound of it, I immediately become defensive. Sara thinks Christoph is a creep, one notch above child molester. She's never even met him, but every time I've so much as mentioned his name, she's become agitated and suspicious. Maybe it's because Sara's dad had an affair a few years ago with some twenty-year-old nitwit he met through the personals, of all places. Her parents worked it out, eventually, though according to Sara they still go to couples therapy twice a week.

"I didn't end *up* with him. We just went to breakfast."

Sara lies back down and turns on her side to face me, one hand propped beneath her head. I can feel her unsaid thoughts like heat-seeking missiles. When she speaks, the words come slowly, carefully, as if I might break at the sound of them.

"Were you high last night?"

I shrug. "A little. Not really. Not bad."

Sara sighs, flipping onto her back and crossing her arms over her chest.

"I shouldn't have ever taken you there in the first place," she mumbles. "I could fucking kick myself, I really could."

There is a tremble in her voice, and even though I'm not looking at her, I know she's gnawing at her bottom lip the way she always does when she's upset. By tomorrow, she'll be able to peel the skin off in strips and will once again be addicted to the small pot of Carmex she always carries in her bag.

"What are you *talking* about?" I prop myself up on one elbow to see her face better. "I would have found it anyway, and if not the club, something else. I don't need saving," I say softly. "That's not your job."

"Then whose is it?" she says quietly.

I fall silent, burying my head in the pillow. The soft cotton smells of the musk of her perfume and of the sweet scent of detergent. The room is heavy with the sound of our breathing, with all that remains unsaid, Sara's chest rising and falling beneath her sweatshirt.

"What about school, Cat? I mean, I don't want to sound like some kind of *mom* or something, but what about the SATs? Have you even started studying?"

"Jesus, Sara, I'll figure it out," I say, unable to keep the annoyance from my voice. "I will," I say more quietly. Even as the words leave my lips, I know they are a lie.

Sara exhales loudly, and when I look over at her, I think I see a tear squeezing its way out of the corner of her eye. I want to reach out and wipe it away, but instead I lie there silent, do nothing.

"You're not seriously considering starting anything with Christoph, are you? I mean . . . he's, like, old enough to be your dad!"

"Gross," I mutter, pulling the blanket up to my neck. "Besides, my dad never takes me to breakfast."

"That's so not what I meant," Sara answers, irritation creeping in little by little. "I know you're pissed at me for saying this, but I'm worried, OK? First that psycho Julian, and now Christoph. Is it *possible* for you to have worse taste in guys?"

"Just chill out," I snap, turning over on my side. "First off, I freaked out on Julian the other day in the hall, and I doubt he'll ever speak to me again anyway. And I just had *breakfast* with Christoph. It's not like he deflowered me on the hood of a car in the middle of Times Square or something."

There's a long pause. I can hear the traffic outside Sara's window start to pick up, the rain hurling itself against the panes of glass.

"Well," Sara says after what seems like forever. "Not *yet.*"

I immediately break into laughter, the giggles bubbling up from my throat like a magnum of good champagne shaken and released from the bottle. When we catch our breath, Sara clears her throat, reaching up to pull her mass of curls farther away from her face so that they're spread out all over the pillow.

"You really freaked out on this Julian kid?" Sara asks, her voice low and sleepy.

"Unfortunately," I mutter. "I'm sure he thinks I'm completely insane."

"Oh, whatever," Sara snorts, kicking my foot under the blanket. "He ignored you the other day! What does he expect? And I told you, his ex was a total psycho. Completely bananas. Loony tunes. I'm sure he's used to it."

"It doesn't matter anyway," I say, my throat an aching hollow tube as my mind floods with the golden hue of his skin, the upward tilt of his dark eyes. The hurt and confusion reflected in them as I walked away. It's so easy to hurt people, just by being alive.

"Guys are so annoying," Sara says, throwing her warm leg across my own and yawning loudly. "You're better off here with me."

My heart somersaults in time with the memory of Julian's face, and I turn toward Sara, my head on her shoulder, our bodies curled together like a pair of bookends, a matched set. As our breathing slowly quiets, fading into the insistent sound of the rain lashing the windows, Sara taps her foot against mine in a code I can neither recognize nor decipher, but which lulls me far from terror and into sleep.

EIGHTEEN

I'M STANDING OUTSIDE the bio lab at break on Monday morning when I see Alexa moving down the hall as if in slow motion, her body wrapped in an enormous black sweater that makes her look more delicate and breakable than usual. She's alone for once, and without her usual entourage she seems smaller, less powerful. When she gets closer, I notice the circles beneath her eyes she can't hide with powder and paint, lavender hollows that hint at just how she spent the rest of her weekend. Even though she's clearly exhausted, a rosy flush decorates her cheeks, her sleepless eyes glittering.

I spent the rest of the weekend at Sara's, safe beside her in the bed, watching movies and stuffing our faces with pizza and the Little Debbie snacks her mother always keeps in the well-stocked kitchen cupboard along with the other junk she buys for Sara but her trainer won't allow her to consume. I wasn't scheduled to work on Saturday, but when I got home late Sunday afternoon, the answering machine showed three hang-ups, the sound of breathing filling the tape with a whooshing sound before it clicked off. As I stood there, Christoph's face filled my mind, making me dizzy, and I had to sit down on the bed and close my eyes, skin mottled with goose bumps that prickled my flesh.

"Hey." Alexa's voice is as breezy as if we're at a garden party in the Hamptons instead of loitering in a vaguely antiseptic hallway outside a stuffy classroom.

"Where'd you end up the other night?" I ask, knowing the answer well before the words even leave her lips.

She smiles. "Oh, you know. Here and there."

I nod, playing it cool. No matter how hard I try, though, I'll never be as unflappable as Alexa Forte. It's just not in my DNA.

"You like him." I say this as a statement, flatly, because it's obvious. If it weren't so amusing, it would almost be sad. I've been clubbing for about a year and I'm like an incurable disease. Alexa goes out for one night and guys are throwing themselves at her feet. All things considered, she could probably do a lot worse. Ethan's gorgeous, and from what I've heard, which admittedly isn't much, he's also pretty smart. The only drawback being that he's also at least twenty-four and working as a barback at a nightclub—something I'm pretty sure Alexa's mother wouldn't find desirable in any sense of the word.

"What's not to like?" She crinkles her brow as if I'm the dumbest human to ever walk the face of the earth, and as far as Alexa Forte is concerned, I probably am. "He's totally hot."

"True," I say with a sheepish smile. I can't even pretend I know what she's talking about. I have no idea what it would be like to roll around in bed with someone you were completely into for an entire weekend, climbing out of each other's arms only to eat bits of stale toast and lick flat champagne off each other's naked bodies. Most of the time I can't even imagine letting a stranger get close enough to touch me. That being said, the experience of trusting another human being enough to let them put part of their own anatomy *inside* me would probably cause my brain to short-circuit entirely, filling my head with a dangerous sputtering electricity. With that thought, I shudder, my shoulders twitching reflexively.

"Are you going to see him again?"

"He wants me to come to the club and hang out on Saturday night while he works." She shrugs as if the thought is pedestrian at best, but the shine in her eyes tells me otherwise. She is seriously smitten, even if she doesn't want anyone to know it.

"So what happened to *you*?" Alexa's expression is mischievous, as if she's just swallowed a delicious secret, one she wants to keep to herself.

"Nothing," I say quickly, my tone offhand and breezy, both because it happens to be true, and to change the subject. Christoph, like everything else in my nocturnal life, exists only in that space. I cannot imagine him doing something as normal and everyday as making coffee or toast for breakfast, then reading the paper. If sunlight touched him, I imagine he'd disappear, crumbling into dust. "We just went to breakfast, then I went home."

"Uh-huh." Alexa nods disbelievingly. "Sure you did."

I laugh, opening my mouth to protest, when Britney and Alison, two of Alexa's minions, begin their slow strut down the hall, their eyes sweeping the hallway and then widening in shock at the incongruous sight of their fearless leader engaged in a conversation with the weirdo who dyes her hair random colors and has some kind of bizarro life that does not involve finding the perfect Jessica McClintock peasant dress to wear to the next senior prom at Dalton or Spence.

Britney turns to Alison and begins whispering something behind her cupped hand, her French manicure flashing in the fluorescence of the hallway, her lips moving without sound as Alison throws her mane of dark hair over one shoulder and dissolves into peals of laughter.

Although Alexa doesn't turn around or acknowledge their approach, their presence registers in her eyes as a subtle flicker, but her expression does not change.

"I should go," she says, barely moving her lips. "Come over tomorrow night."

I nod slightly as the salad girls arrive in a cloud of Obsession perfume thick enough to qualify as a full body assault.

Britney raises one dark blond brow, nostrils flaring as she takes in the black sweater I found in a thrift store on Avenue A, the leggings that end in combat boots covered in spray paint, my hair pulled back in a messy knot. With her excessively long legs and long, aquiline nose, Britney reminds me of a horse. Whenever I see her, I have this urge to put her in a barn and feed her hay until she whinnies appreciatively.

"Slumming it, Lex?" Her tone is cloying, but the look she shoots in my direction is equal parts honey and arsenic.

Alexa's face ices over, her eyes deadened. "Like you'd know anything about it," she answers, her voice clipped and dangerous. "Let's evacuate."

Without another word, the three sweep past me, linking arms with Alexa in the middle, of course. As she glides down the hall, Britney chattering excitedly in her ear, Alexa turns to look back at me over her shoulder, one eye closing in a practiced wink. Somehow the thought that Alexa Forte is now living a double life thrills me in an unexpected way. *Maybe we're not so different after all,* a voice pipes up excitedly inside me, her tone brimming with optimism. Unfortunately, she is answered immediately by the part of me that already knows better, the part of me that is continually disappointed. *This isn't a movie,* she hisses, *and some random encounter isn't nearly enough to demolish the intricate levels of the high school caste system, honey.*

At lunch, I'm sitting on the steps with Molly, this girl from my history class who lives on Eighty-Ninth and Lexington and is totally anorexic and eats the same thing every day for lunch: a carton of Dannon vanilla fat-free yogurt and a bagel. Molly has lank red hair that she's cut in an asymmetrical bob, and she wears wire-rimmed silver glasses and granny boots that lace tightly up her thin ankles. She favors sweaters and shirts with wide lace collars, and when I picture her room at home, I imagine her trapped under a deep pile of doilies, gasping for air. She divides her bagel into strips, separating the soft white dough from the hard, shiny bagel skin. The dough goes in the trash or is tossed to the pigeons swarming the street. Watching her, I begin to crave steak, French fries, chocolate mousse, fried dough covered in powdered sugar and dripping with oil. Eating her bagel takes almost the whole period, and by the time she's finished, I am hypnotized into a stupor.

It's cold out, the trees finally stripped of dead leaves. In ten days or so it will be Thanksgiving, turkeys with all the trimmings, the sweet spicy scent of pumpkin pie permeating the air with cloves and cinnamon. I don't know what's more depressing, the fact that I will most likely be eating ramen noodles on my bed while watching *Gone With the Wind* or that I actually care. I could always go to Sara's, but no matter how much she loves me, I would just end up feeling like a fifth wheel, a charity case without a family, someone worthy of pity.

I'm eating a container of slightly mushy fruit salad I bought at the deli across the street when Julian comes careening down the street on his skateboard, a plastic bag from Subway in one hand. He's wearing dark glasses that hide his eyes, and I can't tell what he's thinking as he begins to slow down, kicking the board up into his free hand as he comes to a stop directly in front of the school.

Without even knowing what I'm doing or why, I stand up, my salad falling to the pavement in a brightly colored mess. Julian just looks at me, his face impassive. Every time I think about the scene between us in the hall the other day, my stomach deflates and I want to die. He might have been rude, but I was tired and sick, and I definitely overreacted. If I can't put things right, I can at least try to explain myself. If he'll listen.

"Julian." My voice comes out as a croak, and I push my hands into the pockets of my black leather jacket, conscious that they have nowhere to go. "Can I talk to you for a minute?"

I walk down the steps, leaving Molly with the remains of her bagel. Julian tucks the skateboard under his arm and pushes his sunglasses on top of his head so that I can finally see his eyes. He looks confused, startled, and suddenly I'm unsure of myself as I shift my weight from one foot to the other, hoping that the pavement will suddenly open beneath my boots like a trapdoor, hurtling me into the murky labyrinth of the Manhattan sewage system. Now that I'm here, I don't know what to do with myself. I bite the inside of my cheek to keep from crying or running away.

"I've gotta go to class," Julian says, his eyes focused somewhere behind my right shoulder.

The small sense of hope I've managed to gather together inside me plummets to my knees, leaving behind a heady mix of shame and disappointment in its wake. Of course he has to go to class. Of course he'd rather go to class than stand outside and have any kind of potentially pointless conversation with me. The blood in my cheeks begins to boil, and even the cold wind ripping down the street isn't enough to cool them.

"What are you doing later?" he asks, finally concentrating my face. His eyes betray nothing.

"Umm . . . later?" I stammer, caught off guard. "I don't know. Nothing, I guess."

"Meet me here after the last bell," he says gruffly, giving me a curt nod before pushing open the door as the bell begins to ring loudly, filling the street with clanging noise.

NINETEEN

I'M STUFFING BOOKS into my bag when the last bell rings, shattering the stillness of the hallway. As I throw my backpack over one shoulder, I'm aware of the excitement coursing through my veins, the wave of giddy pleasure mixed with apprehension. It's obvious that Julian is still mad at me. *And why shouldn't he be?* a voice rises up to ask, cutting through the adrenaline. *You treated him like shit . . . well, after he treated you like shit. But still.* Sometimes I think that's what life really is—the passing of small hurts on to one another, those circular little moments of daily abuse. *You hurt me, I hurt you. Rinse and repeat.*

By the time I fight my way through the crowd to the large red double doors of the school, I'm thoroughly freaked out. What if he just tells me off and then leaves? What if he just wants to humiliate me and then run away? But somehow I cannot imagine Julian, with his kind face and gentle voice, doing either of these things. Even the way he ignored me seems weirdly out of character.

When I step out into the street, a blast of cold air greets

me with a slap in the face, my hair whipping backward, and my eyes immediately fill with water. I blink a few times to clear my vision, and when the street snaps into focus, I see my father standing at the curb. He's outside his idling black Mercedes sedan talking on his mobile phone, eyes shielded by a pair of black Ray-Bans that make him look younger than he really is, his thick hair brushed back from his face. At the sight of me, he raises one gloved hand and waves me over. His trench coat hangs loosely, untied, a suit the color of toasted hazelnuts peeking out from underneath. I don't think I've ever seen my father out of a suit, except right before bed when he'd put on a pair of silk striped pajamas that my mother ordered for him in bulk from Harrods in London. I haven't seen my father in person for three months now, and the sight of him causes my stomach, my blood, the very tissues of my body to lurch, rolling and seasick.

As I approach, he hangs up the call, tucking the mobile phone—the approximate size and shape of a brick—under one arm, his eyes still hidden behind the dark lenses.

"What are you doing here?" I blurt out before he has the chance to speak.

My father coughs, looking down at the pavement before looking up again and meeting my eyes, removing his glasses and blinking into the gusts of wind that sweep over the sidewalk.

"Not exactly the reaction I was hoping for," he says quietly.

I'm silent, staring into his face, wanting him to know just how angry I really am that he walked out on us, replacing my mother with a new model, one that wouldn't cause him any trouble.

"I just wanted to see if you needed anything," my father continues, his eyes that look so much like my own sliding away from my face as if he doesn't recognize me, as if he's never seen me before.

"I'm fine," I say woodenly, my voice strained. I shove my hands inside the pockets of my leather jacket.

"Do you need any money?" he asks, keeping his tone light, as if it's just a random poll, as if he asks total strangers the same question daily. He reaches into his coat and fumbles for his wallet, pulling out a sleek alligator billfold.

"I don't need anything." *Except maybe a new father,* I think sarcastically, even though at night, before my eyes close and I drop into sleep, I still think about him. Sometimes I sit up and stare out the window, sleepless, watching the lights of the city flicker on and off, watching the windows that glow in the building across the street, and imagine the families that lie behind the glass, how they will hold and protect each other in yellow circles of light. When I finally lie down and turn over, my arms hugging the pillow, I ache for what I no longer have.

"How's the new apartment?" His tone is efficient and brisk, as if he's checking on one of his investments, which I suppose I am at the end of the day. This realization causes my heart to sink, even though in some sense I've always known as much. My father has never stepped foot inside my apartment, and standing here on the curb with the distance elongating between us, I doubt he ever will.

Although the car windows are tinted so that the inside of the car and its inhabitants are concealed, there is a rustling from within that causes my father to briefly spin around. He seems surprised to find the car still there, idling at the curb and releasing clouds of white smoke that disintegrate into the air. I realize in a sudden rush that Jasmine is inside, probably gazing at herself in the visor mirror, the silver sliver illuminating the reflection of her exotic beauty. The hatred I feel for her smolders in my brain, even though I'm aware that it's probably unwarranted. After all, it's my father who left, and if it hadn't been Jasmine, it would have been someone else. This knowledge can't override my emotions, and even if Jasmine actually spent her days helping deaf kids learn sign language or feeding Haitian orphans instead of lolling around at Elizabeth Arden getting her butt waxed, I'd find it hard not to despise the very thought of her.

"Well, if you don't need anything . . . ," my father says, his voice trailing off as he shoves his billfold back into his coat, "I should probably get going."

"Sure," I mumble, backing away from the car in case my father tries to hug me. He walks over to the driver's side, raising his hand in a wave, palm up.

"I'll call you soon and we'll have lunch," he calls out before ducking inside the car and pulling away from the curb. I watch the passenger side windows, transfixed, searching the tinted glass for Jasmine's upturned eyes, and imagine she stares right back at me, her expression haughty and entitled. *It's me he chose,* she seems to be saying. *Not you.*

As I watch the car drive away, I feel a tap on my shoulder. When I turn around, Julian is standing there, his skateboard tucked under his arm, his eyes covered by a pair of sunglasses. I shiver, the wind ripping through my leather jacket. For the first time I'm aware of just how cold I am. My nose is threatening to start running from the brisk weather, and I sniff loudly, hoping to avert disaster. I wonder if Julian saw me talking to my father, and, if so, just how much I'll have to explain. The thought of having to discuss my screwed-up family at length fills me with dread, and I offer Julian a weak smile, hoping that he won't interrogate me.

"You ready?" Julian asks, and it's clear from the look on his face—open and guileless—that he's seen nothing. I feel a wave of relief moving through me so strong, I consider sitting down right where I am until it passes. Instead I follow Julian down the block, lagging behind him slightly, teeth chattering, wondering if I'll ever be warm again.

TWENTY

I'M SITTING WITH JULIAN on a bench in Tompkins Square Park, watching a group of black-winged birds attack a half-eaten piece of bread on the pavement in front of us. The clouds overhead are the color of dirty cotton balls, and the wind blows the last crunch of dried brown leaves around the concrete.

Tompkins Square is less of a "park" in any sense of the word and more a haven for drug dealers, leather-clad punks just out of school who want to loiter in groups before hightailing it back to Mommy and Daddy's apartment, and a random lot of assorted freaks. Girls fly by on roller skates, brightly colored sweatbands wrapped around their wrists and foreheads, neon fishnet stockings protruding from their spandex bike shorts. Their laughter rings out into the park, filling the space with light and music. The smell of pot drifts over from the benches beside us and hangs medicinally in the air. Three guys in ripped jeans speak loudly in Spanish, passing a joint of skunk weed back and forth languidly between them.

On the subway, we rode downtown in silence, watching as

a homeless man crawled through the car on two stumps, his legs amputated below the knee, what remained of his flesh wrapped in layers of dingy white fabric tinged with dirt. The metal seats lined with women in suits and men in tastefully striped ties in neutral colors, kids like us just out of school who looked straight ahead. Girls dressed in neon anklets with black pumps elbowed one another in the ribs, giggling, ropes of fake pearls strung around their necks.

When we climbed the long set of stairs leading us out of the tunnel and into the light, the smell of urine and musty smoke from the trains swirling around us, Julian grabbed my hand, the feel of his warm skin shocking me. No words spoken and already we were holding hands. Something in my brain shut down, some mechanism of fear instantly replaced by a longing so intense, it almost stopped me in my tracks. *I want this.* The thought raced through my brain as Julian and I walked out of the station and toward the park. *Let me have this moment, this feeling, just for today.* Unlike my breakfast with Christoph, holding Julian's hand didn't make me feel as if I were cracking open some treacherous trapdoor in my heart, but like I was falling into a cloud of cotton candy, pink and warm, the comforting scent of vanilla sugar rising up like steam.

As we walked down the street, I looked over at Julian, taking shy little glances and noticing the way he nimbly maneuvered us around the punks loitering on the corner, their studded collars glinting in the light, and past CBGB, the doors shuttered and silent, the blare of car horns, yellow taxis flashing at the corner of my eye as we crossed the street. *Walk. Wait.*

Now on the bench, hands in my lap, I'm increasingly aware

of the fact that Julian's leg is so close to mine that I try to fool myself into believing I can feel the heat from his skin radiating through the rough denim and onto my skin.

"So, what was up the other day?"

Julian turns toward me, taking off his shades and shoving them into the pocket of his jacket, a broken-in piece of leather with multiple zippers, the cover from the Ramones' first record painted artfully across the back in red, white and black, the figures slouching defiantly.

"I could ask you the same question," I retort. "The other day in the hall you passed right by me like I was invisible."

"I know," he says, taking a deep breath and looking away. "I'm an idiot."

We are quiet for a moment as a guy on a skateboard rolls by, the sound of the wheels on pavement drowning out any possibility of being heard.

"Sometimes I get really awkward." He turns to face the park, scuffing one foot against the concrete. "Especially when I . . ." He stops, his words hanging in the air like smoke.

My stomach tightens, and a tingling feeling runs through my body, unchecked, racing from my feet all the way to the top of my head.

"Anyway," he says, exhaling loudly, "I'm sorry." He turns to face me again, his expression pained. "I should've definitely said hi, but sometimes you look like you don't want people coming anywhere near you. It's like you're wearing this big sign that says 'Stay the hell away or else.' So I guess I did."

"I know I do that sometimes," I say, my voice shaky. "Too much, probably."

"So what's your excuse?" He smiles, the mood suddenly lightened. "Bad hair day? Or do you have random hallway freakouts every other week or so?"

I'm finding it hard to smile back, and the corners of my lips turn up into something approaching a grimace. Why are real conversations so exhausting? My limbs feel heavy with the weight of everything I've never said out loud. Or to myself, even.

"Well, you ignored me, and then you just walked up the other day and started talking to me like it didn't even happen." I take a deep breath and rub my hands together to warm them, wishing I had gloves. "I'm really sorry. It was a bad day."

"I get it." Julian looks down the street, quiet for a moment. I take in his stillness, the ease in which he lives in his body. The scent of his leather jacket fills my nose, reminding me of horses, of worn leather saddles.

"You live down here, huh?" he asks, changing the subject and jutting his chin in the direction of the street.

"Yeah, for about six months now."

"How do your parents like it?"

"Next time I see them, I'll ask." I fold my arms over my chest, tucking my hands under my armpits to warm them.

Julian looks at me, confusion blanketing his face.

"You don't live with them?"

"Not that I'm aware of," I answer, trying to make my voice light, and failing completely.

"How'd you manage that?" he asks, bemused, maybe even impressed. "I'd give anything to live alone. My house is totally insane."

His face changes slightly, and he looks away and out into the park.

"What kind of insane?" I ask, aware that I'm entering dangerous territory.

"The kind that makes you want to run away on a daily basis."

I nod, looking down at my fingers, twisting the hammered silver band on my index finger that Sara bought me for Christmas.

"So, what's your story," he asks.

"What do you mean?"

My pulse begins to accelerate, my heart skipping every other beat. Do I really want to talk about this? No. Yes. My thoughts are suddenly so muddled that I can't see my way through them. A dense haze creeps into my brain, obliterating everything.

"Why don't you live at home? I mean, don't get me wrong—I'm seething with jealousy, but it's not exactly standard."

I look right at him, enunciating every word.

"My home life is *unsatisfying.*"

Julian cracks up, looking over at me appreciatively.

"*The Breakfast Club,* right? Let me guess—you were all about the Ally Sheedy character, right?"

"Of *course,*" I scoff, like this is not even a question to be taken seriously. "Except for the end where they made her all normal and boring."

Julian laughs. "She *definitely* looked better with all that black shit on her eyes."

Suddenly, even though the wind is still howling through the park, I'm no longer even the tiniest bit cold.

"What kind of unsatisfying?" Julian asks. As he speaks, I'm

watching Emilio Estevez pressing Ally Sheedy to answer his questions, the light from the screen illuminating the blackness of the theater.

"Oh, let's see. My father completely ignores me since he left my mother for a skank half his age who looks like a reject from *Dynasty*, and my . . . my mother . . . she . . ."

My breath catches in my chest. I can't do this. I can't say the words out loud without him pitying me or thinking I'm a bigger freak than he probably already does. My breath becomes ragged and labored, the park tilting crazily, the trees blurring before my eyes. I'm aware that I'm dangerously close to hyperventilating. My mother's face rises up from the jumble of images and detritus in my mind, the tight, controlled expression she wears just before the room explodes, her manicured fingers scratching my skin.

"Hey, hey," Julian says, reaching out to rub my back like something that's damaged, broken, which I suppose is exactly what I am.

"I can't talk about this," I manage to spit out. "I'm sorry."

"It's OK. Seriously. We don't have to talk if you don't want to."

His face is tense with worry, and he pats me uncertainly, not sure what to do. I concentrate on taking big gulps of air until my breathing slows, the world snapping back into focus. I'm too tired and freaked out to even be embarrassed, although the feeling that's taken up residence in my gut tells me that I probably should be.

I wipe my eyes, aware for the first time that they're damp, and try to smile reassuringly.

"You know what makes me feel better after a freakout?" Julian says casually, as if I didn't just lose my shit in public, in broad daylight.

"A padded cell?"

Julian grins, relieved that I'm back to my annoyingly sarcastic self once again.

"No. Ice cream."

"It's freezing out!" I exclaim, pointing at the sky with one frozen hand, my eyes widening in disbelief.

"So what? And I thought you were a rebel. I know your type—all talk," Julian says smugly, so I reach out and push him with one hand, feigning irritation.

"I warn you—I only like Häagen-Dazs."

"And . . . the Upper East Sider in you rises to the surface." Julian grins engagingly, his tough-boy image receding into the warmth of his smile, and my heart flops over in my chest. I have to force myself to take deep breaths just to maintain. I don't know what to do with the feelings that rise up from somewhere deep inside me. They seem so large and unwieldy, it's like trying to shove a semi truck through a keyhole.

Later, standing in front of Häagen-Dazs on Eighth Street, leaning up against a store that sells only custom belt buckles, the very store where Madonna bought her now infamous "Boy Toy" belt, Julian pops the tail end of his chocolate cone into his mouth and tosses a balled-up napkin into the wire trash can at the curb. I'm so cold that my teeth are literally chattering. My hands are sticky with the remnants of a single scoop of butter pecan, and I can't stop trembling.

"What's your number?" Julian asks nonchalantly as I walk him to the subway.

"Why?" I blurt out before I can stop myself. It's good to know that despite having an afternoon that mostly resembled a John Hughes movie, I'm as socially awkward as ever.

"So I can *call* you," Julian says like I'm being ridiculous. "Why else?"

"I dunno," I mumble, red-faced, staring down at the mosaic of crushed cigarette butts littering the sidewalk. "I don't know if I'm ready for this," I say, looking into his face, my eyes wild. I feel trapped and unsure, like I'm in a car driving blindly down the street, an empty space behind the wheel.

"Ready for what?"

"This. Whatever this is. My life is really complicated right now."

Christoph's deeply tanned face swims up from behind my eyelids. I shove my hands into my pockets, my fingers so cold, they feel as if they might just break off at any moment. Christoph belongs to the nighttime, to the hushed hours that fall after twilight, to the black night edging toward dawn. *Go away*, I think, banishing his image to the farthest corners of my brain. *You have no place here in the light.*

"We're friends," Julian says simply, squinting slightly, a crooked smile animating his face. "You can handle *that*, can't you?" He kicks an empty can of Tab on the sidewalk, the iridescent metal flaking off the sides of the can, and shoves his hands into his pockets when I don't respond. My mother loves Tab and buys it by the case. Just the sight of the can makes me uneasy, and I watch as it rolls helplessly into the gutter.

It's weird how such a seemingly simple question leaves me with no easy answers. I nod slowly and recite my number into his waiting ears because it's easier to give in than fight, and I'm so tired of fighting, of being on guard all the time. But as I watch him branding my digits onto the soft skin of his palm in black ink, I'm anything but sure.

TWENTY-ONE

THE PHONE RINGS as I'm walking into the apartment. I throw my backpack on a chair and search frantically under the bedsheets. As soon as I pick up the receiver, cradling it beneath my chin so I can shrug off my jacket, I know it's her. I can almost smell the sharp, animal scent of her perfume coming through the phone in waves with her pulse, fast and erratic, can hear the metallic tapping of her nails as she waits for me to speak.

"Hello, Caitlin."

Her voice is unnaturally cheerful and bright, the way it always is when I haven't spoken to her in a while. Maybe she heard about my father's after-school visit. Maybe it's just a coincidence. Either way, I detect a strange manic quality, as if she's ready to jump out of her skin or burst into tears. This is the flip side of her anger, and it is as wild and unpredictable as the slaps and kicks that bubble up like lava, crisping everything in its path. As I listen to her breathe, there's a familiar pressure in my chest, the feeling of suffocation, an elephant squashing my lungs. Thoughts race through my brain without stopping, and all at once I'm dizzy, confused. Whenever I hear her voice, I completely lose what's left of my bearings, my grip on the world. I sit down on the bed and close my eyes, waiting for her to speak, the imprint of the room flashing beneath my eyelids.

"How are you," she asks in sotto voce, as if she really wants to know. I'm not fooled. The only person my mother cares about is herself. Everyone else is of little consequence.

Before the divorce, when things started to really get bad between my mother and father, between my mother and me, my father made us an appointment with a psychiatrist on Park Avenue, the waiting room filled with ferns and old copies of *Better Homes and Gardens,* the pages creased by a legion of worried fingers. My father, of course, had to conveniently work late at the office on the nights the sessions were scheduled, which surprised no one. The shrink once told me, after a joint session where my mother stared at the wall for an hour refusing to speak, the anger emanating from her pores like steam, that my mother suffered from a combination of borderline and narcissistic personality disorders. What this boils down to is that although she wears an unassuming, beautiful mask in public, my mother is essentially incapable of seeing other people as anything else but an extension of herself. People are pawns to manipulate, convenient things to use to get what she wants. Nothing more.

I remember my mother's eyes narrowing as the therapist asked her a question, the doctor's voice slow and measured as if she were speaking to a child, and my mother's frozen expression as she walked quickly from the room at the end of the session. Her heels clicked lightly on the wooden floor, and I thought of the scurrying of rats, the clatter of tiny nails scraping against pavement.

"I probably shouldn't be telling you this, but your mother has been tremendously devalued by difficult circumstances in her childhood. These issues, as I'm sure you well know, have been undoubtedly exacerbated by the current state of things between her and your father." All I knew of my mother's childhood was that she hated her parents, hated Queens, hated being poor. My mother refused to talk about the past in any detail. "What does it matter?" she'd snap, waving her hands in the air as though dismissing the thought from the premises.

The therapist stared right at me, her face blank as an envelope, willing me to speak.

"She is also one of the angriest people I have ever come in contact with," the shrink said a moment after the door closed, her expression grave behind the glint of her glasses. "She will manipulate anyone to get her way, and she has no empathy for others. Especially you. When manipulation fails, she will use rage and fear. Remember that, Caitlin, every time you speak to her."

Not that I really needed reminding.

"I'm fine, Mom," I mumble, finding my voice in the present moment, the past dropping away in a rush. I clear my throat, picking up an album sleeve that's fallen to the floor and placing it on my bed, Madonna's navel staring at me from the *Like a Prayer* LP. The patchouli emanating from the limited-edition cover wafts through the air, reminding me of Sara and safety.

My mother's voice is silky, practiced, like fingers gently stroking the back of my neck, her words the lashings of a cat's raspy tongue. I hear words cutting through my thoughts. Words like *home* and *proper* and *please,* but the language is garbled and unfamiliar, the signal unclear. I know better than to mention that, however briefly, I've seen my father. What she wants is for me to come home, back to the apartment where my bedroom waits for me like an abandoned child, like clothes that no longer fit, back to the kitchen where she once pushed me against the sharp edges of the wooden cabinets, my forehead splitting open like the overripe skin of a peach. The bathroom where I'd run water in endless rivers to drown out the sound of my tears. Still, her voice pulls at me, encircling me like a web I can't get out of, her words stuck to my skin, my flesh deadened with the freezing sensation that comes after a bad burn. *You're safe here,* I tell myself, repeating the words over and over in my mind. A mantra. A prayer. *Safe, safe . . .*

I feel as if I'm slipping beneath an avalanche, gravel filling my lungs, her words drowning my ears in poison. Claudius creeping through the foliage, pouring the contents of the vial into the King's waiting ear as he slumbers dreamless in the garden. I remember sitting on her lap as a toddler, how safe I felt in her arms. How surprised I was when it started, my body thrown against a wall like so much dead weight, my head hitting the plaster as I crumpled to the floor, motionless. And even before my father left, she had stopped being careful, stopped being careful at all where I was concerned, not even bothering to straighten the house before he came home or to make sure I wasn't still crying but quietly doing my home-work, my head bent over open books, the words swimming black and white and meaningless before my eyes.

"No," I say with effort so great, it makes me instantly ex-hausted, unable to sit up. *Even after six months,* I think, *even fifty city blocks away, she can reduce me to ashes.* Tears squeeze out from the corners of my eyes in spite of the anger boiling just below the surface. "I'm not coming home."

Her tone escalates, the pitch rising through the phone, creeping toward hysteria. When she starts to scream into my ear, my mind goes utterly blank, and it occurs to me that I can just hang up, severing whatever connection remains between us.

"I have to go now," I say, my voice wooden.

"Wait, wait," she says quickly, smoothing down the surface of her anger like the ruffled feathers of a looming black bird, wings outstretched. "Just let me take you for lunch, the way we used to. Don't you remember our lunches?" she pleads, her voice reedy and thin. "We'd always have such a nice time, wouldn't we, Cat?"

Yes, I think. Except for the fact that those shopping trips and lunches were designed to accomplish only one thing: to give her the daughter she always wanted. I'd sit across from her in the restaurant at Bergdorf Goodman, nervously palm-ing my spoon, knowing that one wrong word was all it would take, one glance she didn't quite approve of, and the moment we got into the car there would be a backhand slap across my cheek, my skin erupting in flames, her eyes flashing in the dimness of the limo.

"Tavern on the Green," I hear through the haze crowding my thoughts, a kind of white noise. "Saturday. Noon."

Without answering, I hang up the phone and lie down, pulling the covers up to my chest and hugging them to my body until the shaking subsides and I am warm again. I tell myself that I don't have to go. I begin to shiver violently once again when I picture the hard, dead look in her eyes, the judgment reflected there.

Children should love their mothers, Caitlin.

Her seductive purr creeps into my waiting ears, infecting them, drawing me ever closer until I am floating back aimlessly, dangerously into her grasp.

＊　　＊　　＊　　＊

I PULL THE COVERS UP to my ears, smiling as my grandmother climbs into bed beside me, her fragile weight barely sinking the coiled springs in the mattress. The room smells of her perfume, Shalimar, and the mothballs she keeps in her closet—even though it's lined in cedar—to protect rows of sweaters organized by color and weight. Even with my eyes closed, I'd know this room like the back of my hand: the heavy silver brushes and combs on the dresser, the mirror hanging above, its surface wavy with age. There is blue carpet underfoot, and white curtains that shield the long windows from glare. The weekends I spend here are all I know of safety. Here I sleep unafraid of the door creaking open in the dead of night. Here I fear no footsteps across the polished wooden floors, and my own are steady and sure. Here in this place called Queens, I can breathe. My mother hates the outer boroughs and her own mother even more, so on weekends before my grandfather dies suddenly of a pulmonary embolism and my grandmother is transferred to a nursing home, I am often dumped here when my parents are out of town, my father on one of his endless business trips.

She lets out a large sigh, turning over on her side, the sound of her breathing filling the room, the streets quiet, the stillness punctuated only by the sound of a car skidding down the street or the groan of a truck rumbling past. I love you, she whispers just as I began to fall asleep, dropping down into the delicious nothingness, devoid of pain, never sure if I've dreamed the words. In the morning, there will be slices of wheat toast cut carefully into triangles, the bread coated with butter so yellow that it will mock the sun. I will sit at the table, the top scratched and nicked from the banging of plates and forks over time, my grandfather's old silk pajamas pooling at my ankles, hiding the fine bones of my feet and wrists as my grandmother stands at the stove singing to herself under her breath, frying eggs in a cast-iron pan.

My grandmother with her blond hair the color of the yellowed pages of a rare book and her skin like paper will see my bruises, even at nine years old, and flit her eyes away, placing one hand on my wrist and patting me gently, her blue eyes coated with a film that might be cataracts or tears.

TWENTY-TWO

TODAY I SAT WITH JULIAN at lunch. We shared a turkey sand-wich and an apple I scored from a bodega, passing the fruit back and forth between us, aware that putting my mouth on something his own lips had touched was the closest we'd come so far to sharing a kiss. I could sense Julian trying hard to keep things light, limiting the conversation to bands, TV shows, the new Lichtenstein show at the Guggenheim, sensing just how fast I'd bolt if he tried to shove his way through the scaffolding I've built around my heart. Some moron who just transferred in from a school in Brooklyn attempted to break-dance on the pavement, spinning for a moment on the top of his head be-fore collapsing in a ball, his parachute pants rustling furiously.

Every time Julian's hand brushed against mine, I shivered somewhere deep inside. The more time I spend with him, the more I want to see him again. But whenever the phone rings, shattering the stillness of my apartment, I freeze in mid-step, unsure of what to do. Instead of picking it up, I watch the receiver with the wariness of a rabid animal until it stops abruptly as the machine picks up. Without knowing whether it was Christoph, Julian, my mother—or someone else entirely—I am paralyzed, my feet stuck to the floor. I guess it comes down to the fact that Julian is the choice I *should* be making, who I *should* be with—despite Sara's warning—and Christoph is who I *shouldn't*, but that knowledge doesn't make deciding any easier. Every choice feels wrong, like having no choice at all.

As I walk quickly through the chilly streets, I'm filled with a sense of dread. The last time I was in Alexa's apartment was on her tenth birthday. All I remember of the actual event was that the theme was Versailles, and predictably, there were platters of pastel cakes and cookies everywhere, Alexa standing at the front of the room in a white dress, her hair piled atop her head, which looked delicate and breakable even then, the brightly wrapped gifts dwarfing her small body. Alexa Forte lives in the kind of Upper East Side town house that's furnished like a wing at the Met—Louis-the-whatever chairs and tables everywhere, chandeliers hanging from fourteen-foot ceilings in every room. A fresco of dancing cherubs chasing a flight of doves graces the entry hall, and there are elaborate sconces dripping with crystal on every available wall. Your basic baroque nightmare.

Alexa's mother answers the door, her face unlined and serene. She's wearing a green-and-white-patterned wrap dress that reminds me of cool forests, moss creeping over wet stones. The diamonds in her ears sparkle against the blond hair twisted away from her angular face, and I finger the buckles on my leather jacket nervously, feeling like I've arrived at a black tie dinner wearing a tracksuit. She smiles, asking about my parents but not really listening to the answer, her eyes glazed over with what may be boredom or Valium as she leads me down a long hallway, knocking briskly at a heavy wooden door before opening it.

Alexa sits on a white platform bed, hot-pink wall-to-wall carpet covering the floor. A stereo system takes up most of one wall, the silver dials glowing red, the new Taylor Dayne single playing softly amid frantic bass beats. Above the bed on the creamy white wall hangs what looks like an actual Warhol painting—four square portraits of Alexa hung in a quartet, her face bleached white, her features outlined in bright color, her eyes haughty and imperious. *You like?* she seems to be saying. *Well, too bad. You're not getting any.*

"Took you long enough," Alexa says, glaring hard at her mother before she leaves, closing the door without a word. Alexa grabs a can of Diet Pepsi from her bedside table, sucking noisily on a hot-pink straw shot through with silver glitter.

"The train was running slow."

I throw my bag down on the floor, not sure what to do with myself. Should I sit next to her on the bed? The floor? The uncomfortable pink beanbag in the corner? "Some guy jumped in front of an express and everything was backed up. We sat in the tunnel for, like, twenty minutes."

School's been out for hours, but before coming over to Alexa's place, I needed to regroup, stopping at home to change and eat something before heading back uptown, the train packed with rush hour commuters.

Alexa shudders. "I can't believe you take that thing every day."

"I thought you were so tough," I say, laughing as I walk over to the beanbag, sitting down gingerly, as if it might collapse under my weight.

"Toughness has nothing to do with it," Alexa snorts, picking up a cordless phone trapped in her sheets and tossing it to the floor. She's wearing black leggings and a gray sweatshirt artfully ripped at the neck to expose one shoulder, her hair pushed back from her face with a black cloth headband, a pair of huge white slouch socks on her feet. The combination of tight leggings and big socks makes her legs look like toothpicks swathed in spandex. "I now speak from experience, so listen up: the subway is seriously gross."

I watch as Alexa stands up, stretching her arms over her head, groaning as her back cracks with a sharp snap that reminds me of branches breaking. She comes over and sits on the floor beside me, folding her legs beneath herself, graceful as a dancer.

"So I probably already know the answer to this question, but what *really* happened with Ethan the other night?" I ask, pulling at the pink fibers of the carpet with one hand. It's so soft and plush that I imagine sinking into it for days at a time, the fibers rising up and swallowing me whole. Asking about Ethan feels strained, awkward. The only girl I speak to with any kind of regularity is Sara, and I'm not exactly practiced at girly small talk.

A charm bracelet on Alexa's wrist jangles musically as she reaches up to play with a strand of her hair. Among the dangling charms I catch a glimpse of a martini glass, a small gold spoon and what looks like a credit card.

"Custom-made at Tiffany for my twelfth birthday. My mother said I could have a charm bracelet, but I'm not sure this was what she had in mind." She looks down at the tinkling charms, moving her hand so that they glint in the light. "But she'd already paid for it, so, *whatever.*"

"Don't change the subject," I say, laughing. "What *happened?*"

"Maybe I should be asking you the same question." A smile plays on her lips, one eyebrow raised. My stomach sinks and I exhale for what feels like forever, her words punching the wind out of me. Through my discomfort I can't help but notice how easily Alexa has evaded my question.

"I told you," I say, trying to brush it off, "we just went to breakfast."

"*And?*" She rolls her eyes, and I notice for the first time that her irises are speckled with flecks of gold, the round orbs like painted Easter eggs.

"And nothing. That was it. Boring but true."

"But you like him."

I hesitate, drawing in my breath before answering.

"*Like* probably isn't the right word."

Actually, I've never thought about whether or not I like Christoph at all. I'm trying to figure out if that's a good or bad thing when Alexa interrupts, clearly exasperated.

"*Whatever.* Define it any way you want. But you're interested, right?"

"I guess so." I curl my legs beneath me, shrugging. "Whatever that means. I don't know."

God, I sound like a moron. Any minute she's going to stand up and tell me she's late for ballet class or something.

"He is kind of hot," Alexa says thoughtfully, mulling it over. She holds up one long strand of hair to the light, inspecting it for split ends, but it's predictably perfect. "In an old-dude, Eurotrash kind of way." Her expression becomes distant, and I wonder what she's thinking.

"Wait a minute . . ." Alexa leans forward excitedly, as if someone's just turned on a heating coil under her ass. "Don't you have something going with that weird kid who looks like one of the Lost Boys? What's his name . . ." Alexa snaps her fingers in rapid succession. "Jesse? Jamie? Or is he gay?"

"Julian," I say, swallowing hard. His name in this cluttered room sounds like a prayer, something you whisper to yourself late at night. "And he's definitely not gay."

At that admission, my face turns red, and I can't help but stare, openmouthed, not sure what to say next. Circles of pink color Alexa's cheeks, making her appear fragile, almost doll-like. Like the sun, she is so beautiful that it almost hurts to look at her for more than a few moments without turning away.

"Fuuuuuuck," Alexa says softly, drawing out the word. "So basically, you're a total mess?"

"Pretty much."

Alexa smiles, her grin growing incrementally wider with every second, and we burst into laughter. It's one of those moments that wouldn't be funny at all to anyone not sitting right here with us at this very second, but at the same time it's inexplicably hilarious, and I'm holding my sides, doubled over. Alexa is laughing so hard that she's wiping under her eyes, checking for tears or smeared mascara, and as my voice rings out into the room, only one thought is racing through my head: this is the only time I've ever admitted how screwed up I feel without wanting to cry. Alexa's hot-pink travesty of a bedroom is some kind of bizarre refuge, a panacea from the usual fear and sadness that follow me throughout the day. Somehow, the fact that she's laughing at my insane life doesn't make me want to kill myself immediately.

"So what happened with Ethan?" I ask again as soon as we've managed to compose ourselves. Now that we've just lost our minds together, it feels OK somehow to ask again. So I do.

"What do you *think* happened?" she asks cryptically, her eyes glowing in her face like green embers. She's in love, and it's all over her. I can smell it—the sulfur that lingers in the air after striking a match, the blackness after the flame. Some kind of smoldering left in its wake.

"You slept with him."

Alexa leans her elbows on her thighs, cradling her head between her palms. She doesn't answer me, but then again, it wasn't really a question.

"What do you know about him?" Her eyes meet mine, and I see the naked hunger reflected there, the desire. *This is what love reduces you to,* that tiny voice inside me whispers as I take in the flush in her cheeks. *Remember that.*

"Not much," I say, and it's the truth. I've spoken to Ethan only a handful of times, and I can barely remember what we even talked about. "I know that he lives somewhere near Gramercy Park, that he has about seven roommates crammed into a two-bedroom apartment. One of them—this guy with a Mohawk—came into the club once for one of Sebastian's parties, drank a whole bottle of Jack Daniel's and had to be carried out."

"How punk rock," Alexa deadpans, looking decidedly unimpressed.

"I think he used to have a girlfriend—I'd see her sitting at the bar sometimes, waiting for him to get off work."

"Who?" Alexa asks impatiently. "Ethan or the roommate?"

"Ethan," I say quickly, before she gets the wrong idea.

"What did she look like?"

I close my eyes briefly, trying to remember. Small, dark hair and reed thin. Always in a washed-out black dress that bordered on gray. But what I remember most is the look of sadness on her face, the melancholy she carried around with her, a veil blanketing the bland prettiness of her features.

"It doesn't matter," I answer, watching as the tension stiffens Alexa's angular limbs. "I haven't seen her in months."

With that admission, Alexa sighs in relief, and I realize that while I've been speaking, she's been holding her breath, and her eyes beneath her smooth forehead are subdued and uncharacteristically serious. Whatever is going on is clearly weighty enough to force her out of her usual sarcastic demeanor and into quiet contemplation.

"I brought him back here."

There is a pause, the words hanging in the air between us.

"What did your mom have to say about that?"

I cannot even remotely imagine Alexa introducing Ethan to her parents. Something in the universe would probably shift, then immediately implode.

"Oh, please," Alexa snorts. "Once she's taken her sleeping pills, not even an earthquake could wake her up. And my dad was out of town on business, as usual. I've been sneaking people in since I was fifteen anyway. It's not really all that difficult—even when they *are* home and conscious."

My eyes widen a bit. I'm kind of impressed, not that I would give her the satisfaction of admitting it.

"But this was different." Her eyes glaze over, lost in memory. "It was . . . intense. But he hasn't called and . . . oh, I don't know." She throws her hands up in exasperation, clearly frazzled. "I mean, there have been other guys. Obviously."

I nod, thinking of Alexa back at Dalton, making out with her teacher. Her defiant face in the headmistress's office as she stood up, throwing her mane of blond hair over one shoulder and striding out the door. I'm not sure at all why she's telling this to me. Despite the fact that she came out the other night, despite the fact that I'm sitting here in the inner sanctum, Alexa Forte and I are still not friends. Of *course* there have been other guys—the boys practically snap to attention when she saunters down the hall, leaving a honeysuckle sweetness in her wake. Maybe it's just that I am the only one she can be this vulnerable around, this exposed. No one would believe it. The legend that is Alexa Forte waiting by the phone like any other lovesick girl, her defenses battered and broken down, her heart flayed open.

"He hasn't *called*," she repeats miserably, reaching up and pulling the headband from her head, releasing a cascade of hair. "Maybe it didn't . . . mean anything to him, you know?"

She forces the words from her throat like she's trying to get rid of them. Tears well up in her eyes and she blinks them away, looking off to the side. Despite the armor she's built up around herself, this is the soft candy core of Alexa Forte. I picture her hunched over the toilet in the girls' bathroom, her finger down her throat, the taste of fried dough and disgust lingering on her tongue.

"I've messed around with tons of guys, OK?" She raises one hand and swipes at the moisture collecting in her lower lashes, darkening them. "But this was the first time I . . ." Her voice trails off into innuendo. "Well," she says, looking up at me, her expression tentative, almost shy. "You know."

"Did *he* know?" I ask gently, knowing that we're in dangerous territory, that I could say the wrong thing and she might explode in righteous anger or melt down into a puddle of jelly. "Did you tell him?"

"Not in so many words."

"In *any* words?"

"No, but I'm sure he could figure it out," she adds sarcastically, the old Alexa rising to the surface like bubbles in Perrier. "I mean, really. Hello, Captain Obvious!"

I giggle a bit. She looks so incredulous that it's actually kind of funny, her eyes so wide they're practically bulging out of her head.

"But you're going to see him on Saturday, right?" I ask once I've stopped laughing. "I mean, that's something at least."

"He asked me to come watch him lug ice and empty

bottles," she deadpans. "He probably asks every girl he bangs the same exact thing. I'm sure I'm *so* special."

Sarcasm is clearly Alexa's default mode, a guise she slips into to protect herself from whatever emotional messiness she's feeling, and to this I can relate. Underneath that practiced exterior she's vulnerable as a flower in the August heat. The big difference between Alexa and me—well, not the only difference but a major one—is that I learned long ago just how unremarkable I really am. It's hard to believe you are exceptional in any way when your father abandons you for a girl half his age, calling you only to sign a lease that serves no other purpose than to take you away from him permanently. And your mother . . .

I blink rapidly to clear the thoughts from my mind, erasing them like a damp rag moving efficiently across a blackboard.

"So, why him? Ethan, I mean. You've held on to it this long—why now, with him?"

"Everyone else I know lost it at thirteen," she blurts out. "By the way"—her eyes narrow as she peruses my face—"if you talk about this with anyone, I'll fucking kill you." Alexa pushes her hair back with one hand until the entire mass of it falls sleekly over one shoulder.

"They all look up to me," she spits out as if the words themselves are rotten, and though I don't question her further, I assume she's talking about the salad girls, how they follow her around, worshipful as petitioners at a church service. "You don't know what it's like," she says, taking a deep breath, gulping the air as if she's trying to overdose on oxygen. "The benefits, the dinners—always having to be so goddamn perfect.

At my debutante debut last year, I had to bite my tongue the entire night to keep from screaming, I was so fucking bored. Plus, my dress was kind of hideous. Well, you know," she says, sighing loudly. "You were *there*."

"For about a millisecond," I say, laughing.

My mother forced me to go to Alexa's debut, and I retaliated by showing up in a black dress and pink combat boots. The only reason I was even invited is that I suspect Alexa's mother forced her to ask me, since our mothers are friends in the loosest definition of the word.

"Sometimes I think I'm going to start screaming and never stop." Alexa looks down at the carpet, running a palm over the plush strands as if it's a grassy lawn. "Sometimes I wish I could just run away to Paris or Switzerland and never come back."

"The land of chocolate and cuckoo clocks?" I raise an eyebrow.

Alexa grabs a pillow off the foot of the bed, lobbing it expertly in my direction. It hits me squarely in the face, the soft cotton muffling my laughter. I hold the pillow in my lap, cradling it in my arms.

"So I'm supposed to feel sorry for you. Is that it? Everyone worships the ground you walk on, you can get any guy you want, but you've got it so tough?"

I can't believe that I'm talking to Alexa Forte like this, but somehow I am.

"It's not as easy as you think," she says after a long pause, her eyes squarely locked on my face. The hair on my arms rises as she stares at me, unblinking. "In fact, it's not easy at all."

"Nothing ever is. And neither is being a freak. Even if it's your own choice."

"Trust me, I'd rather be a freak than what I am right now."

Her voice is an urgent whisper, and I can tell that she thinks she means what she's saying, means it desperately.

"You just say that because you think it's easier, and in some ways, it is." Even as the words leave my lips, I can't help wondering if they're really true. "But it's also hell. I don't think you'd like it one bit," I tell her, my voice a low murmur. "Instead of people looking up to you, envying you every time you walk by, they'll either avoid or fear you—sometimes both. Neither is any kind of fun."

I think of all the lunches I've eaten alone since transferring to Manhattan Prep, all the times I've watched Alexa and her group saunter by, their perfume floating along the breeze like an anesthetic, and my eyes grow damp at the corners.

Alexa walks over to her bed, flopping down on her stomach, her face buried in the softness of her pillow. "Maybe you're right," she says after a long moment, her voice muffled.

Alexa rolls over on her back and stares up at the ceiling, strands of blond hair she doesn't push away strewn across her face. I sit there on the floor listening to the sound of the silence that descends, the rush of air animating the room as night closes in, deepening the sky outside Alexa's bedroom windows like the coming of some kind of judgment, rushing toward the dawn.

TWENTY-THREE

THE WEEK HURTLES ITSELF toward the weekend, the question of whether or not I'll actually meet my mother looming over my head like a raven, talons bared and ready to strike. Each time I close my eyes and picture walking through the front doors of the restaurant, toward the corner table she favors by a large bank of windows overlooking the park, my mind goes utterly blank. And don't even get me started on the whole Christoph situation. I don't know what I think about more—my impending date with Christoph or meeting my mother. Neither option offers any kind of solution. I used to think that when I moved out of my mother's apartment things would somehow magically be OK, a wand waved, gold glitter falling from the tip, erasing everything. Now I'm beginning to wonder if it's all been an illusion, if my life has somehow shifted from bad to worse in just a few short months . . .

On Thursday afternoon, Sara and I sit on my rumpled bed, rubbing polish remover over our toenails. It's less than a week before Thanksgiving, the stores full of chocolate turkeys, cloves, cinnamon, the tang of apple cider hanging over the streets. The harsh, acrid smell of acetone fills my mouth as I take a deep breath, releasing my words like a series of cannonballs.

"My mother called. She wants me to meet her for lunch at Tavern on the Green."

Sara's hand halts mid-swipe, poised over her foot. Her eyes widen in shock, her mouth falling open slightly before her lips snap rigidly shut.

"Ha," she says with a clipped, mirthless laugh. "That's funny. Oh, by the way, I'm sure you don't need me to tell you you're not going."

Sara holds my eyes with hers for a long moment before bending back over her foot and removing the last bit of red polish from her toe. It's clear from the way her back muscles suddenly bunch up beneath her thin gray T-shirt that she means business. The guilt rises up in my chest, threatening to drown me. I imagine my mother sitting at a table set with white china and neat rows of silverware, her hair like onyx shot with bronze in the afternoon sunlight. A vase of pink roses sits before her on the white linen tablecloth, the petals the color of an open heart. She checks the gold watch on her wrist impatiently, ordering a third glass of Chardonnay while her eyes search the door of the restaurant, expectant and somehow sure, despite all that has come between us, that I will arrive on time.

I swallow hard, feeling as if there's a Nerf ball stuck in my throat. It's amazing that someone who hates the very sight of me can make me feel so completely guilty for refusing to cooperate. How can I feel so torn about something I should be able to resist without even trying? It is, as Sara would say, a no-brainer.

"I might," I say, clearing my throat and picking up a bottle of blue polish Sara brought with her, turning it over to look at the name stamped on the bottom, Blue Bayou. I picture mossy swamps, the banks of a river running with mud, sucking at my toes as I approach the water's edge, smelling the rich mineral scent of the earth. "I might go." I turn the cap, pulling the brush from the bottle, and bend over my toes, dabbing at them unevenly, my hand shaking with the effort.

"Are you *serious*?" Sara's head snaps up, her expression fierce, predatory. "You're going to meet her after everything she's put you through?"

"It's only lunch," I say in a whisper so faint that even I don't quite believe it.

I close my eyes and my mother smiles as she reaches out to hand me a stuffed tiger, striped golden and black, her eyes crinkling at the corners. A day at the zoo, the smell of roasting peanuts and sun-warmed hay drifting through the air, the promise of something rich and intoxicating, my future hanging like layered gauze in the distance, still mostly unspoiled. I am four.

Children should love their mothers, Caitlin.

"Bullshit, Cat!"

Sara throws the bottle she's holding across the room, red polish streaking the white wall, recasting it as a butcher shop, a crime scene. She grabs my arm, her fingers squeezing my flesh tightly, trying to shock me back into the present. I flinch at the sudden touch, the implicit violence in it, and for a brief moment I see my mother's face staring back at me.

"How many times are you going to let her hurt you?"

Her voice is pleading now, but she is yelling, still yelling, and something inside me begins to shut down and hide, the way it always does when I am confronted violently or with aggression. I see the hurt and fear in her eyes, and I know exactly what she is thinking. It is bad enough that my mother hits me, slaps me in the face until my vision is blurred, the sharp jewels in her rings opening up the tender skin at the corners of my eyes or the rough, chapped fabric of my lips, but the fact that I am willing to go back for more is unforgivable. It makes me what I have never wanted to be, what Sara has never wanted to see me as—a victim.

"Cat, you have to listen to me." She releases my arm and shakes her hands in front of her for emphasis or to shrug off the tension between us, I'm not sure which. "I'm sorry," she says, quietly now, pulling her hair back with one hand and twisting it into a white rope. "I don't want to hurt you. You know I'd never do that. Not to you. Not ever." We stare at each other, unblinking, her eyes glistening with regret. "But she is never going to change and you know it."

"It's not about that," I say, trying so hard to keep my voice calm and measured when it is taking every fiber of self-control I possess not to bolt into the streets, away from everything I don't want to hear and feel. I wish I could push all the rage, fear and pain back inside me where it belongs, safe and locked in the velvet dark of my body, but those feelings have some-how sprung to the surface like an evil jack-in-the-box popping up to surprise me, grinning maniacally at their liberation. *See?* they seem to say with no small degree of elation. *We were here all along!*

I see the incomprehension fogging her sharp features, and I know she will never understand. Sara, with her two loving parents who make sure she is safe in her room at night, studying for finals. Parents who reach their arms out for hugs, not slaps. Sara, who sleeps each night without fear as shafts of rose-colored morning sunlight make their way into her room. Sara, for whom I am—as much as she ultimately loves me—an enigma. My childhood an unfathomable island Sara peruses from a distance, binoculars held up to her squinting gaze.

"I'm meeting her in public. At Tavern on the Green. In broad daylight. Not even she would try anything there."

Reasonable, I am thinking. *This sounds reasonable.* But even as the thought flashes through my brain, it is replaced by another thought entirely, the timbre of a sonic scream or Sara's angry voice. *What are you DOING?* it wants to know. *What good could possibly come of this?*

"Oh, *public,*" Sara says, sarcasm poisoning her words like cyanide. She jumps to her feet and stands over me, grabbing her leather jacket from the pile of clothes on the floor and throwing it on, wrapping her bright red scarf around her neck. "Right. Did that stop her when she slammed your hand in the car door, Cat? Because that technically happened in public, too."

Even in the fading afternoon sunlight her hair shines whitely, her face bloodless as bleached bone. She zips her jacket, collecting herself with a deep breath and exhaling loudly. "I've told you what I think," she says woodenly. "But you'll do what you want. You always do."

"I'm not trying to hurt you," I say. My voice sounds small, like it belongs to someone else entirely. I stare down at my hands, cap the bottle of polish and push it to the side. "This isn't about you. It's something I have to do—for me."

I don't even know if these words are true, but I cannot stop them or take them back. I don't know if it's for me or for my mother, but I know that I am drawn to her like a drug, that I must play out this scene to the end, even if I don't know how or why. I have to see her for myself and face her down, this monster in my head.

Sara leans down and hugs me fiercely, squeezing my ribs so hard that a small, involuntary squeaking sound leaves my lips.

"I love you, Cat," she whispers urgently. "If you have to do this thing, please be careful."

"I will," I whisper back, my eyes strangely devoid of tears, the sockets hot and dry. "I know you don't get it, but . . ." My voice trails off into her hair, the tight curls that lie at the nape of her neck that smell of hairspray and musk. "I haven't seen her since I moved out, and she's my mother, Sara. My *mother.*"

I say these words like an incantation, as if they mean anything at all, and with them I smell the rush of my mother's exotic perfume, feel the touch of her hands on my shoulders. Despite everything that's happened between us, I still hold out hope that somewhere beneath that cold, chiseled exterior there is another mother buried there entirely, one who might, if the stars are aligned, love me.

Sara releases me, stepping back. "Right."

Her face is expressionless. I'm reminded of the dolls my father brought home for me one year after a business trip to Japan, their blank affectless faces and perfect white skin, their bodies folded into kimonos tight as origami. My father was always more comfortable giving gifts rather than hugs.

"Your mother," she repeats tonelessly before heading for the door, her brown-fringed bag slung over her shoulder. "Whatever that means."

∗ ∗ ∗ ∗

MY MOTHER COMES *into my room at night. First, only to watch me sleep, she says, and I get used to waking up to the weight of her presence at the foot of my bed, her eyes on my face as she possessively runs them over my body while I slumber away, her hand reaching under the cover to pull out one warm sleeping foot and marvel at it. I made you in my body, my mother is fond of telling me urgently, and for her I know this means that she controls me, that I belong to her in some way that is unbreakable.*

I made you, she hisses when I disappoint her, which is often. How dare you act this way?

All I am is myself. I am myself so fully from such a young age that it is painful to watch as she tries to remake me in her own image. I fight from the very beginning, choosing my black clothes, my spiky hair like armor, and this is what angers her most of all, it's what sets off the night visits, the door swinging open as she enters, a cloud of rage coloring the room with a dangerous amber light, the sky before a thunderstorm. A low rumbling sound fills my ears as I clap my hands over them, drowning out her words that hum like a hovering of bees. She flies through my room, fingers tearing at the posters of musicians and movie stars pasted up on the white walls, walls I am not allowed to paint. Her nails tear large holes in the paper, gutting it, and with every tear something rips in my heart, my lungs, the very fiber of my being. Somewhere in the core of me someone is screaming, while the me that is present hides in the corner, her arms thrown up over her face to ward off whatever comes next.

TWENTY-FOUR

THAT NIGHT, after Sara goes home, I'm perusing the pages of my history book before I get ready for work, trying to be responsible. But as I flip past the pictures of battles long past, bloodshed and death, of gleaming swords, I begin to feel slightly queasy. I reach one hand up to my forehead, checking to see if I have a fever, but the skin is cool, almost moist. When the phone rings, cutting through the pounding din of the music blasting from my speakers, I rush over to grab it on the third ring, thinking it might be Giovanni telling me that he's going to be later than usual. When I hear Julian's voice in my ear, my stomach contracts sharply. I look over at the mirror on the wall directly across from my bed and I almost don't recognize the girl reflected in the gold frame, her cheeks flushed inside the wavy glass. She looks almost happy.

"So, what are you up to?" he asks, and I can hear his nervousness cutting through the confident exterior he wears like his battered leather jacket.

"Not much," I say, sitting down on the bed and pushing a lock of hair from my forehead. "Just getting ready for work."

"Oh, that's right." Julian exhales loudly, and I can hear his disappointment over the line as sharply as if he were standing right in front of me. "I forgot."

"Yeah," I mumble, kicking at the pile of clothes next to my bed with one bare foot. For the first time since I've started working at the club, I almost wish I didn't have to go.

Maybe you don't, a little voice in my head pipes up, causing my heart to trip ungracefully, beating out of time. Who would really care if I didn't show up? Giovanni would probably convulse at the opportunity to take over the door for a night. *What about Christoph?* that little voice interrupts again. *He's expecting you to be there, right? Isn't he?* I close my eyes and see Christoph's tanned face smiling down at me, his hand reaching up for mine as the bottom drops out of the dance floor, the room spiraling away in a haze of smoke. I don't want to think about Christoph tonight.

"Maybe I can get out of it," I say slowly, cautiously, as if I'm wading into shark-infested waters.

"Really?" His voice is bright and hopeful, and as it fills my ears, I begin to smile, a feeling of warmth suffusing my limbs.

An hour later I'm walking down Eighth Street, past the Häagen-Dazs where we had our first unofficial date, smiling at the couples huddled together over dripping cones. The street is alive with foot traffic, vendors hawking small golden Buddhas and incense wafting in pungent clouds from rickety metal tables, kids standing on corners wearing impossibly high platform shoes and leather coats, their high, childish voices echoing clearly in the night. NYU students stumble down the street wearing long, brightly colored woolen scarves, clutching one another for support, their loud, drunken chatter filling my ears with talk of Godard and Bergman. The air is brisk and chilly, but I'm warm, my feet moving quickly across the pavement, taking me closer to Julian with every step. The stars above are hidden by gathering storm clouds and the light pulsating from the buildings, but on nights like these the city seems almost magical, inhabited by benevolent angels, a symphony of car horns and neon filling the shadows with discordant music and light.

From half a block away I can see Julian standing in front of the Eighth Street Playhouse, shifting his weight from side to side, his hands shoved into his pockets to warm them, hair falling across his face like a shadow moving over the sun. When he sees me, he tosses his head back so that the dense curtain of hair falls away from his eyes. His face breaks into a wide grin that makes the blood rush to my cheeks, my skin flushing with the sudden heat of his smile.

"Hey," he says as I approach. "You made it."

Standing there in front of him, I begin to believe maybe for the first time that he just might really like me. It's in those eyes, the way they take me in—not just my body and face, but all of me. Even the parts I don't want anyone to see. It makes me feel nervous and exhilarated all at once.

"I can't believe you've never done this." He gestures toward the marquee lit up in red and white like a Christmas tree flashing softly in the dark. "And you call yourself a New

Yorker," he scoffs, elbowing me in the side playfully as we make our way to the ticket booth.

"It always seemed like such a touristy thing to do," I say as Julian pulls a wallet from his back pocket, holding up two fingers at the girl inside the booth. She resembles Pippi Longstocking with her fire-engine-red pigtails and the smattering of cinnamon freckles that run across the bridge of her nose. She blows a huge pink bubble with a wad of gum before distractedly pushing the tickets at Julian. When he turns toward me, his almond skin illuminated by the neon light, the clarity of the bones in his face breaks my heart a little. Whether I like it or not, something is happening between us, something I'm not sure that I want to stop, and that knowledge scares me more than anything else.

"*Rocky Horror* isn't touristy at all," he continues. "It's classic."

"Like you?" I ask, looking into his face as he pulls me inside the theater. I take in the high ceilings and faded red velvet seats. He grins, his face alight, and at this moment I could die, just drop dead right here amid the scents of popcorn and hairspray, and not care one bit.

The space is crowded with people dressed in costumes, an homage to the characters in the film. An impossibly tall guy wearing fishnets, a corset and bright red lipstick is obviously Frank-N-Furter, and out of the corner of my eye I spy Magenta perched on the stage in front of the huge screen, laughing. Her bright red curls stream past her shoulders as she throws her head back in delight. Janet is two rows in front of us wearing a suit of the palest lavender, pearls encircling her throat, her auburn hair perfectly coiffed. Even though I've seen *Rocky Horror* countless times on video and late-night TV, I've never seen it in a theater, and the packed room, the laughter that surrounds us, not to mention Julian's hand in mine, enthralls me.

Even after the lights dim and the film flickers across the screen, after we stand up awkwardly to do the Time Warp, laughing, our hips bumping against one another and the other people in our row, even after the clouds of pot smoke hanging over our heads dissipate and the last grain of rice is hurled at the screen, Julian doesn't let go of my hand. As Tim Curry sings his final song, the stage is crowded with audience members swaying and singing along with the music in a perfect pantomime.

Don't dream it, be it . . .

At that moment, Julian leans close to me, our shoulders touching, his hair brushing my cheek. When I turn to look into his eyes, he slowly lowers his lips to mine. I close my eyes and breathe in the scent of shampoo and Ivory soap as he cups one hand under my chin, his fingers reaching up to brush the hair back from my face. At the feeling of his hands on my skin, all my nervousness falls away. We are kissing softly, Julian's hands touching me tentatively as if I might bolt. Something in his kiss, in the way he looks at me, makes me feel worlds away from the girl I know that I am, the girl with the screwed-up family and the weird job, the girl who can't feel much of anything except disappointment and fear. When we finally come up for air, I open my eyes to find his lashes fluttering as if he's just woken from a dream, the kind you try to find again after waking in the morning light.

"Wow," he whispers, dropping my hand for the first time all night and pushing his dark hair back from his face. I bite my lower lip in response, afraid to speak, and then he leans in again, kissing me with urgency this time. When his lips release me, I'm breathing fast, my chest tight with all that remains unspoken between us. I look away, not sure if I can trust the rush of heat in my veins. As the lights come up, I blink, adjusting to the sudden glare that flattens everything out, bringing us back to reality.

"Hey," Julian says softly. I can't look at him. "I'm sorry. That was probably way too fast for you."

It's strange how he knows me so well, without really knowing me at all, the way he can anticipate my reaction. It makes me feel disoriented, off balance.

"Maybe a little," I answer, watching as the crowds make their way up the aisles of the theater as slowly as a herd of cattle.

Outside on the street, I take big gulps of rain-freshened air as we walk through the late-night crush of pedestrians crowding the streets of the East Village. The sidewalks are alive with chatter, yellow cabs crawling down the wet black asphalt, headlights reflected in puddles like the orb of the moon. As we walk toward my apartment, my stomach begins to jump nervously, my heart skidding away like cars on the wet pavement. Every block or so, Julian shoots me little side glances, smiling encouragingly, his hand once again in mine.

We stop in front of my building as I point to my stoop, which is currently occupied by the weird guy from the first floor who is always wearing the same pair of black parachute pants, his pet parrot Chico perched on his shoulder. Chico squawks loudly, flapping his brightly colored wings, and we laugh awkwardly. Julian shoots me a look of disbelief as if to say, *Why is some weird dude with a psychotic bird on your stoop?*

"Well, this is me," I say, dropping his hand and trying to smile. In a sudden burst of impulsivity or downright insanity, I realize that I don't want him to leave, that I don't want the night to be over so soon. I feel like a complete dork when I ask, "Do you want to come up for a minute?"

Julian coughs once, looking at the sidewalk and trying to mask his astonishment by playing it cool. "Sure," he says, shrugging. "If you want."

Inside my apartment, I bustle around in the kitchen getting two glasses of water so I don't have to watch as Julian walks around, taking in the mismatched furniture, the heavy black curtains that cover the long windows, the sloping ceiling and wooden floor covered with heaps of clothes. The bedroom door is open, the closet bursting with racks of Giovanni's creations, a heap of tulle and sequins. The twin bed shoved in the corner, the lilac sheets rumpled.

"This is great," he says, walking over to one of the end tables beside the couch and picking up a crystal paperweight my father gave me when I was eleven. There is a white rose suspended inside, petals opening hopefully within the sparkling glass. I used to think that paperweight meant something, that inside its transparent depths lurked a message from my father, silent and pure, but there all the same. Now it just looks like a paperweight.

"It's OK." I blush, handing him a glass of water. I'm sweating nervously, the material beneath the arms of the long-sleeved black T-shirt I'm wearing growing damper by the minute. Julian sits down on the couch, drinking his water in a series of rapid gulps, wiping his mouth with the back of his hand. He shrugs off his leather jacket. Underneath he's wearing a navy sweater, the color underscoring the blue highlights in his dark hair.

"Seriously," he says after putting his glass down on the floor. "I'd give anything to have this place. You win: you are officially the luckiest person I know."

I laugh, perching on the rolled arm of the sofa. Somehow this feels safer than sitting next to him.

"It's pretty cool. But it can get kind of lonely." It's the first time I've ever said as much out loud to another human being, and the admission makes me feel like my skin has been peeled away in a series of long painful strips.

"I can see that." Julian nods thoughtfully. "It would still be better than living at home, though."

"Are things that bad?" I take a sip of water, mostly to have something to do with my hands, which I'm sure are shaking. I get up for a minute and switch on my turntable, and the sound of Jane's Addiction's "I Would for You" drifts into the room, softening the rough edges of our conversation and soothing my nerves.

"Right now they are." Julian takes a deep breath, smiling wanly before training his gaze on the opposite wall. I sit back down on the arm of the couch, waiting for him to tell me more. "This . . . thing happened with my ex-girlfriend a few months ago, and ever since then they've been on my ass basically all the time. Her parents called mine, and it was a huge fucking mess."

"What happened?" I ask, remembering what Sara said about the girlfriend, the suicide attempt. "I mean, I've heard some things, but—"

"Yeah," he says, cutting me off and exhaling heavily. "It's a fucking small city in some ways."

He looks away for a moment, and when he turns back, his eyes are glistening and I can't tell if he's angry or if tears will momentarily spill over his cheeks. When he speaks, his voice is a low mumble, as if he'd rather swallow what he has to say than spit it out.

"When we first started seeing each other, we were . . . really into it. In deep, like, right away. It's funny. It feels like a million years ago now, like it happened to someone else." Julian pushes his hair back from his face, and the pain I see there makes me want to take his hand in mine and squeeze it tight. Instead, I do nothing.

"Anyway, the more we got to know each other, the more I started to realize she was seriously screwed up. I mean, she'd cut herself all the time for no reason, just gouge her skin with a razor every time she got angry or sad. It got to the point where I was scared to fight with her, or even just disagree about a movie or some dumb bullshit without worrying that she'd hurt herself."

I watch his face as he fumbles for the words to explain. I hold my drink very still in my hands, cupping them around the cold glass as if it can somehow magically warm them.

"By this time we were sleeping together, and I wanted out even though I was worried that she'd freak if I broke up with her. I couldn't help her, and she didn't want to tell her parents or see a shrink or anything. But I didn't know what else to *do*, you know?" He holds his hands out in front of him in exasperation, confusion and anger distorting his features. "She started following me around everywhere, trailing my every move as if she was afraid I'd disappear if she let me out of her sight. I could barely breathe anymore, so I told her it was over, that she had to let me go. A few nights later her father found her passed out on the bathroom floor. She'd taken a bottle of her mother's Valium and carved my name into her leg with a razor blade." Julian is practically whispering now, and I lean forward so I can hear him. "Her parents sent her away somewhere, some hospital upstate," he says, bitterness coloring his voice. "I don't know where."

"Shit," I breathe, not sure of what to say or how to comfort him. I slide down onto the couch next to him, my feet tentatively touching his leg. "Are you OK, now? I mean, I know that's probably a dumb question, but . . ."

Julian laughs, a short bark that bounces off the walls, utterly mirthless. "I don't know," he mutters, looking away. "I feel responsible, like I could've done something different, like I could've saved her."

"From what?"

"Herself." Julian looks back at me, and the shame and intensity in his eyes burn through me. I feel dizzy, like I'm going to pass out, and I force myself to keep breathing, Sara's words echoing in my head like a skipping record.

Sooner or later you're going to end up in the goddamn hospital. Or the morgue.

I need to keep talking, to move away from these awful

thoughts crowding my head, leave behind that image of my own gray, bloodless face, limbs splayed out against the cold slab, eyes fixed uncomprehendingly on the ceiling.

"Do you miss her?"

"I don't know." He lets out a sigh, his narrow shoulders shaking. "It's more like I miss the way she used to be before she got so screwed up, you know? When we first started seeing each other, she was happy. And I was, too. I miss that. That feeling. I haven't felt that way since, well—until now." He takes a deep breath and looks at me, his eyes watery with unshed tears. "I like the way I feel around you," he says softly. "You make me feel like things are going to be all right for some reason."

"I don't know why," I say, my emotions caught in my throat in a large, unwieldy ball of stopped-up tears and hopefulness. "I mean, I have no idea why you like me." I swallow hard, looking away. "I'm probably just as screwed up as your ex-girlfriend."

"You don't *need* anything from me," he says, looking at me until I meet his gaze. I can see the hurt and disappointment so clearly, the part of him that doesn't want to trust anyone again. "You seem so, I don't know . . . *contained*. Like you don't need anyone at *all*."

Before I can answer, he pulls me to him and his lips find mine once again, the room dissolving around us in a crimson swirl, his words turning around in my brain over and over, the absurdity of them. If Julian knew how vulnerable I really am inside, where no one can see it, he'd walk out my front door right now and never look back. It's easier to pretend that you need nothing and no one, that you're an island surrounded by miles of water, uninhabitable, than it is to let your real feelings out where they can be trampled on. Sometimes I wish I were made of something impermeable and hard like wood or metal. Something that would keep the core of me locked away, encased in a thick, glittering shell.

Julian slowly pushes me down on the couch, stretching his long body over mine, kissing me deeply, my hands pulling him closer, his strong, wiry body under my palms. His fingers, tangled in my hair, begin traveling slowly down my torso, reaching beneath my T-shirt and gently pulling away the soft cotton. But at the feel of his warm hands on my bare stomach, the rush of cool air on my skin, I freeze, my body going rigid as a metal ruler. This is too much, too real. The shock of his hands on my skin, the exposed underbelly, the softest bits I never let anyone close enough to touch. My mother's smile as she pulled a leg from beneath the covers at night, pinching the skin of my calf in her tight fingers. *You belong to me.*

I feel as if I'm drowning under the weight of Julian's body, so comforting and delicious a moment before. I push him away, my thoughts spinning out of control. *Too much, too close,* they shriek, drowning out the music, the noise of the street outside my windows, Julian himself, who is looking at me and speaking, his mouth moving soundlessly. I cannot hear a word he's saying. The blood pounding in my ears erases everything.

"I can't do this," I say, sitting up. "You need to leave."

The urge to be completely alone comes over me in a vast wave, the need to sit by myself in my empty apartment, the refrigerator humming maniacally in the silence. Right now my apartment feels about as big as a cubicle, crowded with heat and flesh and a kind of emotional messiness that I can't seem to decipher, written in a language I don't understand.

"What did I do?" he asks, clearly worried. "Cat, talk to me!"

"Nothing," I say, standing up, crossing my arms over my chest. "I'm not ready for this." The room is moving rapidly. Things are speeding up, and all I want is for him to leave me alone. "I told you that day on Eighth Street."

"I know," he starts, walking toward me, "but then you asked me up here, so I thought—"

"I don't *care* what you thought," I say, and the look that comes over his face as the words leave my lips is enough to break what's left of my heart. Still, I can't seem to stop myself, even as I know I'm ruining everything, even as I can see it all slipping away from me. "You need to go."

Julian's face is alive with anger, his eyes steaming as he pulls his leather jacket on roughly.

"You and I both know this is bullshit," he says in a low voice. "And I *know* that what happened here tonight was real—even if you won't admit it."

He stares at me for a long, uncomfortable moment that makes me wish I could disappear before he walks to the door, slamming it loudly behind him.

As the silence grows in his absence, I begin to breathe normally again, my heart slowing. But along with relief, what I feel most of all is a potent combination of sadness and disappointment—disappointment in myself for chickening out, for making him leave when all I really wanted was for him to stay. I sit back down on the couch, one foot kicking over Julian's empty glass, which shatters against the wood floor, the fragments sparkling like crystal. As I bend to pick them up, I cut my finger on a long, sickle-shaped piece of glass, red blood bubbling up to the surface of my skin. And when the tears begin to stream from my eyes, it's not only from the pain in my finger, sharp and smarting, but at my inability to connect, to live my life in any other emotional state except fear mixed with detachment. As I cry, I put my finger in my mouth, sucking on it to stop the bleeding. Julian's hurt and confused face rises up in my mind until I am seized by the overwhelming desire to feel nothing, nothing at all anymore.

I walk into the bedroom, rummage for the blue velvet coat I wore to the club a few nights ago, fingers searching for the plastic baggie at the bottom of the front pocket. I pull out a large rock of cocaine, breathing a sigh of relief as I dump it onto my bedside table, chopping it into fine pieces with an American Express card I find there next to the phone, my mother's name printed in raised letters along the bottom. After the first line disappears up my nose, I feel markedly better, the powder shimmering in my bloodstream like a million tiny lights, the familiar, bitter taste of baby aspirin dripping down the back of my throat.

I look over at my closet, at the bustle of tulle and brightly colored satin sticking out from the open door, and feel the club pulling me closer. I get up and grab the first thing I see, a gold skirt embroidered with tiny sequins like stars. I hold the rough material up against my body, a bandage, a tourniquet, the taste of blood suspended in my mouth like an iron curtain.

TWENTY - FIVE

EIGHT A.M. AND I'M STILL WIDE AWAKE, pacing the floor of my apartment as if I'm trapped here, the walls closing in around me. I've already called school and told them I have a migraine, which I'm sure will put me in detention for the rest of my natural life, if not get me expelled completely. I sniff hard, looking into the mirror, paranoid that the residue from the coke I've been snorting for most of the previous evening has crusted around my nostrils. My eyes are bloodshot and ache in their sockets. I stare longingly at my bed reflected in the glass, the soft pillows urging me to collapse on top of them and rest. I would give anything to lie down and sleep until next week, falling into a land of oblivion without thoughts or dreams. Sleeping Beauty lying motionless in a glass coffin, trapped for eternity until a kiss set her free, blue eyes blinking open in sudden light, a face as blank and empty as a plastic doll's. I think of Christoph's face as he leaned toward me last night, whispering in my ear. *You are so beautiful* . . . That sense of danger as his arm slid up the length of my own and up to my face, cupping my cheek in his hand, holding my breath until he released me. Unlike Christoph, I don't see any beauty reflected in the mirror this morning. I see a pair of bulging red eyes and a nose that is moist, pink, and twitchy as a rabbit's.

The coke still in my system has made sleep an impossibility, and the four walls of my apartment stare down on me malevolently, crowding me in. I throw off my gold skirt and top and pull on a pair of leggings and a long black sweater, stuff my feet into boots and grab my leather jacket, the zippers glinting cruelly in the morning light. I search the detritus on the couch until I find my backpack, pulling a Sony Walkman from one of its bulging pockets and checking to see if there's a tape inside. As I make my way down the stairs of my building, shoving the headphones over my ears, I don't know where I'm going, just that I need to move fast, to walk through the maze of the city streets until I'm lost, then found, then lost again. I walk through the East Village, past groups of NYU students hurrying to classes, past the Rastafarians on street corners selling incense and T-shirts embossed with Bob Marley's likeness, and down Eighth Street, turning left at Sixth Avenue. When I reach the subway, I don't hesitate as I duck inside. The A train is just pulling into the station, and before I know what I'm doing, I'm aboard, the silver doors closing behind me, a voice squawking authoritatively over the loudspeaker: "This is a downtown A train to Far Rockaway. Please stand clear of the closing doors . . ."

The stations flash by and I sink onto a bench, grateful to find an empty seat during morning rush hour. My head feels heavy on my neck, and my eyes dart around the car, unable to settle on anything in particular. As we move through Manhattan, into Brooklyn and beyond, the car begins to empty out. The train comes up into the light aboveground as we enter Queens, the view out the windows displaying rows of tightly spaced, single-family homes in red brick or covered in aluminum siding. At the next-to-last stop I get off, the train almost empty now. As the doors close behind me, I stand on the platform for a moment, breathing in the cold air. I walk down the flight of metal stairs and onto the street. I've done this walk so many times, I could perform it in my sleep. The pavement is hard under my feet, and I'm grateful for one thing that feels substantial right now. Crowds of people shove by me in a hurry, the noise of traffic deadened by the music in my ears, the singer warbling in a tuneless monotone about a black planet, a black world.

When I reach the nursing home, I'm annoyed to see the front of the building has been tagged, white paint marring the redbrick exterior in a series of unidentifiable squiggles. I push through the glass doors and step into the lobby, my cheeks red from the cold and the exertion of the walk. The walls are painted a wretched shade of green that could only be called institutional. It falls somewhere between lime and mint, and makes everyone look awful, even if they haven't been up all night hoovering drugs.

"Well, hello, stranger! Long time no see."

Mary, the plump black nurse behind the desk, smiles up at me, a pencil stuck behind one ear, her mass of braids falling over one shoulder. Her soft Jamaican accent is so soothing that I want to put my head down on her desk until she pats me on the head like a child. She smells of Chanel No. 5 and baby powder. A red scarf is knotted jauntily at her neck today, the color illuminating her brown skin.

"No school today?" Her forehead is creased, her eyes narrowing.

I shake my head, mumbling "Uh-uh" as I reach for the pen, my hand shaking.

"Is she up there?" I nod toward the ceiling.

"And just where else would she be?" Mary laughs good-naturedly, her voice filling the air with a throaty richness.

I blush, rolling my eyes in embarrassment.

"OK to go up?" I point at the clipboard, my signature a meaningless scrawl on the white paper. *At least I've managed that much for today,* I think, as tiredness begins creeping slowly into my bones.

"Yes, yes," Mary clucks, waving me through. "Go on up there now. And give the lady my best, you hear?"

I nod and walk toward the elevators.

Outside my grandmother's room I stop for a moment and smooth my hair back from my face, aware that it is matted and tangled from last night. When I enter, she is sitting propped up in bed, three fat pillows behind her back. The walls are covered in framed pictures of me at every age—newborn in her arms, at my christening, a floppy white dress hiding my small, pudgy legs. There are photos of her and my grandfather when they were first married, a mink coat draped around her shoulders, snapshots of my grandfather young and handsome in his army uniform, medals glinting on his chest. There are no pictures of my mother anywhere in the room. It's as if she has been erased entirely.

As I reach the bed, her eyes open, clouded by cataracts. Her eyes move restlessly, sensing my presence in the small space. Her arms extending from her pink satin nightgown are bony and frail, marked by prominent veins, and her hair frames her face in a cloud of white, her skin deeply lined around the mouth and eyes.

"Who's that?" Her voice trembles, and her eyes move from side to side, searching for that which she can no longer see. No matter how many surgeries she's endured, the cataracts grow back with a vengeance.

"It's me, Nana." I sit down on the bed beside her, taking her warm hand in my own. She smells of Ivory soap and Shalimar, of home and safety, and I close my eyes, breathing deeply.

"Who's *me*?" she says, chuckling, squeezing my hand.

"Caitlin. Your granddaughter?"

"Oh, yes," she says happily. "*Caitlin.*"

These moments of clarity are happening less and less frequently as the months pass by, and I sigh loudly in relief, reaching up to smooth her hair back from her face. Today she recognizes me, if only for an instant, and that's enough for now.

"Did you eat breakfast?" I ask, searching the room for the empty tray.

My grandmother looks at me, a mischievous expression on her face, although her eyes are unfocused.

"I cheated," she says, her voice dropping to a whisper. "I had prunes, but I hid them under the napkin! They'll never find them there!"

Her tone is triumphant, and I smile, glad to see that she's

taking little rebellions wherever she can. It means that her spirit is still mostly intact, that she's still fighting.

"How's school?" she asks, patting my hand as if I'm the one in the hospital bed needing to be consoled.

"Not so great." My voice breaks a little, and I blink back tears. Something in my chest folds in on itself, breaks free, and I long to just rest my head in her lap and sleep.

A confused expression distorts her face, and she begins patting my hand quickly, more rhythmically.

"There, there," she murmurs. "You never did have a knack for schoolwork. You always had your head in the clouds, Diana."

I freeze, my body going rigid.

Diana is my mother's name.

"Nana," I say softly, afraid I will break down completely if I speak any louder, "it's *Caitlin*."

No matter how many times this happens, I never get used to it, the unsettling feeling of being thrust into my mother's skin, suffocating under the weight of her heavy perfume, her life itself. My grandmother's love for me is the only sacred thing I possess, something that cannot be marred by time or history. She is so much a part of me that I don't know where her frail body ends in this hospital bed and I begin. Her hand resting in mine is a mirror image of my own, the same long, slender fingers and olive skin.

"I *know* who you are," my grandmother snaps, dropping my hand and turning away, seemingly miffed. But I can tell by the way she stares defiantly at the ceiling that it isn't true. I think of how terrifying that must be, to be having a whole conversation with someone who thinks they know you well enough to hold your hand, but whom you don't recognize. I know from what her nurses have told me that these moments will begin to happen more and more frequently, that she will lose more of her memory with every passing day until she slips away from me for good, unable to recall my name or what I mean to her.

Meant.

Past tense, I tell myself over and over like a mantra, the words reverberating in my brain. *Get used to it.* But I can't, don't want to.

"Where's my nurse?" She looks around indignantly, her hands gripping the sheets white-knuckled. "Who are you?" she barks at me, staring in the space above my head. I recognize the note of hysteria creeping into her voice, and I get up, walk to the door and flag down a nurse at her station. The nurse has tired brown eyes, and it looks like someone has flung handfuls of what appears to be mashed peas at her blue scrub top.

"Is she acting up again?" She raises one eyebrow and doesn't wait for a response, just strides into my grandmother's room as if she already knows what she'll find there.

"Now, now, Martha," the nurse says in a patient, soothing voice. "Let's lie back and take your medicine, OK?" The nurse draws a syringe full of clear liquid, injecting it into the thin skin of my grandmother's arm. I watch as she flinches at the stick of the needle, turning her face away from me, her lips moving soundlessly.

"She'll be all right now," the nurse says, patting me on the shoulder as she exits the room, her cotton-clad legs swishing together as she moves.

I pull up a chair and sit there for a while next to the bed, watching my grandmother sleep, the way her eyeballs move beneath her eyelids, which are vaguely purple, almost bruised looking. I hold her hand in mine, knowing it could be anyone's hand that she holds, that it takes two to hold hands and right now, I'm the only one really holding on. I know that when she dies, the good memories I have of my childhood will fade and die along with her, and the thought shatters any small bit of hope I have left.

I watch her chest rise and fall with every breath she takes until sunlight creeps across the walls of her room, bouncing off the pictures in their gold frames, until I am hardened and dry as an empty husk.

TWENTY-SIX

THE NEXT MORNING, I wake at 11:15, adrenaline flooding my body as I crack one eye open to glance at the clock. My mouth is so dry that when I move my lips apart, I actually hear a sucking sound as the flesh comes unglued. Standing at the refrigerator chugging a glass of ice water so fast that I sink to the floor, my head filled with blinding pain, hands pressed to my forehead as if I could somehow blot everything out— Julian, my mother, sitting on Christoph's lap in the Chandelier Room the night before, a cold bottle of champagne tucked between my knees. My pulse racing each time his tanned skin brushed against my own, the feeling of falling, vertigo, the air rushing by my face as he leaned closer, his citrus cologne tickling my nose with the scent of sun-warmed beaches. The strained look on Giovanni's face as I bent over the mirror repeatedly, my reflection rising up to meet me.

Standing in front of Tavern on the Green, I pace the sidewalk, glancing up at the red awning over the door as if it will somehow magically change into a place I actually want to enter. After ten minutes, I take a deep breath and force myself to walk through the front door, my heart hammering in my ears. The restaurant is full of well-heeled families settling in for brunch, gold and crystal chandeliers dangling from the ceiling like huge, expensive earrings. The scent of freshly cut flowers and imported coffee mingles with a myriad perfumes: hot-house roses, violets and the animal growl of musk.

I duck quickly into the ladies' room, stand at the marble counters and breathe, filling my lungs with gulps of air. In some kind of attempt to appease my mother and thwart her anger and disapproval, I am wearing what could be considered my most nondescript articles of clothing. A black pleated skirt with gray woolen tights, and a tailored white shirt topped with a navy pea coat. A feeling of hopelessness comes over me as I take in my boring clothes, hair scraped back into place with a patent-leather headband—a cheap facsimile of the daughter my mother always wanted. Even after all this time, I am still trying to cater to her wants and desires, to please her in some way. Sara was right: It's ridiculous. Pathetic.

When I walk into the main dining room, I see my mother right away. She's in the back, where I knew she'd be, at her favorite round table set for four near the huge glass windows. As I move toward her, I'm numb, taking in the frosted hair combed back from her face and secured at the base of her long neck. She's wearing a beige silk dress, the material artfully draped at the bust and waist. Gold chains glitter at her throat, and diamond studs shine in her ears, as compact and neat as twin seashells, treasure glinting at the bottom of the sea.

As I slide into the chair across from her, my mother looks me up and down with a tight smile, bringing a glass of champagne up to her red lips, the crystal flute gripped between her fingers. I can tell from her expression that, as usual, I've failed some important test, disappointing her once again.

"Hi, Mom," I say, careful to keep my expression neutral.

"Thanks for coming," she says, turning to rummage in her purse, pulling out a gold cigarette case my father gave her on her thirty-fifth birthday. She extracts a cigarette, lighting it with her gold Cartier lighter. Smoke envelops her face as she exhales, momentarily disappearing until the smoke fades, drifting in lazy circles above her head.

I fidget with the silverware as the waiter approaches, smiling at me expectantly.

"She will have the eggs Benedict and an orange juice," my mother says before I can speak. "Just the champagne for me." She hands him the menus with disdain, as if talking to waiters is a necessary evil, something she merely tolerates in the course of her daily life. At the mention of eggs, my stomach begins to turn in protest, a wave of nausea sweeping through my body.

"Very good," the waiter says, collecting the menus and wine list, which is as thick as a Manhattan phone book. As he prepares to walk away, I manage to find my voice.

"Actually, I'll just have a cup of black coffee and some wheat toast," I say. My mother glares at me, clearly annoyed.

"Caitlin, you love the eggs Benedict here," she protests, an icy note in her voice. The subtext? Do. Not. Argue. With. Me. "It used to be your favorite."

The waiter glances at my mother, then me, his lips held in a thin smile, his eyes glazed over in either boredom or annoyance.

"When I was ten," I say carefully. "I haven't eaten eggs in years."

The waiter smiles, then walks away, the menus tucked under his arm, leaving me to deal with this mess on my own. My mother shakes her head in irritation.

"We've only been here five minutes, and already you're arguing with me." She stamps out her cigarette in the ashtray with an angry jab of her wrist, shaking her head from side to side.

Through the wall of windows behind my mother, I watch a little girl in a puffy winter coat walk by the restaurant holding her father's hand, a pair of bright red mittens clipped to her coat sleeves. She looks up at her father as she walks, her face full of wonder and delight, her corn-silk hair curling gently around her small face.

"I'm not arguing with you," I say, still staring out the window, my voice a monotone. "I just didn't want eggs. That's all." Somehow it feels less dangerous to not look her in the face, but I know that if there is even a chance she thinks I'm ignoring her, it will seriously piss her off. I tear my eyes away from the window and take a sip of the water in front of me, ice clinking painfully against my front teeth.

Sensing my restraint, she switches tactics, smiling with a warmth you'd think was sincere unless you knew my mother the way I do. It's the kind of smile that makes you feel like the sun has just burst out of the clouds after a long, interminable winter of gray skies and drizzle—if you fall for it, that is, which

I stopped doing some time ago. Still, the sight of her face alight with pleasure and maybe something like love stops my heart entirely.

"I wanted to talk to you about your living situation." The waiter approaches again, carrying my toast and coffee, the bread cut into precise triangles, the edges so sharp they could puncture an artery. He sets down a silver tray of butter along with tiny jars of French jam. The smell of toasted bread and the acrid burn of coffee makes my stomach recoil, and I close my eyes for a moment. *You will not throw up,* I tell myself sternly.

"What about it?" Despite my attempts to keep things neutral, I cannot stop an edge from creeping into my voice. I pick up the coffee cup and bring it to my lips, steam flooding my face.

"I'm sure you know that I don't think it's at all appropriate." She picks up her champagne glass, draining it and signaling the waiter for another.

"For who?"

"For anyone, Caitlin," she snaps, annoyed now. "It's been six months, and people are starting to talk."

"And whose fault is that?"

After the words leave my mouth, I become rapidly aware that they were a mistake. My mother's face closes off like a door slamming shut, her eyes narrowing as she calculates her next move.

"Have you seen your father?" she says, changing the subject expertly, dodging and weaving like a prizefighter. The problem with prizefighters, I know from experience, is that they often wait for you to drop your guard before they hit you.

"Barely."

"And what does that mean?" She raises one finely arched eyebrow as the waiter returns with another flute of champagne, setting it gently before her on the snow-white tablecloth.

"It means I've barely seen him. He showed up at school a few days ago and stayed for approximately five minutes. Three months ago, when he forgot to send the rent, I dropped by his office to pick up a check. Besides that, I haven't seen him since he signed the lease on my apartment."

"You know," she says, leaning forward conspiratorially, as if she and I are in this together, "your father never wanted you. He said that children would be too much trouble. Personally, I think he was afraid it would cramp his style." She smiles with false brightness as if she's just told me about a sale at Bloomingdale's. My throat immediately goes dry. She is always cruel, my mother, but one never knows when that cruelty will make an appearance or what guise it will take. She has the rare talent of putting into words one's deepest fears and insecurities, going right for them like a lion at the kill. I can't swallow, the moisture in my mouth evaporating with her words. I blink rapidly, desperate to keep tears from falling in front of her. My chest aches. An open wound.

"In any case, it's not appropriate for you to be living all the way downtown in that *hovel*," she says, pleased that her admission has had the desired effect. My mother shudders in revulsion as if the apartment itself is the real problem, changing the subject again as easily as switching the channels on TV. "Your father agrees with me, by the way."

"Well, he didn't say anything about it to me when I saw

him," I say, picking up a piece of toast, then laying it back down, brushing crumbs off my fingers.

"Caitlin." She is all business now, pushing her glass to the side and folding her hands together on the table like we're at a board meeting. "You need to come home."

There is a long silence. *Home.* That word as foreign as my name in her mouth. The trouble with words is that they never mean what you want them to mean. I am thinking about the last night I called my mother's apartment *home.* The quiet in the kitchen broken only by the ticking clock as I warmed a frozen dinner in the microwave, my mother entering the room soundlessly, her hands grabbing my hair from behind and yanking hard, my skull aching for days, the way my eyes focused only on the pink veins in the marble floor as my head made contact and my eyes closed, bracing myself against pain. How everyone stared at me in school the next day, my eye purple-black as a wilted pansy, the look on the headmistress's face as she called me into her office, the room spinning with tentative, probing questions that left me dizzy and unable to speak. Sudden vertigo. My face deadened. The social workers who arrived unannounced later that night, and the hardened look in my father's eyes as he pressed crisp bills into their waiting hands, his mobile phone ringing endlessly. The car waiting downstairs ready to speed him far away from us. My mother glowering in the corner, her face half in shadow.

"I don't think so," I say slowly, my words as heavy as lead. "It isn't really home anymore."

My mother sits back in her chair, observing me with eyes that glisten with moisture at the corners, her face unreadable.

All around us the restaurant bustles with life, waiters walk back and forth on the plush carpeting with silver trays held high above their heads, the sound of laughter ringing in the air mixes with the noise of eating as glasses are clinked together, plates scraped with the sharp metal tines of a fork.

"I'm still your mother," she says quietly after a few minutes.

I bite my bottom lip, focusing on the pain that blooms on the surface of the tender skin there. I force myself to concentrate on the breath going in and out of my lungs, aware I am fighting to keep those breaths regular and even, fighting to breathe at all.

She looks down at the tabletop, her mouth quivering, and for a moment I think she might cry. I know rationally it is most likely an attempt to manipulate me into doing what she wants, but if tears actually fall from her eyes, it will undo me completely. Something irrevocable will happen, my brain breaking apart, a mass of ice cracking on a rooftop, loosening before crashing headlong to the pavement.

But when she looks up, I see the hint of a smile in her eyes, a brightness that tells me this is part of the act. If she makes me believe she's sorry, maybe I'll give in, give up and follow her home like a whipped dog reunited with its owner. I'm not sure what I wanted, what I hoped to find here in this place with clinking silverware and the careful squint of her eyes across the table, but the idea of that kind of submission makes my blood burn, my skin suddenly prickling with heat. *How dare she,* I think, the anger building like a piece of music, a rising crescendo. *How dare she.* But what makes me angrier still is my own reaction, the fact that even after all I know of her lies, her manipulation, I could almost fall for the guile of her manufactured tears. The only reason she wants me back is that she cannot have me. The only reason she covets me at all is that it doesn't look "right" to be living on my own, without her looming over me.

"Caitlin, you have to think about your future. You simply cannot run and play your whole life! Your guidance counselor mentioned that—"

I stand up, a strength I didn't know I had rising up inside me, the momentum and heat of dry leaves catching fire, a blaze that threatens to obliterate everything. How can she lecture me about a future that she never prepared me for, a future she never gave me the tools to handle? All I know is pain and fear, how to survive the day-to-day-ness of life by putting one foot in front of the other and looking straight ahead. My mother's mouth falls open in surprise as she watches me gather up my things, jerking my coat on with angry movements, my arm catching in one sleeve before I pull it free, the lining tearing with an audible rip.

"Caitlin!" my mother hisses under her breath. "Sit down! People are looking!"

She reaches out one hand and grabs my wrist, her fingers tightening around my skin, scratching me with her nails in a way that feels so familiar, I almost scream. I jerk my arm away roughly, aware that the whole restaurant has stopped to watch us, that forks piled with food are being held motionless in front of open mouths, that the women directly across from us are whispering behind cupped hands.

"I don't care!" I yell out, my voice surprising me with how

loud it sounds in the hushed room. The spot on my wrist where she scratched me pulses hotly, and I rub it with my other hand, my eyes never leaving my mother's face as I lean down. This close we are mirror reflections of each other. The face that looks angrily back at me is my own, lips the same fleshy pillows. But the expression in her eyes is flat and dead. Snake eyes, devoid of any kind of real feeling, and as I look at my mother, I make a silent promise to myself; I swear that I will never become her, bitter and full of rage, obsessed with what other people think, that in spite of genetics, a physical resemblance is the only thing we will ever share between us. At this moment I am so angry, so full of urgency that my entire body is vibrating like the buzzing whine of a chain saw.

"If you ever touch me again," I say, my voice barely above a whisper, "I will hit you back. And it will hurt."

Her eyes widen further, and in them I see not only anger but, for the first time, fear, and I know she has heard me. She nods almost imperceptibly, dropping her gaze to the floor.

I walk out of the room, all eyes on me as I move farther away from my mother, every step sealing my fate. Even though I can't see her, I imagine the apologetic smile that is surely plastered all over her face, how she will raise one hand to ask for the check, and I am inexplicably filled with a sadness so large, it threatens to swallow me completely. She's cruel and dangerous, but she's also my mother. As much as I hate to admit it, I'm only seventeen, and I still need mothering. Whatever that means. What makes me saddest of all is the crushing knowledge that she will never be able to love me the way I need her to, that maybe she cannot love at all. And it feels like a kind of death. I thought if I finally stood up to her, I'd feel better. I was wrong.

When I push open the front door and the cold wind rips through my coat, I begin to shiver violently, the adrenaline finally giving way to exhaustion as I begin to make my way through Central Park, the bare branches of the trees overhead offering protection against nothing. The world feels like a Xerox of itself, two-dimensional and unreal. I know I will meet Christoph tonight because there is no longer any reason not to. No matter how much I fight against it, I'm always inevitably drawn to the worst of everything. That kind of darkness.

I force myself not to think about Julian, love, or any other kind of fake salvation, my shoes clicking against the path as I move myself forward, pedestrians walking blithely by me in a blur of wool and laughter as tears finally begin their slow, icy crawl down my face.

THE SCENT OF FRANKINCENSE and myrrh drifts by my head as the priest shakes the incense burner, the brass swinging from a chain flashing like a prism in the sunlit stone room. I am sitting between my grandparents, my small hand wrapped in my grandfather's large, meaty palm, the skin roughened by long hours spent in his minuscule garden plot. When he releases me, I know my hand will smell of the tomato vines he tended before we got in the car, of sunlight and the dark, loamy tang of turned earth.

Every Sunday I spend with my grandparents is the same—church in the morning, followed by a long lunch at the worn kitchen table, tomato sauce simmering in a blue speckled pan licked by a gas flame. Sometimes a barbecue, my grandfather carefully flipping seasoned pieces of chicken on the grill, smoke billowing up and engulfing me in its sweet meaty scent. I watch as he raises one hand to his heart and stops, momentarily, his face creased with pain. I lie on a hard wooden swing, aimlessly turning the pages of a book, entranced by the leaves of the trees overhead, their green carpet hiding the sun. The pages draw me in, and between the stark *black type and white pages, I see safety in fantasy, that the removal of the self from the world is the only thing that might save me. In those pages, I am not the girl who hides under the bed waiting for her mother to go to sleep, or the girl who tugs on her father's sleeve as he strides purposefully out the door. I am a fairy princess, a magician, a warrior.*

At church, the priest reads from his leather-bound Bible and we follow along, repeating the words that hang heavily in my throat, words like God and love and faith. Words that ring falsely in the air, echoing in the enormous room, words that have no meaning. Just three years from this moment, my grandfather's mahogany coffin will be carried down the aisle and I will watch as the priest performs a blessing, making the sign of the cross over the hard wooden surface, my heart empty. My grandmother will sit in his chair at night, refusing to lie down in the bed that they shared for more than forty years, her eyes blurred and unfocused. If there is a God, he is for other people. Even at seven, I know that if there is a man up there, hanging suspended in the sky, he cannot possibly love me, that there is no salvation in this life but the world you make for yourself.

TWENTY-SEVEN

SATURDAY NIGHT, and I'm standing outside of Chaos, the first snowfall of the year drifting down in large, fat flakes that land softly on the sidewalk, blanketing it in whiteness. The snow lands in my eyelashes, caught there, and I blink it away, exhaling my breath into the cold air. At midnight, the streets of Alphabet City in front of the abandoned buildings are lined with addicts waiting for a fix. They tap their feet against the sidewalk, their voices wailing out into the night, causing me to shiver violently. This is where people come to buy not only crack, but heroin, tearing open small glassine bags that feel like waxed paper and snorting the contents in empty doorways or the safety of phone booths, patrol cars passing by lazily in the night.

On my right hand I wear Giovanni's onyx poison ring, its depths packed with white powder that reminds me of the gently falling snow. I bent over it repeatedly during the short ride from my apartment, the driver's eyes meeting my own in the rearview mirror once and flitting away silently as I sniffed loudly, beyond caring. The club's pink neon sign and the trio of black limousines parked at the curb waver like some kind of gaudy mirage, and I duck inside the front door, which shuts heavily behind me with a loud thump. I'm wearing a tight black dress that ends short of my fingertips. My hair is pulled back, ropes of vintage rhinestones glittering at my ears and wrists. On my feet are heels so high, I must walk carefully just to stay upright. Black feathers spike from my head toward the stars dangling in the night sky.

"Very Holly Golightly," Giovanni murmured an hour earlier, invoking Audrey Hepburn's stylish New York grace, nodding his approval, arms crossed at the chest. "He's gonna love it." But now, standing just inside the doorway, I'm not so sure. The more I look in the mirror lately, the more unsure I am of what is reflected there.

Even though it's only midnight, the club is packed. Most of the women are working the large, sparkly-earring Eurotrash look more often on display at intimate clubs like Nell's, where people sit perched on couches talking quietly over glasses of Merlot: tight black clothing, slicked-back hair and violently red lips. Everyone looks like an extra from a Robert Palmer video, with pouting, glossy mouths and vacant stares, their cigarette smoke trailing softly to the ceiling. These are not club kids, but a more upscale, well-heeled crowd that doesn't flinch at shelling out hundreds of dollars for bottles of cut-rate champagne and top-shelf liquors swirled into small glasses, and strangely enough, in the outfit Giovanni fashioned for me this evening, I fit in just fine. The first floor is painted in wide stripes of magenta and black, dominated by cushy white sofas in shapes beamed straight from outer space.

The music pounds through the room, silencing the sound of my heels against the ebony-stained hardwood as I make my way toward the bouncer standing behind a velvet rope, clipboard in hand. He's wearing a silver jacket and expertly cut dark pants, his black hair combed into a pompadour that offsets his high cheekbones. I don't recognize him, but he squints as I approach, sizing me up. At moments like these I feel like a steak on display in a butcher shop window or the last cold piece of pizza at the bottom of a soggy box. The fact that I perform the same ritual nightly at Tunnel doesn't make it any easier when I'm stuck on the other side of the fence.

"Yes?" he says as I walk up, not unkindly, but his voice isn't exactly friendly, either. I smile to myself as I observe his cool detachment. I could be looking at my own face in the mirror, my expression blank, with a slight edge of condescension. From the frosty vibes he's sending my way, it's doubtful that we're going to end up having weekly slumber parties or sharing a line in the bathroom. He glances down at his clipboard, waiting for me to speak.

"I'm Caitlin," I say quickly, swallowing hard and adding, "I mean, Cat. I'm here to meet Christoph. From Tunnel?"

I am not unaware of the fact that I sound like a stammering moron or that I'm suddenly inexplicably sweating at the mention of Christoph's name. *What are you doing?* I think as I wait for his expression to change, for the rope to magically swing open as it always does at moments like these. *What the hell are you even doing here?*

He looks up from the clipboard, his eyes widening as a flash of recognition sweeps across his face, which breaks into a slow smile the moment Christoph's name leaves my lips.

Bingo.

"Right this way," he sputters, all sugar and sunshine as he hands the clipboard to a hugely muscled black guy who is clearly in charge of either crowd control or breaking legs, his biceps straining beneath a dark suit. Rope Nazi takes my arm, leading me through the pulsing crowd that ebbs and flows like the sea. Laughter shatters my ears, more beautiful than music, and I am light-headed as we push through the crowd, then through a door marked EMPLOYEES ONLY and up a flight of stairs.

"We've put you in a private room because of the weather." He turns to me, offering up an apologetic smile.

My blood is pounding in my ears as we reach the door I know will lead to the place where Christoph waits for me, and the stairwell begins to swim dizzily before my eyes. When I close them to get my bearings, my mother's face emerges and a small cry escapes my lips. I put one hand on the wall, steadying myself, my heart racing beneath the spandex shell of my dress, my breath coming fast and ragged. Rope Nazi looks at me, one hand on the door marked PRIVATE, his brow wrinkled in concern, a look in his eyes I recognize immediately as fear.

"Umm . . . are you OK?"

He leans toward me, patting my arm as if he's afraid

I might fall apart right here in the stairwell, and then how would he explain *that*?

I lean my forehead against the wall. The white plaster is cool against my skin. I breathe in and out, willing my heart to slow its rapid ascent. After a moment I straighten up, offering him a weak smile, checking that my hair is still smoothly pulled back from my face. Without even looking in the mirror, I know my skin is waxen, sweat breaking out along my temples.

"I'm fine," I say, and even though he knows I'm lying, he shrugs once, then opens the door, and suddenly the lights of the city are strung out like jewels through a wall of windows. The effect is instant vertigo, the sky opening up in front of me, snow swirling in front of the glass, purifying everything in hushed silent whiteness. Low music drifts through the room, candles bathing everything in a soft glow. Christoph sits at a table in front of the largest window. China and silverware gleam on the table, and the scent of lilies in the air is intoxicating. The room is full of flowers in hammered silver vases, and the open petals mix with the plastic smell of the dripping wax.

I take a deep breath and walk toward Christoph as if I'm going to my own execution, my heels clicking against the floor as the door shuts tight behind me. I try to glue a cheerful expression to the lower half of my face, my jaw clenched tight as a fist. I'm so high that I notice for the first time I've been grinding my teeth for what seems like forever, my jaw sore and overworked. My teeth feel as soft and insubstantial as soapstone, and I run my tongue over them just to make sure they're still in there, anchored to the fleshy pink heat of my gums.

As I reach the table, Christoph jumps to his feet, grasping me firmly by the shoulders and leaning in to kiss me on both cheeks, his lips lingering against my skin. He smells of a cologne that manages to be both musky and bracing at the same time, like an animal pelt washed clean by rainwater and left to dry in the sun. The smell of his body, the floral tang of laundry detergent emanating from his clothes—it all makes me dizzy, and I'm grateful for the leather chair I sink into the minute he releases me.

"I wasn't sure you'd come," he says, sitting down across from me and balling a white cloth napkin in his fist. His skin is dark in the candlelight, and I wonder if he went to the tanning salon this afternoon before our date. The thought makes me feel sad for some reason, and I clear my throat to steady my nerves, the sound echoing over the music piped into the room by invisible speakers. My throat feels raw and red, a ribbon of blood candy. Christoph looks at me expectantly, and I realize he is waiting for me to speak.

"Yes you were," I say, my words hollow in my throat.

Christoph's smile returns, and he leans back in his chair, confidence restored as a white-jacketed waiter enters the room and approaches the table, pouring champagne from a dewy-necked bottle. The golden liquid spills into my glass and I reach for it before the waiter is even finished pouring, bubbles frothing over my wrist as I raise it to my mouth, gulping frantically. *I need this,* I think as it slides down my throat, tickling the inside of me like silent fingers. *I need something.* My heart is still hammering away in my chest, relentless, and when I put my glass down on the table, Christoph nods almost imperceptibly at the waiter, who refills it, his face impassive. After topping off Christoph's glass, the waiter disappears, the door closing noiselessly behind him.

"I wasn't sure it was a good idea," I say, even though my throat seems to be closing up. I offer him a weak smile. I can feel the sweat standing out on my forehead, and I wonder if I can somehow wipe it away without him noticing. I also begin to realize that I've done way too much coke, that the drugs swirling through my system like snow have become an uncontrollable blizzard, coating my insides in a dense, suffocating fog.

Christoph laughs, his eyes crinkling at the corners, revealing tiny lines etched into his tanned skin. "Funny. I tend to do most things precisely *for* that reason alone. Life is an adventure, no? It is to be experienced." He leans forward in his chair, resting his arms on the table. His suit tonight is jet black, the material soft and expensive. I know if I reach out and touch his sleeve, it will feel like butter, the wool fine-spun as a spider's web. The words coming from his lips could be my own, that pull toward the abyss.

"I mean, you only live once, right?" Christoph reaches across the table and takes my hand, running his index finger slowly across my palm, making me feel as though I'm squirming without moving an inch.

The waiter enters the room again silently, carrying a large silver tray with a huge dome. He sets it down carefully in the middle of the table, removing the dome with a flourish of his wrist. There on the shiny silver surface is a large pizza. I stare down at the pie, dumbfounded. The waiter nods at Christoph, then slinks out again. When I look up, Christoph is watching me carefully, waiting for my reaction.

"You did *say* it was your favorite food."

There is something in his voice—the gentle teasing lilt—coupled with the gesture he makes as he points toward the pie, that exposes his own nervousness. Christoph is trying to impress me with this room, with a stupid pizza, and the thought makes me so depressed that I am having trouble opening my mouth to speak. Circles of pepperoni dot the surface of the steaming cheese, and I think of Julian, that first day outside school watching him eat a slice, the way he strode defiantly across the street to claim me, his hand grasping my own.

I close my eyes and images flash through my mind: Alexa's smirk framed in the bathroom mirror at school, Julian's eyes searching mine for some kind of answer. My mother at Tavern on the Green, the nonchalance of her fur thrown over the back of her chair, her hard stare that impacts my bones like a fall onto cold concrete. Her imperiousness as she calls things forth to do her bidding, the universe ordering itself around her as neatly as stacks of folded paper. Sitting here with a man who is old enough to be my father, a man who possesses that same smug sense of entitlement as my parents, I know that I have become my worst self, a girl who will do anything to avoid looking at her own frightened reflection in the mirror. A girl who runs away, straight into the dark of an eclipse, just to have someplace to go.

But I can't remember who I am, I think frantically, my eyes opening on the candlelit room, the pizza, and above it,

Christoph's face. *Then isn't it time you found out?* an unfamiliar voice from what feels like the depth of my being whispers. It is a voice that might be Sara's, or it could be my own, a voice so hoarse and raspy from disuse that the sound is foreign to my ears. I don't want to be this person anymore, but I've been running for so long, I don't know how to stop, how to stand still, how to begin again. If there was a map, could I follow it? Could I make a new start? A new life out of the haze of ghosts and ashes, so much burnt-out terrain? *Maybe it's time you tried,* the voice whispers again without judgment or sarcasm, but with so much compassion that a ragged, tearing sound escapes my throat before I can contain it. I pull my hand away and stand up, knocking the chair over with my sudden movement, the imprint of Christoph's fingers lingering on my skin like a chemical burn.

"I'm sorry," I say, though I don't think I really am. "I have to go."

Christoph stands up sharply. "What? You just got here!"

"I know," I mumble. "But I can't stay." Christoph's face colors a deep red, his arctic-blue eyes narrowing dangerously.

"What?" he says again. *"Why?"*

There is no reason I can give him that will make any kind of sense. I've woken up in the middle of a dream in the wrong house, the wrong city, the wrong country.

"Just who the hell do you think you are?" he asks through gritted teeth. "No one walks out on me, you ungrateful little brat—you'd still be getting tucked into bed by your parents every night if it weren't for me."

He pulls me roughly toward him so that I am pressed

against his chest, his face inches from my own, his hands pinning my wrists to my sides, fingers encircling my bones like handcuffs. He snakes one hand over my stomach and I stop breathing entirely. His palm encircles my left breast, first gently, then pinching the nipple hard so that my mouth opens in pain. I am stunned, my heart stopped dead, stillborn. Christoph's lips curl into a cruel twist, moving closer to mine. If he kisses me, something will sputter and die inside me. I can feel his breath on my skin, smell the champagne mixed with the heat of his mouth, something vaguely metallic, and my stomach turns violently. The strong scent of his cologne fills my throat and I almost gag, my gut heaving, the room drenched in a haze of candles and the purity of white flowers, petals outstretched.

I channel Alexa as hard as I can, imagine I am inside that perfect body and blond waterfall of hair. I look Christoph dead in the eye with the last bit of strength I have left. I can see the light stubble on his cheeks and chin, the gray in his hair. When my voice exits my mouth, it is measured and cool, the voice of someone whose pulse never climbs above fifty beats per minute, the voice of someone who doesn't take crap from anyone.

"Good point. I mean about the fact that I'm still *young enough* to be tucked into *bed*. I wonder what the cops would have to say about that little tidbit of information. Or my parents, for instance."

There is silence as I stand as still as I can, one eyebrow raised for emphasis. I know it is just as likely that he will knock me to the floor, throwing his body on top of me, as it is that he will let me go. A dead look crosses his face, an iron door sealing off his emotions, the anger contained deep inside his body.

"Get the hell out of here," he says, removing his hands from my wrists, his eyes sliding away as he turns his back on me to face the window. "Before I lose what's left of my patience." It's snowing harder now, and the fat flakes are coating the window in a layer of frost, obscuring the glittering night.

As I walk quickly toward the door, I don't turn around to see if Christoph is watching me. I concentrate on the sound of my shoes, the rush of wind that hits me squarely in the face as the door opens, the musty, damp smell of the hallway in my nostrils, the mutiny in my guts as I bend over the first flight of stairs, dry heaving, my stomach churning spasmodically.

TWENTY-EIGHT

WHEN I WALK into the Tunnel basement fifteen minutes later, the night is in full swing, the dance floor teeming with energy. All I want is to be somewhere safe and familiar, somewhere I belong. Smoke drifts above my head, and my nose fills with the smell of sweat mixed with spilled liquor and perfume. I push through the crowd, stumbling a little in my heels and swaying queasily as a guy wearing a vinyl catsuit grabs me by the elbow until I'm upright once again.

"Steady there, girl," he says, yelling above the music and patting me as though I am a horse. I grab my midsection as if I can somehow stop it from rebelling with this small pressure alone. I keep moving until I reach the bar, arriving just as a girl seated on a bar stool gets up, moving off into the crowd with a vacant look. I sit down on the stool gratefully and try to catch Ethan's attention. Since almost puking I feel a little better, but not even remotely approaching good, or even OK. Now that I'm back in familiar surroundings, my heart is pattering away normally in my chest and I feel a little less like I'm about to keel over and die, which I guess is an improvement, all things considered.

"Are you OK?" Ethan stands above me behind the bar, his golden-brown hair hanging to his shoulders in waves, biceps chiseled beneath the rolled-up sleeves of his black T-shirt.

"That seems to be the question of the night," I mutter. "Where is everyone?"

My eyes sweep the room, but Giovanni, Sebastian and the usual crew of club kids are nowhere to be found.

"I think they're all in VIP," Ethan says, jerking his head toward the back of the basement, where a red velvet rope sections off the VIP room. "You want a drink? You look like you could use one."

"Tequila shot," I yell over the din as a cheer roars up from the dance floor when a hard-hitting house track segues into Blondie's "Rapture."

Ethan places a shot glass in front of me, filling it to the top with Herradura Silver tequila. I gulp it down and he holds the bottle over the empty glass, looking at me questioningly, but I shake my head and he places the tequila back on the bar.

"Are you going to Alexa's party later?" Ethan yells, cupping his hands around his mouth so the sound will travel farther.

"*What* party?"

"I guess she rented out some swanky hotel suite all the way uptown. I'm actually getting off early tonight, for a change, if you can believe that." He grins, and I remember just how good-looking he is, which of course causes me to blush hard. "You going?"

"I don't know," I mumble. "See you later," I yell. I get up

before he notices how red my cheeks are, and walk purpose-fully toward the small VIP room located at the very rear of the basement.

When I get to the velvet rope, an unfamiliar girl with a blond, high ponytail is standing behind it, clipboard in hand. Rhinestones sparkle in a heavy column around her throat, and her face is adorned with a slash of red lipstick and a pair of the heaviest false eyelashes I've ever seen. Despite all of this, or maybe because of it, she is ravishingly beautiful, her breasts mounded up beneath a black lace bustier that shows off her tiny waist.

"Yes?" she says. Her voice is a deep growl that hints at some sort of an accent, the vowels clipped and staccato.

"I'm Cat," I say brusquely, itching to get inside already. "I work here."

Her face breaks into a small, cruel smile.

"Not anymore you don't." Her nails are lacquered a bold red, and she taps them against her clipboard.

"What are you talking about?" I ask, my blood rising.

"Christoph called a few minutes ago. He said that if some-one named Cat showed up, I should tell her she was fired." She runs a tongue over her lips as if this bit of info is delicious, a tasty morsel. Watching her, I feel nauseated again. She re-minds me of a lion licking the last drops of blood from its own mouth.

"That's bullshit," I snap, reaching for the rope to unlock it, the metal cool under my hand.

"Don't make me have to call security, OK?" Her voice is a lazy drawl.

"Call them," I say, stepping inside and pushing past her. "Knock yourself out."

The VIP room is packed, and I push through the mass of bodies, furious that Christoph would pull this kind of crap, my arms shoving random limbs out of the way, contorting my body like an elaborate game of Twister as I slide through the crowd. But inside I am scared. Without the club, what do I have? I could move over to The World, or Save the Robots, maybe even Nell's, but if Christoph blackballs me, I'm pretty much finished. My eyes fill up with hot salty tears, and I angrily blink them away.

Alexa is holding court on the red velvet sofas in the back of the room, a huge mirror on the wall behind her reflecting the bottles of Cristal strewn across the top of a gilt-legged coffee table, the legion of club kids at least three feet deep who are listening raptly to whatever she is saying. Alexa throws her head back as she laughs, her voice pealing out into the room. Giovanni and Sebastian sit on either side, and Sebastian in particular seems dazzled, looking up adoringly as she reaches out to refill his glass. A mirror piled with white powder sits on top of the table, and Alexa watches as her followers snort long lines from a rolled-up dollar bill, sniffing loudly.

When she notices me watching her, she stops dead, her body going momentarily rigid. A look passes over her face that might be something like guilt, but it disappears as quickly as it arrives. Her face is smooth again, poreless under the colored lights. As I approach, Giovanni turns to face me, his eyes widening at the very fact of my presence.

"What are you doing here?" he hisses, pulling my arm so

that my ear is now flush with his lips. "Shouldn't you be hand-cuffed to some strange S-and-M torture device that we both *know* is in Christoph's apartment?"

Giovanni is convinced beyond all reason that Christoph's apartment is some kind of bizarre den of iniquity, complete with whips, chains and an assorted array of shiny silver hand-cuffs. Giovanni giggles uncontrollably, and the glassiness of his eyes and the shrillness of his voice tell me that he is very, very high. "You still look fierce, by the way," he adds, blithely downing the remaining drops of champagne in his all-but-empty glass.

Alexa looks over at me and smiles, leaning over to whisper in Sebastian's ear.

"What's going on?" I ask Giovanni. "Since when does Alexa hang out in VIP?"

"I guess she came to see Ethan, but once Sebastian saw her, he dragged her back here and made her buy champagne for everyone. Not that I'm complaining. Did you really get *fired*? What did you *do*?"

"Whose is *that*?" I ask, changing the subject and pointing at the rapidly disappearing blow. "And now that we're on the subject, who the hell is working the door?" I glance toward the Soviet vixen behind the rope, who glares right back at me.

"Well, I got here after it was already out, but I'm assuming it's Miss Thing's." Giovanni nods at Alexa. "I think we both know that if it were Sebastian's, I wouldn't be allowed to so much as *breathe* on it, much less hoover it up my nostrils at such a terrifying rate. And that's Svetlana. I think she's from Ukraine or some other underdeveloped Eastern European

country where they still stand in line for bread every morning." He sniffs loudly, reaching up and pinching both nostrils
together.

"Svetlana?" I ask incredulously. "Sounds like a Russian
hooker."

"Honey, *please*," Giovanni deadpans. "Aren't we *all*?"
Giovanni leans over the mirror and does another line, wiping
his nose and sniffing hard as he comes up for air.

"Russian?"

"No, silly—*hookers*." Giovanni laughs, leaning back on the
red velvet cushions of the couch.

"How much blow have you done, anyway?"

"Enough." He laughs again, the sweat on his neck shining.
"Although that's the funny thing about drugs, coke in particular—there's never *really* enough, is there? Not for me, anyway."

Giovanni is still laughing, but his eyes are somewhere far
away, and his expression is startlingly sober.

"Cat, are you just going to stay there talking to that fat
queen all night, or are you going to come over and say hello?"
Sebastian yells out, standing up and placing his hands on his
narrow hips, every move exaggerated to sheer comedy. There's
nothing Sebastian loves more than having center stage. You're
no good to him if you aren't paying strict attention to his every move. Tonight he's painted his entire face in those round,
blue, entirely stupid spots that make him look like he's con-
tracted a flesh-eating disease.

"I believe I've been *summoned*," I stage-whisper in
Giovanni's ear.

"And the Academy Award for best actor goes to . . . ,"

Giovanni says, staring at Sebastian with a smirk. I walk over to Sebastian, watching as Giovanni grabs a bottle of Cristal, emptying its contents into his waiting glass.

"Hey," I say to Sebastian and Alexa, as Sebastian air-kisses both of my cheeks, my tone conveying a brightness I don't even remotely feel. In fact, since the cab ride to Tunnel, I feel less than nothing. Deadened. All the coke, or maybe the emotional burnout of the past day, has finally rendered me numb.

"Somebody's in trouble . . . ," Sebastian drawls, a mischievous glint in his eye. "Girl, what *happened* with you and Christoph? He's *seriously* pissed!"

"I don't want to talk about it," I say, looking over at Alexa, who looks on silently, taking in my shaking hands.

"I thought you'd be at the bar with Ethan," I say to Alexa, who immediately sits down on the sofa, smoothly crossing her legs sheathed in sheer black stockings.

"Well, I *was*"—Alexa flashes me a quick, almost apologetic smile—"but then I ran into Sebastian and—"

"And she looked so *fabulous* that I absolutely *insisted* she come in here and join us," Sebastian interrupts, his cherubic face flushed and agitated. "You *are* fabulous, you know," he says, grabbing her arm, his voice a low, satisfied purr. Alexa tries her best to look humble, but like a frog in a trench coat, it really isn't her style.

"In fact she's SO fabulous, I'm going to tell Christoph to hire her ass as soon as he gets here tonight," Sebastian babbles on, his fingers tightening against Alexa's slim, pale flesh. Alexa rolls her eyes in mock exasperation, but I can tell that she's loving every minute of the attention. Sebastian leans his head closer to

Alexa's, and my stomach flips over again as he whispers something quietly in her ear. My head is filled with so much static that my thoughts are a blizzard of disconnected images mixed with rage and panic. My hands at my sides curl into fists, nails scraping against the meat of my palms.

"What do you mean, *hire* her?"

My voice comes out louder than I wanted it to, and manages to arrive precisely over a break in the music. All heads in the VIP room turn to face me, expressions somewhere between quizzical and bemused, hands over mouths, glasses stopped dead before parted lips. Sebastian looks up with a shocked expression, his blue eyes growing larger by the second. I can tell by his face that he thinks I'm a fool, that I've somehow stepped over some invisible line of coolness by reacting emotionally not only in public, but at the club, of all places.

"Well, like I said, she's fab, and Christoph could do much worse than to let her throw a party or two. We were talking about starting out small," Sebastian gushes, his words coming faster as he talks, "just something in the Chandelier Room, maybe a kind of mock society event . . . Oh, I know!" Sebastian jumps to his feet as if he's been electrocuted. "What about a coming-out party? But instead of debs in white gloves, we'll have all kinds of white food and drink, white orchids everywhere, and oh, I don't know . . . maybe a drag queen cotillion?"

"Yes!" Alexa squeals breathlessly, and the high-pitched register of her voice makes me dig my nails deeper into my skin until I'm sure it's flayed open, streaming blood. But when I uncurl my hands, the flesh is still white, pocked with tiny red half-moons.

"And don't forget those names we talked about earlier, dollface." Sebastian giggles conspiratorially, reaching out and nudging Alexa with one pointy finger, his nails painted a neon yellow that glows under the black lights.

"No problem," Alexa says, shrugging her slim shoulders that might look bony if not for the swanlike grace of her neck. "I'll invite my whole Rolodex."

At this, Sebastian's eyes widen, and a smug, satisfied expression comes over his face. I realize that it's not just Alexa's beauty that impresses him so deeply, it's also her pedigree, the impressive roster of names she can potentially bring to his parties. I've always known Sebastian is a shameless social climber, but now with Alexa, he's got a way in—and up—to her level. Just watching the way he's hanging on her every word, it's obvious he's no longer satisfied with playing in the sandbox alongside all the other club kids. And now, because of Alexa, he doesn't have to.

I watch as Alexa smiles, blushing prettily, her face open as a fresh pink flower, and I can feel the anger rising up inside me, threatening to burn the room, the building, the whole goddamn block to the ground. My chest is tight and dry, a mass sticking in my throat like a dry, rotten piece of bread. *How dare she,* I fume. *How dare she come in here and take my life when I have so little, so very little that I care about in any real way?* Everything I have left is swirling away, down an empty street like trash picked up by the wind. I cough once and try to clear my throat, my rage a ball of black sludge blocking my windpipe. If I don't spit it out, I'll stop breathing entirely.

"Since when do you care about throwing parties?" I ask Alexa, a thin sheet of ice coating my voice like a shield. "Or anything below Fourteenth Street, for that matter? Just last week you were scared to even come down here in broad *daylight,* and now you're the new It Girl? *Please.*"

My voice is coated in sarcasm as thick as motor oil, and my eyes narrow as I watch Alexa's expression change, watch it seal itself off expertly. Vacant and expressionless, the remnants of a small smile still on her lips, she reminds me of a doll, her eyes glittering faintly in their sockets, skin emitting the reflective sheen of smooth, coated plastic. If I moved closer, she would smell like a combination of sickly sweet vanilla and toxic chemicals. I realize I'm shaking like a leaf shuddering in the wind. I feel like I'm actually *vibrating. Too much coke,* I tell myself. *Too much, too much. Isn't that what the Mad Hatter said to Alice? Or was it "your hair wants cutting"?*

"You're not really mad, are you, Cat?" Alexa asks, her eyes widening innocently. She's good, I'll give her that much. She knows enough to back down in the face of a potential explosion, so that if and when it happens, she won't look responsible. "It's just a few tiny parties. It's not like I'm trying to take your *place* or something!"

"Not *yet.*" My words are as taut as wire.

Alexa and I stare at each other, transfixed, and I see a gleam of recognition in her eyes.

So. You're on to me.

"Now, ladies," Giovanni says smoothly as he saunters to my side and places an arm around my shoulder, "why are we wasting time on this stupidity when there's champagne to consume?" He holds up a bottle of Cristal in front of me, and I wave it away, glaring at him. "Among other things," he finishes, looking at the table, still covered with blow.

"I don't even know what you're *doing* in here!" Sebastian yells at Giovanni, cocking one hand on his hip, his face twisted into a scowl. "You are *so not* VIP material!"

"Well, *honey,*" Giovanni says, smiling sweetly, "I may not be VIP 'material' but at least I don't look like some second grader's *art* project, or the *main attraction* at a fucking *freak show.*" Giovanni points at the bright blue spots on Sebastian's cheeks. "What are those, anyway? Leprosy?"

The crowd erupts in laughter as the skin around Sebastian's dots turns increasingly red. If smoke could come out of his ears at this moment, it probably would. After the laughter dies down, Sebastian smiles grimly, grudgingly, and I can tell that he'd like nothing more than to snatch the bottle from Giovanni's hands and smash the top, twisting the broken end into Giovanni's flushed, smirking face. But outnumbered and now ridiculed, he retreats, until later, when he will no doubt exact his revenge by spreading some kind of noxious rumor guaranteed to embarrass Giovanni down to the core of his being, or at the very least, dream up some way to get him permanently eighty-sixed from the VIP room.

Alexa reaches over and grabs my arm, pulling me closer to her. I can smell the strong, cloying perfume she is wearing, Calvin Klein's Obsession, and the smell of it, the musky base, makes me feel dizzy, my head light.

"Look," she whispers urgently, "I'm not trying to steal your thunder or anything. I'm really not. He asked if I would do some parties with him, and he just wouldn't take no for an answer." She lets go of my arm, throwing her hair back and smiling winningly over my shoulder as Ethan approaches, walking past the velvet rope. He leans in, kissing her on the cheek as she closes her eyes, her lashes dark as insect legs.

"You off?" she says softly as he wraps his arms around her, nuzzling his face in her neck.

"Mmm-hmm," he mumbles, lost in her flesh. "Way off."

Watching the two of them, I remember Alexa crying on the floor of her bedroom, and it's all I can do not to burst out in peals of laughter. From what I can see, she doesn't have much to worry about where Ethan is concerned. He seems to like her just fine—more than fine, really.

"This scene is *tired!*" Sebastian yells out, picking up a forgotten bottle of champagne and holding it to his lips, tilting his head back as he drains it.

"I have the cure for that." Alexa grins, looking up and winking at me expertly, the skin beneath her cheekbones dusted with powder that glows dangerously under the lights.

I stand there as the room gathers up its jackets and shoes, as Sebastian tosses the empty champagne bottles on the floor, the glass crushing like ground diamonds under his shoes as he dances among the glittering shards, the bass pumping through the room like an earthquake. As I watch him, I can feel my pulse slowing for the first time all evening, the drugs winding down in my system like a worn-out mechanical soldier. I'm so tired that all I want is to lie down right there amidst the shattered pieces of my life and sleep for a hundred years. Instead I know I will follow Alexa and Sebastian out the door and into a limo, that on the way uptown I will finish the coke in my poison ring, my fingernails scraping the metal bottom to get at the last of the white powder, staring dully at the city streets as the lights go flashing by, snow sparkling against the cold, frosted windshield.

TWENTY - NINE

WE PULL UP in front of The Plaza hotel, past the shine of Columbus Circle, the row of flags out front swaying in the night breeze. Thanksgiving hasn't even passed yet, but I swear, Christmas comes earlier and earlier every year. There are lights and trees covering every square inch of Manhattan already, the boughs sparkling with silver.

I remember coming here with my mother for my birthday when I was eight. The tables in the restaurant piled with elaborate, gold-dipped centerpieces of pinecones and holly. The huge tree in the center of the room, draped in twinkling white lights. My mother's face as she plucked a small cake from a silver tray, placing it carefully on my plate. In the lobby, the portrait of Eloise smirking down at me, her plump, rounded figure dressed in black and white. It hurts to remember these things.

At the curb, the doorman opens the limo door and Giovanni tumbles out, lying in the gutter faceup and cackling like a demented snow angel. Someone throws Giovanni's black duffel bag out of the limo and it lands squarely on top of his face, muffling his laughter and high-pitched shrieks. The red-carpeted steps stretch before us like a tongue, and I uncurl my legs, stepping over Alexa perched on Ethan's lap. As I exit the limo, I reach down and grab Giovanni's hand, pulling him to his feet. He sways there dreamily for a moment before grabbing his bag, throwing it over one shoulder. On the way here, I watched as Giovanni drank two bottles of champagne in quick succession, the bubbles moving down his throat effortlessly as he leaned into the bottle.

"You are a MESS." I laugh, brushing snow off the back and shoulders of his long black coat.

"Look who's talking," he snaps, brushing past the doorman, chin lifted high. "You did enough blow in the limo to stun a small elephant into submission."

I sniff loudly in response, the inside of my nostrils caked in concrete. I've reached the point in drug consumption where the coke no longer makes me feel spastic, but almost mellow. The cold air hits my lungs like a plunge into ice water, and I crane my neck upward to search for stars, but all I see are the drifts of snow spiraling down to the ground, waiting to cover us all.

"Are you going to stand there all night staring at nothing?"

There is a low voice in my ear, something between a growl and a purr, and it sends shivers down my spine. Alexa's ruby lips are so close to my skin that her words are almost a kiss. When I tear my gaze away from the night sky and turn to face her, she is beside me holding on to Ethan's hand, a wry smile on her face. She's on her turf now, and I watch the confidence with which she strides into the hotel lobby, her fur coat thrown across her shoulders like a cape, her heels clicking purposefully across the marble floor. She removes her platinum AmEx from a Louis Vuitton wallet and pushes it across the counter.

Club kids file into the lobby in droves, posing insanely with the potted palms tucked into corners, legs wrapped around the trunks, heads thrown back. One black drag queen in a tight-fitting cocktail dress begins voguing through the lobby, using the marble floor as her own personal catwalk. Sebastian enters wearing huge, dark sunglasses and immediately starts rating the queen's performance, screaming, "Ten, ten" and "Work it, bitch" at the top of his lungs while clapping wildly. I watch as the desk clerk, his face flushed with embarrassment, registers the queen's antics, then looks away.

The suite is on one of the top floors of the hotel, and the carpet underfoot is a luxurious beige pile that seems to creep up my ankles as I walk. Most of the club kids immediately commandeer the living room area and begin raiding the minibar and calling room service, ordering bottles of Cristal and tequila. Alexa smiles triumphantly, sitting down on the long white couch, her body framed by a row of windows. She pulls off her heels, flexing her feet against the carpet with obvious pleasure. Ethan turns on the stereo and music floods the room.

"You're not still mad at me, are you?" Alexa yells over the music, grabbing on to my arm and holding on tight. "Don't be mad," she continues with a hard look. "It's boring."

"Yeah, don't be *boring*," Sebastian parrots affectionately, pushing me to the side so he can sit in the middle of us, next to Alexa. The two of them immediately begin chattering like magpies, locked in their own private world, and after a few minutes of this, I begin to feel stupid and unnecessary. I get up, pushing past Giovanni and a bunch of club kids I've never seen before who are in the process of turning the living room into a makeshift dance floor, moving coffee tables and lamps out of the way, and walk toward the bedroom. Despite the fact that the suite is crawling with people, some of whom are supposedly my friends, I am suddenly lonely.

When I push the bedroom door open, I see Ethan sitting in a pool of light in the middle of a king-sized bed covered in gold silk, his legs crossed beneath him. When I close the door behind me, he looks up hopefully, his face falling slightly when he sees that it's only me. At that moment, Aria and Amy come stumbling out of the bathroom clutching bottles of champagne, and switch on the large TV at the end of the bed. They settle down on the floor in front of it, giggling at the videos filling the room with color and light. Amy has a long blue ponytail that reaches her waist, and wears matching blue fake eyelashes. Aria is wearing a yellow tutu with a black unitard underneath. With her bright yellow tangle of curls, she reminds me of a bee or some other winged insect complete with poisonous stinger. I sit down on the bed and face Ethan, drawing my legs underneath me.

"Hey," I say. "What are you doing in here? All the action is out there."

"I could ask you the same question."

He smiles, showing rows of even white teeth. I remember Julian's slightly crooked smile, and regret clutches its fingers around my throat, stopping my breath momentarily.

"But you won't," I manage to say when it passes.

"No," he says, reaching over to the bedside table and lighting a cigarette. Smoke drifts up, obscuring his face. "I won't."

"I thought you came here to hang with Alexa." I pick at a loose thread on the bedspread and breathe in the scent of lilies in a gold vase on the dresser. Their sweet, cloying scent makes me think of Christoph, his face when I got up and walked out, how quickly it erupted in anger and resentment. INXS's "Need You Tonight" flashes onto the screen, and Aria lets out a large whoop, immediately cranks the volume, points at Ethan, who more than resembles the lead singer, and whispers loudly into Amy's ear.

"I guess she's busy." He exhales, and smoke drifts toward the ceiling. Although his face is impassive, I can see a glint of hurt in his eyes, and I know from working at the club for as long as I have what it must've cost him to get off so early.

"You really like her, don't you." My voice is flat, emotionless. Maybe it's the coke, but I feel like I can talk to Ethan now without nervousness. Right now I feel like I could say anything.

"I thought I did," he says, crushing out his cigarette in the ashtray. "But if she's really that into all of this"—he gestures toward the other room and the crash of music and broken glass coming through the half-open door—"then I'm not so sure. For me it's a paycheck, you know? This whole scene makes me fucking restless, if you want to know the truth. I mean, it's not *real*."

"And you *want* something real?" I ask, incredulous.

"Sure." He looks at me levelly. "Don't you?"

I think about the club, how in the beginning it made me feel so free, like nothing could touch me, all the weight of the day falling from my shoulders like a heavy coat sliding to the floor. Flitting through the fractured light on the dance floor, my skin shimmering and so alive I was giddy with it.

"I used to think I didn't. Now I'm not so sure."

Ethan smiles softly, waiting for me to continue.

"I've never been too comfortable with reality." I look over at Aria and Amy, who are passing a bottle of champagne back and forth between them. "It kind of sucks in a lot of ways."

"What do you mean?" He draws his knees up, grinding his black boots into the bedspread.

"My realities aren't always that great," I say in a voice that comes out gratingly, as if I'm about to cry, and I realize that I actually am. I blink back the tears and look up to watch Ethan's expression change. He says nothing, but his eyes dare me to tell him everything.

"Alexa and I are a lot alike, weirdly enough," I begin, the words falling hesitantly, jaggedly from my lips. "On the surface, at least. We're both from the Upper East Side—"

"I thought you lived downtown," Ethan says, clearly confused.

"I do now, but I grew up on the Upper East Side. I even went to Alexa's coming-out party."

"What the hell is *that*?" Ethan laughs.

"Don't ask. It involves white gloves and whole lot of pretension."

"So I'm not missing anything?"

"Not by a long shot," I say, laughing. "Anyway, I moved

downtown six months ago because my mother . . ." My voice trails off the way it always does when I try to talk about my family. Watching Ethan as he waits for me to speak again, I have gone suddenly mute. But this time something's changed, this time there's an urgency building up inside me, a kind of heat, and I know that for once, the words are going to leave my lips whether I like it or not. For once, I'm going to say the truth out loud. I don't know why it's happening here in this room with Ethan, whom I barely know. Maybe it's the simple fact that it's easier to share things with someone you have no real relationship with, where nothing is at stake. Or maybe after all this time, I'm just *ready,* unable to hold it in any longer. I'm too tired of keeping it all inside, where no one can see, and for the first time, I don't *want* to anymore. I want to hear the words out loud.

"Your mother *what?*" Ethan prompts gently.

I take a deep breath, and the words fly out all at once like air rushing out of a deflated balloon. "She hits me. She's always hit me, ever since I was little. It was never any one thing . . . It was *everything*. It didn't matter how good I was or how well I did in school. It was never *enough* to make her stop, to make her . . ." The words stick in my throat and my cheeks are suddenly wet. "Love me. That's why I moved out. My father just watched it happen, and divorced her when he met someone else. I don't know why."

Ethan nods, his face solemn. He reaches for another cigarette.

"Why don't you live with him?" he asks, but before I can answer, he jumps in again, the answer already written on my face. "Oh, I get it. She doesn't like you, right? The girlfriend?" He raises one eyebrow, tapping his cigarette ash against the ashtray. "Is that it?"

"Well, no, she doesn't. And the feeling is kind of mutual." I look out at the buildings across the way, and notice that they look almost blue. "But I guess I don't live with him because . . ." Words fail me once again, and I wish more than anything that I had a glass of champagne or a line to make it all recede far into the distance, to make everything hazy and unreal again. "Because he just doesn't care."

When I can finally look Ethan in the face, he's staring at me through the gently curling smoke rising in the air. He doesn't say anything at all, and I realize that the thing I dreaded seeing most on a person's face when I finally was able to tell them about my family was pity. But there's none of that in Ethan's expression, just some kind of understanding. As we look at each other, it's as if a veil has fallen away and I can breathe again, and I realize that the person I most want to hear the words that have just left my mouth is Julian.

"Hey, guys." When I look up, Alexa is standing in the doorway. She walks over to the bed and slides down next to Ethan, curling her lithe body around his, her golden hair falling over his black sweater. "Guess what I have?" She looks up with an impish grin and opens one hand. Inside are three large capsules filled with white powder.

"X?" Ethan asks, reaching out and plucking one from her palm, holding it up to the light. "Where'd you get it?"

"Sebastian." Alexa laughs. "Where else? He's in the other room giving them out like candy."

Ethan calls out to Aria, tossing her the X in his hand. She lets out a squeal of delight as she pops the pill into her mouth, drinking greedily from her bottle of champagne.

"I think I'm OK with plain old reality tonight." Ethan stares at me, a faint smile on his lips.

"Party pooper." Alexa pouts, screwing her face up adorably, a two-year-old on the verge of a tantrum. Any minute now she will stomp her foot.

"Are you going to?" I ask her.

Alexa looks down at the two pills still reclining in her palm. "I never have," she whispers, looking at me intently. "I will if you will." She leans closer to me, and I can feel the heat coming off her skin in waves. "Please, Caitlin. I don't want to do it alone."

I remember my first hit of X, Giovanni at my side. How the warmth of his skin made me feel safe, like everything would be all right one way or another if I could wait, if I could just learn, somehow, to be patient.

I tilt my head back, plucking the pill from her hand and swallowing hard. Alexa grins, bringing the pill up to her lips, and Ethan's eyes cloud over, go blank, and I watch as he turns away, grabbing a beer bottle from the bedside table.

Forty minutes later, the world has gone hazy, the sharp edges of the night softened and pure. The music is streaming through the suite like shreds of shiny tinsel, and when I close my eyes, I think I can see the notes leaping beneath my closed lids in a golden parade. I sit on the couch next to Ethan, watching Alexa dance with Sebastian, the way she throws her hair back and unabashedly shimmies her small hips to the beat. I think of Julian, his shaggy hair falling into his eyes, how much I might have hurt him. I don't know what to call the feeling that springs up inside my chest when I think of him, that small ache, a candle growing steadily brighter.

"Have you ever been in love?" I hear myself asking. My mouth feels funny and stiff, the words coming out slurred, floating somewhere above the music.

"I don't know," Ethan answers, staring straight ahead. His profile glows, sharply etched, the curve of his jaw so clean, it's almost heartbreaking. Even through the haze of the X flying through my blood, I'm aware of the fact that Ethan is most likely the only vaguely sober person in this room. "I can't seem to stay still long enough to find out."

With Ethan's words still ringing in my ears, I'm filled with a desire so intense that it levitates my body off the couch and into the bedroom. I want to talk to Julian, to hear his low, steady voice in my ear. Aria and Amy are curled up in a heap on the bed, huddled together for warmth and comfort. A group of five or six club kids sit on the floor, a mirror between them, long lines of coke laid out on the glass.

I walk past them and into the bathroom and pick up the phone I knew would be mounted on the wall next to the toilet. I sit down on the seat and dial Julian's number, grateful that he has his own line, listening as the phone rings once, twice, three times, leaning my forehead against the cool wall as I wait. The wallpaper, strewn with birds and pink ribbons, swims before my eyes.

"Hello?"

Julian's voice fills my ear—warm, scratchy, and full of sleep.

"It's me," I say into the receiver. "Caitlin."

There is a pause, and I hear a rustling of bedsheets, then the click of a light being turned on.

"I'm sorry for the other night. I feel like . . . I feel . . . like I'm always apologizing, but I am. Sorry, I mean."

Am I speaking out loud? The thought flashes through my mind so quickly that I don't have time to stop it. If I've ever been this fucked up before, I don't remember it. In the lull in our conversation, the music in the other room is turned up sharply, and there is the sudden sound of cheers and laughter.

"Where are you, anyway?" he asks, fully awake now.

"Plaza. Hotel. With Alexa Forte. And some other people."

I'm vaguely aware of just how surreal my words sound. How disjointed. It's getting hard to speak, to form complete sentences. Is my heart still beating? I reach one hand up to my chest and rest it there. My pulse throbs beneath my fingers, slow and erratic. A misstep. A stumble.

"Alexa *Forte*? How did *that* happen?" He laughs uneasily. "And why are you at The Plaza?"

"Long story." I sigh, closing my eyes. "I want to tell you something. I do."

There is a pause, and I hear the breath catch in his throat.

"What's that?"

"I'm sorry. I am. Sorry."

"You already said that." Julian chuckles, and I wonder if he's warm from sleep, his hair tangled against the pillow.

"Also . . ."

"Yes?"

"I like you."

The blood rushes to my face, heating my cheeks. I can't believe I've just said it, but I have. And now the words are out there in the world where I can't take them back. So I say them again.

"I like you. And . . . I'm sorry I've been such a freak. There's a lot . . . so much . . ." My voice trails off as the heaviness in my limbs begins to pull me down. "There are things . . . I should say. Tell you. I want to."

"So tell me," he says simply.

A wave of intense sensation crashes through me, my stomach dropping without warning, and I'm dizzy, the lights overhead as bright as stars. I realize that I might not be able to stand up and walk out of the bathroom, and the thought terrifies me.

"Soon," I manage to get out, my eyes closing.

"Cat? Cat, are you still there?"

Julian's voice sounds miles away, I'm on a boat, drifting further and further into rough currents, bobbing and dipping in the water, my body weightless. My head is too heavy to keep up, and I feel myself sliding down to the tile floor, the receiver slipping from my hands. *Maybe this is it,* the thought flashing through my head in a moment of clarity. I see Sara standing over the small, polished wooden box of my coffin, her face streaked with tears and regret. *Wait!* I struggle to sit up again, to focus. *Not like this. Rewind the tape.*

Go back.

"Cat? CAT!"

I hear Julian's voice somewhere in the distance, but I'm too tired to answer. Everything is slow motion, drawn out, each moment elongating endlessly, the trails of smoke lingering after a cigarette. I know I am falling to the floor again, but my legs are icicles. Immobile. My eyes are leaden, and I keep them closed as the tide rolls in, covering me with white froth that clings to my skin like a million tiny seed pearls, a myriad sucking mouths pulling at my flesh until it falls slowly, softly away from my bones.

THIRTY

MY TEETH CHATTER, my head shaking. Snowbanks and icy ponds. I'm so cold that I can't feel my body. I know it's there, but I can't feel it. A sharp pain on my cheek snaps me awake, and my eyes creak open like a curtain rising moments before a performance, the room wobbling unsteadily into focus.

Ethan stands above me, and for the first time I'm aware that I'm wet and shivering, floating in ice-cold water that fills the enormous tub. Standing under the gold chandelier dripping with crystals, Ethan resembles an angel, the soft waves of his hair framed by a yellow nimbus of light.

"Cat, are you OK?" he asks, pulling me up so that I'm sitting. My dress is stuck to my body, another layer of skin. I shake uncontrollably, my teeth clacking against each other like a mouth full of marbles.

"I'm sorry I slapped you, but when I came in here to see if you were OK, you were passed out on the floor, so I threw you in the tub. That didn't wake you up, so I had to give you a smack." He looks at me apologetically as he grabs a handful of towels from the heated rack on the wall and wraps them around my shoulders.

"How long was I . . . out?"

"I'm not sure. Maybe a half hour?"

It feels like years. I stand up carefully, the water sloshing beneath me, grabbing on to Ethan's arms for support. When I step out of the tub, he hands me a terry-cloth robe, and when I stare at it stupidly for a long moment, he pulls it from my hand and wraps it around me. The phone is still on the floor, and I can hear a busy signal coming from the receiver. *Julian,* I think, closing my eyes again. My legs buckle beneath me, and Ethan steadies me so that I don't go tumbling into space. My feet rest against the cold tile floor, and I'm grateful for the feeling, grateful to be feeling anything at all. *I don't want to die or be out of the present,* I realize with some astonishment. *Not even a little bit. I want to be right here, feeling whatever I'm feeling, even if it's messy or complicated, even if it hurts.* I let the realization stream through me, and it's like sitting in the sun on the first real day of summer, the heat opening every pore of my skin. My eyes spin in their sockets, and I drift back down to the floor. Thirty minutes ago I could have died, and yet, I've never felt as alive as I do right this very moment.

"I think we should get you to a doctor," Ethan says, his brow crinkled with worry.

"No, no," I protest, sitting down on the toilet seat and hanging up the phone. "I'll be OK. Where is everyone?"

"Well, some people left a while ago, but Alexa, Giovanni,

Sebastian and some other stragglers are still here in the other room. Actually, Giovanni's kind of freaking out, if you want to know the truth."

"Freaking out how?" I ask, looking in the mirror. My skin is unnaturally pale, my hair and brows standing out in sharp contrast. I can see my collarbones in sharp relief above the robe, and I wonder how much weight I've lost lately.

"He's been telling people that he wants to jump out the window."

"WHAT? Seriously?"

I turn around and face him. All at once I am almost sober. The drugs are still coursing through my veins, but they seem far away, trampled by a rush of adrenaline.

"Yeah." He shrugs. "Not that people are paying him any attention or anything. But, yeah. He says that he's homeless, that he doesn't have anyplace to go."

I think back over the last few weeks and could kick myself for noticing, but not *really* noticing the black overnight bag Giovanni had started taking with him everywhere he went, stashing it behind the bar nightly, the tight smile on his face each morning after work when I said I had to go home, how that very word itself must have hit him in the pit of his stomach, deep as a sucker punch.

I force my feet to move, and open the bathroom door. There are empty bottles everywhere, and the floor is littered with clothes, soda cans and broken glass. Aria and Amy are nowhere to be found, and the deep beat of house music still pumps through the suite.

When I walk into the living room, Giovanni is standing by

the large bank of open windows, shouting at Sebastian, who is egging him on. Giovanni's dusky skin is streaked with tears and sweat, his corkscrew curls are hanging limply around his face, and his black sequined jacket is ripped at one elbow. Alexa is, unbelievably, passed out on the couch snoring loudly, her face mashed into a pillow, her red lipstick smeared like a gunshot wound.

"I'll do it!" Giovanni screams, pointing at the row of open windows, his eyes wild. He is as intoxicated as I've ever seen him, and God knows what he's been ingesting while I've been passed out.

"Go ahead," Sebastian says with a smirk. "Do the world a favor."

This kind of behavior isn't exactly new. Giovanni and Sebastian have always disliked each other heartily. But add in a cocktail of drugs and alcohol, the anonymous space of a hotel room, a life where there are no rules, no limits, and anything can happen.

Anything.

Sebastian gives Giovanni a small shove, and Giovanni stumbles and falls, grabbing on to the sheer white curtains, the material ripping with a sound so fierce that I clench my jaw, my teeth scraping against one another.

I walk over to Giovanni and grab his arm, hoist him back up to his feet. Once standing, he pulls away. His pupils are black and bottomless, and I wonder if he even knows who I am.

"What did he take?" I shout into Sebastian's insipid, passive face.

"How the hell should I know?" He shrugs. "Who cares?"

"*I* care," I spit back, pushing him in the chest so that he falls backward in his platform shoes. Sebastian gives a disgusted snort, pulling himself to his feet and brushing off his pants with pissy, exaggerated movements before stalking out of the room.

"Oh . . . So now you *care*?" Giovanni says slowly, the haze clearing from behind his eyes. "You don't know anything about me!" he screams. "You never *ask*!"

The words stop me dead. I think of all the clues I've missed, the hints he may have dropped, wanting me to ask, to give some small sign that he mattered. That I cared. The unshed tears clouding his vision as we stood on top of the speaker suspended over the dance floor at Tunnel.

Home? Where's that?

I try to grab his hand and pull him toward me, but he yanks his body away, out of reach.

"Gio," I say, pleading now, "I'm sorry. I didn't—"

"You didn't WHAT?" he yells, backing up, his expression frantic. "Sorry you didn't *care*?"

"But I do care," I say. "I really, really do."

Giovanni spies a broken bottle on the floor and leaps at it, holding the jagged end above one wrist, the tender skin exposed.

"Do you care if I do this?" His eyes are hardened and defiant, but the mouth trembling beneath them belies it all.

Before I can react or grab the broken glass away from him, he slashes blindly at his own arm, blood dripping over his hand. The sight of the crimson stream rolling over his flesh, falling onto the carpet, makes me stop right where I am, bringing one hand to my mouth as if by covering it, I can somehow stop this from happening. But somewhere inside me I know I can't stand here stuck to the floor, that I have to act right now before something even worse happens, before that shard swings down again and everything is lost.

"Giovanni, drop the bottle." He stares at me, his expression uncomprehending. "Drop it," I say again, my voice low and pleading. There is a moment where all is still except for the music pumping incessantly through the room before the bottle slips from his fingers, falling soundlessly to the floor.

I reach out again for his hand, and this time he lets me. He starts to cry, hot salty tears falling over his cheeks, and I brush them away with my free hand.

"You should've told me," I say quietly. "You could have stayed with me as long as you needed to. I love you, you know."

When I say the words out loud at last, they lose all their power to hurt me and I can see for the first time how true they really are. I've been silent about the things that are most important for too long, for my whole life, really, and I want to hear my own strong voice saying the things I know are the truest to the people I love best.

Giovanni collapses into sobs, sinking down to the floor and mumbling incoherently.

I sit next to him, cradling him in my arms and rocking him slowly back and forth the way I wish I could still be rocked to sleep, safe and sound. I grab someone's T-shirt left behind on a chair and wrap it around Giovanni's arm, stanching the flow of blood. It covers my fingers with its wet, primal heat, and I feel a corresponding tug in my heart as the blood in its chambers pushes through tiny valves and crevices, pumping endlessly. *I'm here, I'm here, I'm here,* it seems to shout, racing faster through my veins. I can hear sirens approaching outside the window getting closer, and Ethan is suddenly standing above me, his hand on my shoulder.

"I called for help," he says, looking unsure, and I can see that he is sweating, probably ruing the day he decided that leaving work was a good idea. "I cleaned up the best I could," he says, and I know he's referring to the cornucopia of drugs that have been littering the suite all night long. Giovanni is quieter now, but he's still a total mess, sobbing and smearing what's left of his black eyeliner all over his face.

"Where's Sebastian?" I ask, looking around at the almost empty room.

"He took off. I'm going to get Alexa out of here, too," he says, walking over to the couch and picking her up so that she curls into his arms as if she was born to fit there, her arms hanging limply around his neck.

When the paramedics burst in wearing blue-and-white down jackets, they immediately pry Giovanni away from me and he collapses onto a gurney, where they begin checking his pulse, wrapping a blood pressure cuff around his uninjured arm so that it squeezes the skin tightly. *Don't hurt him,* I think over and over, my hands reaching out toward his motionless body, hovering over his flesh.

"What did he take?" they keep barking at me. Giovanni laughs once, a staccato hiccup, and promptly passes out. I watch the faces of the paramedics tense as Giovanni slips into sleep, his eyes closing.

"I don't know," I say because it's true. "Some coke, and he drank a lot of champagne. Maybe some X, but I can't really be sure."

In the ambulance I hold on to Giovanni's hand and watch his face, so pale in spite of his bronzed skin, his eyes moving rapidly beneath closed lids. I know he's dreaming, that he can't hear me at all, but still I lean down and whisper to him that he's safe, that I won't leave him. I tell him all the things I've longed for someone to murmur to me at night, just before I fall over the precipice into sleep.

Safe. Love. Home.

At the hospital, I sit in a green waiting room full of people with bleeding heads and extremities, drunks wailing in the corner, babies crying restlessly. The sun is just beginning to paint the sky with streaks of magenta and gold, and my skin feels clammy, makeup painting my cheeks with long black rivulets. I'm still wearing the bathrobe, my damp dress underneath, and my feet are cold and bare against the chipped linoleum. The X is wearing off, and my body feels like a wet washcloth, wrung out and left to dry.

I get up and walk to the phone, dropping a quarter into the slot, and dial a number I know by heart but never use. It rings and rings on the other end of the line, and I picture my father and Jasmine curled companionably into each other in their oversized bed, the morning sun shining through sheer white curtains, the white princess phone on the bedside table waking them out of their reverie. When I hear my father's voice mumble a sleepy hello, I break down into tears, my breath heaving in my chest.

"Daddy?" I say. "It's me. Caitlin."

I'm aware, even as I speak, that I haven't called my father "Daddy" in a very long time. I close my eyes and see us sitting together on the stoop of our apartment, eating ice cream, and I wonder if he remembers that little girl who loved the simple pleasure of his undivided attention. I wonder if he ever thinks about me, or if I remind him so much of my mother, their failures, his dead marriage and the violence that came with it, that he can hardly bear to think about me at all.

"Caitlin, what is it?" I can picture him sitting up in bed, shrugging Jasmine's arms from around his torso so that they flop onto the silken coverlet. "Are you OK, honey?"

There is a concern in his voice that I haven't heard in so very long, and it melts what is left of my already rocky composure. I sink to my knees in the hallway, hugging the receiver to my chest for a moment before bringing it back up, tears running hotly down my cheeks, thawing me to the core.

"I need help," I say. The words feel alien and strange leaving my mouth, but I know they are the truth. I do need help. And I need my father, maybe more than I've ever needed him before.

"Where are you, Cat? I can send a car."

"You need to come," I say through the haze of my tears. "*You* need to come and get me."

When we hang up, I just sit there, clutching the receiver to my chest, and I wait, watching the sun as it makes its way across the chipped linoleum floor until it reaches my legs, creeps up my torso, warming me from the outside in with its soft yellow rays, the sunlight moving through my flesh and into the cells of my body, the very marrow of my bones, like a kind of baptism.

THIRTY-ONE

I NEVER THOUGHT I'd live somewhere as normal as New Canaan, Connecticut, but I've been here for a month now, and so far no one's chased me out of town with a bunch of torches or anything. The grounds of my father's estate are framed by rolling hills hushed and blanketed in whiteness. Through the frosted panes of my bedroom windows I can see dappled gray horses in the distance, and the drifts of snow that press against the house make me feel safe and hidden away—especially when I sleep huddled under a pile of blankets. And sleeping is mostly what I did for the first few weeks I was here, my face pressed into a wide, soft pillow.

When my father showed up at the emergency room, his long black coat spotted with snow, I collapsed into the heft of his body, falling limp. As his arms encircled me, I heard the tears in his voice and along with them, his regret. My father isn't perfect, something he's recently admitted during one of our joint therapy sessions, but we're trying. *I'm* trying. With every session, I'm coming closer to someday forgiving him for abandoning me, for turning away from my mother's abuse. Sometimes the anger still claws at me when I look at him, but I'm learning to wait for the moment to pass. It always does, eventually. Maybe I'll even talk to my mother again someday, although right now that seems as likely as visiting the moon. I'm not back at school yet, but my father says that it doesn't matter, that what I need now is rest, that I have all the time in the world for history and algebra. It probably isn't really true, but it makes me feel better each time he says it.

Even living with Jasmine hasn't been that bad. Since I've been here, she's left stacks of Godiva chocolate bars on my nightstand, stocked my freshly painted white room with extra pairs of pajamas and slippers, and filled the bookshelf with classics like *Jane Eyre*. This gave me pause for a second, until I realized that she'd probably never even read it, that she had most likely asked a bookstore clerk what books were appropriate for a seventeen-year-old girl, that in all likelihood she probably wasn't leaving some tome about a crazy lady locked away from the world lying around just to torture me. That would be going a little far—even for Jasmine.

At night we sit around the kitchen table and eat the dinner that Marta, the cook, has prepared, or we'll order in Italian or sushi. "NO avocado in the California roll," my father will bark into the receiver while giving me a slow wink. "My daughter hates it." I have to grudgingly admit that my father and Jasmine seem kind of perfect together. I like to watch them when they don't know I'm looking, mesmerized at the tenderness between them as he leans in to her hand resting on his cheek, or pulls her to him as they cuddle together on the couch watching a movie on HBO. Sometimes, though, when I'm watching them, I can't help thinking about my mother, how my father would walk past her in the kitchen after work, oblivious, and I hurt a little inside for what we've all lost. Still, it's obvious that Jasmine makes him happy, and for the first time in years, I actually *want* my father to be happy.

From what I hear through her letters, Alexa is now the reigning queen of downtown, and her parties, thrown in tandem with Sebastian, have become almost legendary. Her debutante ball at Tunnel broke some kind of record in attendance, and there were club kids and Upper East Side debs lined up all the way around the block waiting patiently to get in. Diana Ross's "I'm Coming Out" was the track of the evening, and the drag queen cotillion that took over the main dance floor is still talked about in clubs and on street corners. Ethan left the scene as quickly as he'd entered it, leaving Alexa behind and moving, I've heard, to Los Angeles. Sometimes when I can't sleep at night, I picture him out there among the palm trees and platinum-blond starlets, pouring drinks in some fancy bar with oak-paneled walls. I like to imagine the sound of the surf pounding outside his window at night as he sleeps, his tanned body turning in clean white sheets, his hair tangled on the pillow. I hope he's found what he's looking for out there in that la-la land of perpetual sun I know only from movies. I hope it's something real.

Alexa is dating Christoph now, and weirdly enough, she confirmed to Giovanni's endless delight that he really *does* have a round bed in his apartment, complete with pink, fur-lined handcuffs permanently attached to the headboard. Apparently he gave her a pair of five-inch patent-leather high heels for her eighteenth birthday and a gift certificate to Elizabeth Arden. I've written to her, asking her to be careful, that I know the terrain she is treading so intimately that I could walk it blindfolded, but Alexa pushes away my concerns with the brush of her elegant fingers. And maybe she's right. Alexa Forte was always much stronger than I am, more sure of herself. But when I think of Christoph's grip on my body, his hands snaking possessively over my flesh, I shudder, and I can't help but worry just a little. The envelopes she sends are the lightest shade of pink imaginable, sealed with the precise imprint of her glossy mouth.

I can't lie. When I read her letters, a part of me misses it all. The crowds, the power of that velvet rope in my hands, the lights flashing over the sweaty bodies littering the dance floor. How after a line I'd feel invincible, diamonds exploding like fireworks in my brain. I long for that feeling the way you mourn a lost love, how the drugs let me release everything pent up inside for so long, the way they made me feel bigger than I actually was and more numb than I ever want to be again.

Whenever this happens, I call Dr. Goldstein for a session. Sometimes I call Sara. Sometimes Giovanni, who now lives in my apartment on Third Street and spends the majority of his days in an outpatient rehab program for substance abuse. Even though we've spoken on the phone multiple times, we haven't yet talked about that night. It sits between us like a shadow or a sword, waiting patiently. Most evenings, he tells me, he stays in, working on his designs, drawing blouses and dresses in his distinctive, flowery hand. He's been talking about applying to Parsons or maybe Pratt if he's lucky enough to get financial aid or a scholarship. I've heard that the gash on his arm is mostly healed except for a long, twisted scar that will eventually turn white, a souvenir permanently tattooed on his skin. A reminder. A warning. "I love you, girl," he says, chuckling softly before getting off the phone, and each time I hear those words in my ear, I'm careful to actually say them back.

But today I'm nervous, pacing the wide wood floors of my father's house before settling down on my bed, hugging a purple pillow to my chest as I wait for the doorbell to ring. I've been growing out my dyed black hair, and an inch of walnut-brown roots peeks through at my scalp. My nails are bitten down to nubs, and I've taken to leaving my face free of makeup. It's devoid of color, but it's all mine. I've gained some weight back—around five pounds—and my clothes no longer hang so loosely on my bones. It feels good to be getting stronger, and sometimes, during one of the aerobics classes Jasmine drags me to on Tuesday mornings, when I'm contorted into some ridiculous position that would make Giovanni burst out laughing, I begin to smile, feeling the joy of my body working all on its own without any kind of chemical enhancement, just the way it's supposed to.

When I see Julian and Sara walk through my bedroom door, I jump to my feet. It's been a month since I've seen them, and I'm nervous. Sara walks in front, striding purposefully in her combat boots, and when she reaches me, she opens her arms wide. Crushed against the familiar weight of her body, I close my eyes as her weird hippie perfume inundates my senses, her hair flattened against my cheek like strands of pale cellophane.

"How's my girl?" she whispers in my ear, hugging me so tightly that I can barely breathe.

"Better," I answer, fighting the tears that tremble beneath my lashes. I step back and look at her, at the shock of crazy white-blond curls going every which way, her serious eyes, the way she is just so completely *Sara,* and I am flooded with something like happiness. "I've missed you," I say after a minute of silence in which I take her hands, squeezing her cold fingers tightly.

"Ditto," she answers, choking back the tears in her voice and rolling her eyes so that we both burst into peals of laughter. But I am feeling so much at this moment that I can't tell whether I'm laughing or crying. I am inundated with raw emotion, the weight and responsibility of being fully *present.*

"Hey, you."

I'd forgotten how Julian's voice is even huskier in person than it is over the phone, and he looks at me bashfully, his hands shoved deep in the pockets of his well-worn jeans. He is wearing his Ramones leather jacket and a black sweater, and just standing there, he is the most beautiful thing I have ever seen in my entire life.

"I'll get us some sodas from downstairs," Sara says, letting go of my hands, her gaze taking in the obvious vibe between Julian and me. "Don't go anywhere." She winks at me before walking off, the buckles on her leather jacket jingling as she moves.

"Ask Marta," I call woodenly after her, my eyes never leaving Julian's face.

His hands are still in his pockets and I want to reach out

286

and touch him, but I'm scared to make the first move, take that first irrevocable step.

"So I guess you were wrong about me." My voice is gravelly and strained with everything that's been left unsaid.

"How's that?"

"When you said I seemed like I didn't need anyone." I look down at the floor, terrified that if I keep speaking, he'll walk out that door and never come back. I take a deep breath and force myself to look up. "I guess I'm pretty screwed up."

"Who isn't?" Julian shrugs. For the first time I notice that he has a tiny dimple in his chin, the smallest of indentations, and I want to run my fingers over it.

"I'm not so different from your ex-girlfriend at the end of the day."

I watch the emotions flitting across the bones of Julian's face like birds skimming the rippling water. *Breathe,* I tell myself, focusing on the air moving in and out of my lungs. I picture my therapist's face, his round little glasses and red beard that shines softly in the lamplight. *Stay in the present moment.*

"Sure you are," Julian says quietly, taking his hands from his pockets and pulling me to him. "You're *you,*" he whispers, burying his face in my neck. He is so close that I can smell the scent of his skin: leather, musk, Ivory soap, the blue cold of fresh snow and the bright tang of laundry soap all mixed up together. "And what could be better than that?"

He nuzzles my neck, drawing his nose up my skin until I turn my face and his mouth is inches from mine. We stand there, just breathing each other's breath, and I'm looking steadily into his eyes as if there is something in there I've lost.

If my heart is still beating, I can't feel it. The blood roars loudly in my ears as his lips brush against mine and I close my eyes.

Later, as I sit between them both on my bed, the white duvet piled up around us like fallen snow, Julian and Sara fill me in on all the latest gossip as the tension falls out of me, my limbs loose and pliant. Julian presses his leg against mine, squeezing my hand in his, reassuring me with every joke, with every word that falls from his lips. And even though I'm grateful for their presence, I know that each day I'll wake up and start all over again, that there will never be a time when I won't be tempted to fall into the void, reaching out for a line of cocaine or the wrong pair of arms to blunt the pain of existence. For the first time, I know that whatever happens tomorrow, whatever happens with me and Julian, I will be all right, that if I got through the past seventeen years, I am strong enough to make it through anything.

But all that seems far away in this warm room with the hiss of the radiator punctuating our conversation and snow falling gently outside the windows. Julian leans in for another kiss, and I catch Sara's smile as she rolls her eyes at our blatant PDA. This time when his lips touch mine, I don't shut my eyes. Instead I memorize the planes of his face, the warm skin beneath my fingers, and as he begins to kiss me more deeply, I don't think or hesitate when I begin to laugh right into his open mouth, my lips stretched into a wide smile.

ACKNOWLEDGMENTS

Stacey Barney, editor extraordinaire, who single-handedly restored my faith in publishing. Thank you for taking a chance on me and believing so fiercely in *White Lines*—your friendship and support mean the world to me. My agent, the incomparable Lisa Grubka, who always has my back. Lisa stuck with me tirelessly through two years of drafts and edits, and would not rest until she found the perfect home for this book. I owe her everything. Ryan Thomann for a kick-ass page layout, and Linda McCarthy for a cover design that was so much more than I dared ever hope for. Jessica Koslow, my rock, who showed me the true meaning of friendship and family. Robin Benway, for wine and whine, who graciously read the manuscript at a critical juncture. My therapist, Ari Davis, who holds me up. Claire Mittleman, for our beautiful relationship. And most of all, Willy Blackmore, for his unfailing love and support, for believing in me when I didn't—couldn't—believe in myself, and who read every word as if it were the first time.